SANTA FE
MOURNING

ALSO AVAILABLE BY AMANDA ALLEN

**Elizabethan Mysteries
(written as Amanda Carmack)**

Murder at Fontainebleau

Murder at Whitehall

Murder in the Queen's Garden

Murder at Westminster Abbey

Murder at Hatfield House

SANTA FE MOURNING

A SANTA FE REVIVAL MYSTERY

Amanda Allen

CROOKED
LANE

NEW YORK

Published in the United States by Crooked Lane Books, an imprint of The Quick Brown Fox & Company LLC.

Crooked Lane Books and its logo are trademarks of The Quick Brown Fox & Company LLC.

Library of Congress Catalog-in-Publication data available upon request.

ISBN (hardcover): 978-1-68331-547-6
ISBN (ePub): 978-1-68331-548-3
ISBN (ePDF): 978-1-68331-549-0

Cover design by Lori Palmer
Book design by Jennifer Canzone

Printed in the United States.

www.crookedlanebooks.com

Crooked Lane Books
34 West 27th St., 10th Floor
New York, NY 10001

First Edition: March 2018

10 9 8 7 6 5 4 3 2 1

CHAPTER 1

We cannot express the depths of our disappointment, Madeline. We had hoped that your madness
had passed and that you were willing to return now
to your home and your proper position. You have
been gone much too long. Your grief for Peter was
once unfortunate, though understandable, but is now
quite beyond the pale. Dr. Hoffman says if you come
back to New York permanently, he can see to it you
get the care you need and can thus be restored to us.

We can do nothing if you insist on returning to
such a distant and barbarous place as Santa Fe. It is no
fit home for a young lady of your name and breeding.
You have wounded us greatly by your abandonment of
your duty.

Sincerely, Mother.

Madeline Vaughn-Alwin crumpled the fine cream sta-
tionery and stuffed it into her handbag. *Duty, duty,*

duty. The clatter of the train wheels that carried her farther and farther away from New York seemed to chant the word, mocking her.

What a fool she had been to think she could go back to her family for a visit and explain herself to them face-to-face and they would then understand. They would *never* understand, and her pleading had only made matters worse. If she had stayed any longer, Dr. Hoffman would have had her locked away at Pleasant Pines Hospital, never to be seen again.

She was running back to Santa Fe now, running home as fast as she could. New Mexico had saved her once; it would again.

She closed her eyes and listened to the clack and clatter of the train, the faint shrill cry of its whistle as it pushed on through the night. She could see again her mother's face—Cornelia Astor Vaughn with her classical cheekbones and cool blue eyes, her ever-present pearls and silver chignon, her lips pursed as she shook her head at her only daughter. *Your duty . . .*

Her duty. The duty of a Vaughn, of an Alwin. It had been drummed into her since the cradle, through governesses and cotillions, tea parties and Newport balls. She was an aristocrat; she had to lead by example, to hold to certain standards and never let her true thoughts and feelings be seen.

Yet it had never fit, as if the white gowns, patent leather shoes, and pearls were just an uncomfortable costume. A masquerade disguise, but one she could never shed.

She had only ever found escape in a paint box. A blank canvas gave her a new world, one where she could call anything into existence. She wasn't Madeline Vaughn anymore, daughter of a lady who had once curtsied to Queen Victoria and granddaughter of shipping and steel millionaires. She was a fairy in a green meadow, a bird soaring over ocean waves, a princess in a castle tower. Every color, every shape, every emotion her brushes could evoke—it was all hers to command, a way for her to speak out at last.

And painting was acceptable, even to her mother. To a degree, anyway. Many young ladies sketched and created watercolors, and it was a most genteel pastime, a way to show off her fine education and artistic taste. And a pretty scene of the Roman Colosseum was a good thing to display after European voyages. Madeline even inveigled a few lessons at the Art Institute and a season of instruction at the École des Beaux-Arts in Paris.

But when she dared to want to exhibit her work in a public showing with other artists—that was most unacceptable. Unthinkable. She was a lady, a *Vaughn*, and it was time she behaved like one—marrying well, having children, becoming a Society hostess. Her own feelings did not matter, should never be shown. She was shut in a box again after that tiny taste of freedom.

Only Peter had rescued her from the stultifying life of her parents' Fifth Avenue house. Pete, sweet Pete, who had once shyly danced with her at their childhood cotillions. Who brought her flowers and books of poetry and walked with her on the beach at Newport. Who let her sketch his portrait, the day before their Grace Church wedding. Pete, who didn't care that she hid away in her attic studio when he went to his law office in the mornings, who didn't care that she didn't want to host grand dinners or answer calls when ladies left their cards in the brass bowl in the hall.

Then Pete went to war, to the muddy, bloody trenches of Flanders, and he never came back. And her whole world had turned black and cold.

She had felt as if she would drown in the darkness until she swam upward to the light. The pure, bright-blue, blinding light of New Mexico, a place she had barely even heard of before she'd seen it. And she'd found her art again. Through art, maybe one day, she might find herself again too. Might dare to find a new spark of happiness.

But not if her family had their way. They would lock her away, snatch away the light if they could.

"Mrs. Alwin?" A soft knock sounded at the door, the train porter waking passengers at last. Madeline hadn't been able to sleep at all and had been sitting up waiting for the dawn for hours. "Breakfast in fifteen minutes."

"Thank you, Oscar!" She quickly made sure her dark hair was still in its neat twist at the nape of her neck and her mauve travel suit was as tidy as it could be on a long voyage, then opened her handbag to look for a lipstick. Her mother's letter was still there, crumpled amid the compacts and train ticket stubs. She shoved it under a handkerchief and tried to forget it was even there. She was almost home now.

Maddie made her way out of her tiny sleeper berth and into the narrow corridor, looking toward the dining car. She was used to the constant swaying by now and wondered if she would even be able to walk on steady ground again. She couldn't wait to kick off her heeled shoes and feel the gritty dirt of her garden under her feet, the uneven plank floors of her little house.

Just thinking about it, about how close it all was now, made her feel a little lighter. The dark oppressiveness of the Vaughn mansion was falling away, layer by layer, like woolen winter cloaks and sweaters when the summer sun came out.

She smiled as she swung open the door to the dining car. Usually she was very first to breakfast, wanting to rise as early as she could to see how the landscape had changed in the night, how they passed from the green rolling hills of the East, to the flat plains, into the desert. She was surprised to see she wasn't alone this morning.

A man sat at a table at the far end of the car, reading a newspaper as he drank his coffee. He didn't seem familiar, so he must have gotten on at the last stop, when Maddie was tucked up in her berth with a book of Rembrandt etchings. He didn't glance up as the door opened; he seemed to be deep in his own world, his own melancholy thoughts. Maddie could tell they were melancholy because she often glimpsed just that expression in her own mirror. A faraway, hazy look.

She thought with a pang that perhaps he was struggling with some old mourning pain, just as she carried her sadness for Pete everywhere she went.

But, she was startled to notice, he was also quite interestingly handsome despite that sadness. Tall, lean, with broad shoulders beneath his tweed jacket, he had light-brown, close-cropped hair, just turning silvery at the temples, a short beard that emphasized his strong jaw, and lips that were almost too pretty for his rugged looks. It would be a challenge to sketch him.

Madeline hadn't really noticed men, handsome or otherwise, since she lost Pete, even though a few of her old friends had tried some tentative courting in the early days of her widowhood. It made her feel strange and nervous, almost schoolgirlish, to realize she noticed now. She ran her hands over her skirt.

"Your usual table, Mrs. Alwin?" the porter asked.

"Thank you, Oscar," she answered with a grateful smile, happy Oscar was there to interrupt her silly thoughts. She had gotten to know him rather well on the voyage, enjoyed his stories of his wife and four children in Atlanta, his grandmother who had once been a slave and who he now tried to give a comfortable old age. She had sketched him, drawings he could send back to them.

"Tea and toast?" he asked. "Maybe some eggs? We'll be at Lamy soon. Won't be time for lunch."

"Oh, yes, thank you, Oscar. Eggs would be lovely," Maddie said as she sat down at a small table across the narrow aisle from the strange man. "Just think—I'll have dinner at my own home tonight!" Dinner at home, made by Juanita, her lovely housekeeper, and eaten at her own table. Heaven.

"I bet you'll be happy to sit in your own chair, Mrs. Alwin," Oscar said, snapping out the linen napkin.

"Indeed, I will! Not that the train journey hasn't been excellent," Maddie said. "You'll be home soon yourself, won't you?"

"After California, I can turn around and head back."

"Don't forget to give me your address. I want to paint your portrait from those sketches so I can send a nice oil painting to your wife."

Oscar's smile widened. "Very kind of you, Mrs. Alwin. She'll sure like that." His smile faded a bit as he leaned closer to her to whisper, "I really shouldn't say nothing, Mrs. Alwin, but you've been so nice to me on this trip. I feel like I ought to warn you."

Maddie felt most alarmed at this uncharacteristic seriousness. "Warn me?"

"There was a bit of trouble last night. The train had to stop for a while. Did you not feel it?"

Maddie frowned as she tried to remember. There *had* been a bit of a jolt, but she had thought it was just part of a dream and had rolled over to go back to sleep. "What sort of trouble?"

"Just some bootlegging stuff along the track, I think, Mrs. Alwin. But it's all been getting worse lately. I just hope you'll be careful, a fine lady like yourself. No telling who might be causing trouble these days."

"Of course." Maddie nodded, a bit worried. There were bootleggers in Santa Fe, of course; everyone knew where to go to get their supplies. But there had rarely been any violent trouble, like there was back East, and never this far out of town. She hoped nothing bad was building up. "Thanks for the warning, Oscar. I promise I am always careful."

His smile returned. "Good. Now let me fetch you your tea."

Oscar left the car, and Maddie was suddenly all too aware she was alone in the dining car with the looker—and that there had been some kind of mysterious trouble in the night. The sunshine hadn't yet lit the scene beyond the windows, so she could see only looming shadows there.

To keep from fidgeting like a schoolgirl, she took her small sketchbook from her handbag and flipped through its pages. There were a few scenes from her visit to New York—towering buildings, narrow vistas down busy streets, a girl in the park with an ice cream. Then she reached her earlier drawings, rough images of her own garden, Juanita in the kitchen with her shy smile, the mountains rising up like protectors in the distance.

"That's very good," the man said, the sudden, deep velvet sound of his voice startling her so she dropped the book. He picked it up and handed it to her with a small smile.

"Thank you," she said, feeling shy and uncertain as she took it back.

"Are you a professional artist? Show in any galleries?" he asked, and she noticed he had a faint English accent that made his consonants crisp. It made him even more attractive, damn him.

"Not yet, but I hope to very soon." Olive Rush, a wealthy patroness of the arts and an artist herself, was organizing a show of local artists at the new Museum of Fine Arts, and Maddie had also had some interest from a gallery on Madison Avenue. She had her fingers crossed for both. "I do still have a lot to learn."

"It looks perfect to me. But I don't know very much about art, I'm afraid—not real art. Just what I like."

"That's really the only gauge as to whether art is good or not," Maddie answered. "Much like wine! My father is a great connoisseur, but I only know if it tastes good to me or not. But I'm sure you must see so much great art in London. The National Gallery, the British Museum . . ."

"I'm from Brighton." His smile faded a bit, and he glanced away. "Or was. I haven't been back there since before the war."

"Oh. I am sorry." Maddie smoothed her hand over the cover of her sketchbook, feeling flustered. She never wanted to bring up painful memories of the war to anyone. She remembered too well the haunted look in Pete's brown eyes when he came home for one last leave. "Where do you live now then, Mr. . . . ?"

"Doctor. Doctor David Cole. I was at a hospital in Washington, DC. Now I'm on my way to Santa Fe to do some work at the Sunmount TB hospital. I also have a friend who works as coroner; he could use some help, and I did a lot of that in the war."

"Santa Fe! That's where I live," Maddie said. Against her will, she felt rather excited that he would be there. It was a small place, only about five thousand people. Surely she would see him there. "I was just visiting my parents in New York and am on my way home now. I do hope you like it. There's no other such town in the world, I think. So much history in the buildings and the streets, and fascinating people. Artists and writers—they have parties all the time. And the mountains . . ." She realized she was babbling, *could* babble on for days about the beauties of her chosen home. "I'm sorry. I'm afraid I do get carried away sometimes by my—enthusiasms. My brother says I must be half mockingbird, chattering all the time."

Dr. Cole smiled, and tiny creases formed around his bright-blue eyes. "Not at all. I'm glad to meet someone who can tell me a bit about the place. I've never been this far west. I'm rather disappointed there are no tepees, like the paintings I saw at the Smithsonian."

Maddie laughed. "The natives here have never lived in tepees. And I can tell you far more than you would ever want to know about how lovely it is living here. I'm Madeline Vaughn-Alwin, by the way."

"How do you do, Miss Vaughn-Alwin? I don't think I've heard such a grand name since the last time I was at the Savoy."

"It's just Madeline Alwin, really. Mrs. Alwin. I lost my husband in the war."

His smile turned to a frown, that sadness back in his eyes. "I am sorry. Truly."

Maddie looked away, still unable to bear sympathy. "It—well, my parents do still insist I use their name as well.

Some sort of old family tradition. It's silly, really. Everyone in Santa Fe just calls me Maddie—my friends, anyway."

Oscar returned with her tea and breakfast just then, a steaming plate of eggs, toast, and bacon. Maddie smiled at him and chatted for a moment about when they would arrive, and as he left, she took a sip of her tea. *Earl Grey, lovely.* She did miss that about her mother's home, a fine tea every day.

As she buttered her toast, she realized that Dr. Cole was giving her a quizzical look from those lovely blue eyes of his. As well he might. She had been very chatty, which was not at all like her lately, no matter how her brother once teased her. She gave him a wary glance over the gold edge of her teacup. Surely he, an English doctor, wouldn't be involved in any bootlegging trouble, but Oscar's warning did reverberate in her mind.

"You do have a gift, Mrs. Alwin," Dr. Cole said.

"A gift?" Maddie answered curiously. She always thought she was very ordinary. Not pretty nor ugly, not tall or short, her artistic talent good but not great.

"Yes. You seem to be able to make friends with everyone."

She did wish she could make friends with *him*, but she didn't dare admit that. Not even to herself. "Do I?"

"A strange man at breakfast, an African train porter . . ."

"Oh." Maddie set her cup down with a rattle. She did hope he was not one of those people who dismissed everyone not like themselves. "Oscar has been very kind to me on this trip. And people are always fascinating. They all have such stories, such secrets. Don't you think?"

"Indeed I do," he muttered, looking away.

"Oh, look!" she cried, gesturing to the window, wanting to get away from such a conversation. Away from secrets. "The sunrise. It looks like we really are in New Mexico now."

The train was gliding along the crest of a mesa, giving passengers who dared to be up so early a transcendent view. The towering mountains in the distance looked like blue-purple shadows, hazy as the bright coral light peeked over them before bursting into the twilight sky in a blaze of gold, orange, and magenta, swallowing the fading stars.

The wild, fauvist light turned the desert around them to gold as well, the pale, mellow yellow and shell pink of her grandmother's old pearls. Veins of darker charcoal brown ran through the undulating pink sand sea, and a line of twisting, graceful willows in the distance showed a river was near. Their green-yellow-tipped branches waved like feathers, delicate against the hardier, scrubbier olive green of the cactus and chamisa.

"Just watch," Maddie said, entranced as she always was when she came back to New Mexico. She felt her soul go peaceful inside of her, and the clamor and confusion of New York, of her family and their pressures and exhortations, faded away. "Once the sun is up and the clouds clear, you'll only see blue. The bluest blue ever, bluer than the sea." She should know—she had tried to capture that very blue with her paintbrush so many, many times, only to end in frustration when paint could not match the vision in her head. The perfect blend to make that blue—she would surely never find it.

"It seems to vibrate. The sky," Dr. Cole said quietly. "As if the colors are alive."

Surprised at his wondering tone, Maddie glanced at him. He stared out the window as if entranced. "Yes. It's the light here. Scientists say it's the altitude. To me, it just makes the colors more vivid, more full of contrast. The brown and gray and green of the desert, the tan houses against the vast blue sky that never ends." The infinity of the horizons seemed like a refuge after being closed up in the city. This was a place of quiet beauty that always welcomed her.

"There is a strangeness to the beauty, though," Dr. Cole said. "A danger that humans will just be absorbed into it and never be seen again. I've never seen anything like it, and I've been to lots of places."

Maddie smiled as she looked at him. She had been right—people were always fascinating, always surprising. The English doctor had poetry in him. "Some people hate it here, can't get away fast enough. My housekeeper, Mrs. Anaya, is from San Ildefonso Pueblo. She says that the mountains here will either embrace a person or spit them out, if they don't truly belong."

He looked at her with a quizzical smile. "Which do you think will happen to me, Mrs. Alwin?"

Maddie studied him carefully, mindful of Oscar's warnings, of the fact that she didn't even know the doctor at all. "I think you'll be just fine here, Doctor. But I thought I said I was Maddie."

"I thought that was only for your friends."

"I have hopes for the future. It's easy to make friends here, Doctor. We all long for new faces, new stories. This is a small town. Just don't try to dig too deep for secrets. We all have lots of those too, I'm afraid." Santa Fe was indeed a town of black sheep, people cast far from their families by artistic desires, or romantic ones, or financial woes. She was sure Dr. Cole, with his sad smiles and pretty eyes, was no different.

"I can't imagine you have secrets all that dark—Maddie."

She just smiled and reached for her handbag. "I need to pack away my clothes. We'll be at the Lamy station soon."

"Maybe we'll meet again one of these days."

Maddie laughed. "There's only a few thousand people in Santa Fe, Doctor, and only a few hundred Anglo artists. I'd say we're bound to meet again. Everyone gets together on the portal at La Fonda most nights, unless someone is having a party. You should come. Unless you're too busy? There surely aren't enough doctors around, and lots of work for them to do." And she knew how hard doctors worked when there weren't enough of them. She had volunteered with the Red Cross when the boys came back from war, and then the influenza hit.

"Even doctors need a bit of fun sometimes. Just like artists, right?"

"I do hope so." She made her way through the now-crowded dining car. At the door, she glanced back to find Dr. Cole watching her with that unreadable little smile on his lips.

She hurried on her way, feeling rather pleased—and then very flustered. She hadn't felt that way about a man since Pete—that fluttery little nervous feeling deep inside. It was strange, exhilarating. And just a little scary.

CHAPTER 2

Maddie stepped down from the train car, pulling on her gloves as she studied the chaos around her at the Lamy station. It was the last stop before Albuquerque and the one closest to Santa Fe, so all the tourists got off there, as well as the patients headed for Sunmount and their nurses. People, all shouting and laughing and hugging, swirled around her, along with baggage carts, barking dogs, and vendors selling silver-and-turquoise jewelry and painted pottery. Nearby waited the long wagons from the hotels and resorts and a few exotic motorcars.

"Miss Maddie! Over here!" she heard someone call, and she turned to see Eddie Anaya waving at her. Her little terrier dog, Buttercup, was with him, and she barked and twirled in a white blur at the end of her lead, getting herself tangled up. The boy Eddie had been talking to, a tall, skinny lad with distinctive bright-blond hair, slipped away into the crowd. Eddie laughed and scooped up the dog as Maddie hurried toward them, full of happiness to see their familiar faces again.

Eddie was the oldest son of Maddie's housekeeper and gardener, Juanita and Tomas Anaya, and at fourteen, he was on the cusp of manhood. Maddie thought he would surely be a heartbreaker, with the glossy black hair that was roughly cut and unruly, the aquiline nose, and cheekbones as high and sharp as a mountain ridge. He hadn't yet grown into himself, though, and he moved with a self-conscious awkwardness she remembered too well from her own youth.

There was also a new bruise on his cheek, bright purple against his olive skin, and she knew she daren't ask what had happened. Not yet.

"Eddie, how lovely to see you!" Maddie cried. "And you, Buttercup. I hope you've been a good dog while I've been gone."

"She hasn't, Miss Maddie," Eddie said with a grin. "Ma's been at her wit's end."

"I'm quite sure that's not just because of Buttercup," Maddie said with a stern look. She did remember now that before she'd left Juanita had been worried that Eddie was getting some bad friends and she was concerned, though she didn't confide the details to Maddie. Maddie wondered if that was where he'd gotten the bruise.

Eddie kicked at the dusty ground, his expression abashed. "I've been watching myself. Someone has to look out for Ma now."

Maddie frowned in concern. Could Juanita be ill, or maybe one of the twins? "Is Juanita . . . ?"

"Ah, don't worry about us, Miss Maddie. We're all right. Us Puebloans always are, aren't we? We take care of ourselves." It was obvious that whatever the problem was, she wasn't going to find out from Eddie. "The pony cart's over here."

Once away from the noise of the station, the quiet seemed to close around Maddie like a comforting, familiar quilt. The road they jolted down was rutted and dusty, but the scenery to either side was beautiful, all light brown and dark green, enclosed by the all-encompassing azure sky. The cool, clear air smelled of piñon and maybe the fresh hint of a recent rain. They climbed slowly, creakily, up a hill and then slid down as Buttercup barked from Maddie's lap.

She cradled the dog in her arms, letting the slowness of the place lift her up. She smiled at the way the brilliant sunlight turned everything around them to a shimmering gold, and she couldn't wait to get to her studio, to pick up a paintbrush to capture it all again. But there was still that nagging concern about her friends.

"How is your mother, really?" she asked Eddie.

"Can't wait for you to get home," he said as he flicked at the pony's reins. The slow creature wouldn't be hurried, though, and kept placidly to her path. "She doesn't have enough to do with you gone. Drives the twins crazy, starching and ironing their dresses and hair bows so much they can't move in them. Your floor's so polished, you'll slide right down on it."

Maddie laughed to think of seven-year-old Pearl and Ruby, who loved digging in the dirt for worms and climbing trees, trussed up in lace frocks as she once was. They were like butterflies in little cocoons, struggling to break free and fly. "Poor Pearl and Ruby. I'll be sure to make a great mess to distract Juanita from them."

"Ma wants them to go to the Sisters of Loretto school, if they'll take 'em," Eddie said tonelessly.

Maddie was surprised. The girls, at a Catholic school? "Would the sisters take them? If that's what Juanita wants, I'd be happy to help with school fees, but it seems like the girls wouldn't like it."

Eddie shrugged, but Maddie could tell he was holding his real feelings tightly closed. "Ma thinks with some education they could be proper ladies someday, take care of themselves by teaching or typing in an office. The sisters do take some of us Indians. They think they can whiten our souls." He gave a harsh laugh. "And Ma's been going to church at the cathedral a lot lately. She's been talking to that new Irish priest there, Father Malone. He's helping her."

Maddie bit her lip before asking, "What does your father say?"

Eddie gave another laugh, a sarcastic sound too old for his years. "Oh, you know my dad. Ma doesn't say much about it to him. Says he'd never understand. And he wouldn't. He's not a churchgoer."

Maddie nodded, thinking of Tomas Anaya. Tomas was a silent man mostly, a harsh one to his children sometimes, and proud. Like everyone else in Santa Fe, he seemed to be a man of secrets. "How can he not know?"

"He hasn't been around much lately, that's how."

"Has he been going back to the pueblo?"

Eddie shrugged, trying to seem careless, but Maddie could see the expression in his eyes. That wary watchfulness, that hidden face she remembered from her own youth, when she thought grown-ups would never understand her thoughts and desires. "How do I know?" Eddie said. "He doesn't take me with him if he does. I haven't seen my grandma in ages, or my uncles, Ma's brothers."

"Well, I would miss you if you were gone, anyway," Maddie said, nudging his shoulder with a laugh, trying to distract him from his own painful, adolescent brooding. The Anayas were like her own family; Juanita and the children had done more than anyone except the mountains themselves to pull her out of the dark pool of her grief. She had to find a way to help *them* now. "No one else can get your sisters to settle down and let me work."

Eddie gave her a reluctant smile. "Only because I read them *Princess and the Pea* over and over. You should never have given them that book, Miss Maddie. They make the salt cedar tree their princess castle and won't sleep unless they have at least ten blankets under them." The cart creaked over the crest of a hill, and suddenly Santa Fe was spread out before them, a rolling field of pale adobe houses, shining tin roofs, and in the distance, the square towers of the French-style cathedral. "Almost home now."

Home, home, home. The sweet song of it almost drove the horrible patter of *duty* out of her mind. She hugged Buttercup closer and smiled.

It was a winding journey to her place on Canyon Road, where her little house and studio waited. The roads twisted in a puzzle she could never quite decipher, a warren of old donkey trails formed decades ago that constantly got her lost. But she recognized some of the shops and houses now and waved at the people they passed.

They turned at a dusty intersection, where dogs slept in the shade of an ancient horse chestnut tree and chickens clucked their way across the dirt lane. Maddie wanted to wave at the familiar houses as she had the people, the old brick school with its Victorian white cupola, the little general store where old men napped on the portal, the family houses with their open doors, their tethered goats and bright flowers. But she made herself sit calmly so she wouldn't look *too* crazy.

It was the middle of the afternoon now, the sun sliding overhead in a brilliant yellow-white blaze, and most people were indoors where there was cool shade.

Her own house, the precious little place she had bought with money that Pete had left her and thus was untouchable by her family, waited for her just beyond Garcia Street, across from a tiny grocery store. A tall adobe wall fronted Canyon Road, hiding her portal—what her parents would have called a veranda—and the large garden behind a gate painted bright blue. The blue shutters of the narrow windows were closed against the sun, and it all looked silent, sleepy.

But as soon as the cart rolled to a stop, the gate swung open, and two little girls flew out, their hair bows coming unraveled. "Miss Maddie, Miss Maddie, you're home!" they shouted. She had barely climbed down from the seat when they flung their arms around her, knocking off her velvet cloche hat and making her laugh. Buttercup leaped down and ran into the house, away from their noise, as Eddie set about unloading the baggage.

"You were gone *so* long," Pearl said.

"Did you bring us presents from New York?" Ruby demanded.

Maddie laughed harder and kissed the tops of their rumpled heads. They were getting taller now but still had their childhood lankiness in their wrinkled white frocks. She inhaled their powdery sweetness. "I did bring you something, but you'll have to be patient until I unpack."

"Is it chocolate?" Pearl, the one with the constant sweet tooth, cried.

"Or dolls?" Ruby said. "We've been writing a play, but we need dolls to act it out."

"Girls, stop that right now," their mother called. Juanita Anaya stepped out of the gate, wiping her hands on a dishcloth. Like the girls, she was tall and thin, with large, dark eyes and Eddie's fine cheekbones, and her shining black hair, flecked with gray now, twisted atop her head in braids. She smiled, but she looked tired, shadows turning purple under her eyes. "Where are your manners? Señora Maddie just got home and must be tired. She doesn't need your tomfoolery yet."

"Oh, I missed tomfoolery a lot," Maddie said, thinking of the silence in her parents' house. "I missed you all a lot."

"I hope everything is kept up all right for you," Juanita said. "Eddie, take that cart back to the livery stable, then come right home. There are chores."

"Ma . . ." Eddie began in a whining tone.

"Right back home!" Juanita snapped. Her abrupt tone was not like her, Maddie thought, and she remembered Eddie's vague hints of trouble and the bruise on his cheek.

As the cart creaked away, Maddie let the girls tug her under the portal and through the gate into her front courtyard, a flagstone space dotted with blue and purple pots filled with red, yellow, and white flowers, vivid against the pale-brown stucco walls. The front door was open, and beyond was the cool dimness of her house. Her *own* house, her refuge, not the stuffy, Victorian darkness of Fifth Avenue.

Maddie had loved the old house since the first time she'd seen it, with its whitewashed walls, its long drawing room with dark viga ceilings, and a fireplace at each end faced with bright-blue tiles. Narrow corridors radiated out from it to lead to bedrooms, sitting rooms, and the dining room. The furniture was sparse, painted chairs and sofas from Spain, scattered with embroidered cushions, shelves filled with books, bright artwork on the walls. Gray-and-red woven rugs were scattered on the polished floors. It was her refuge. She had added new electricity and plumbing but left the old character of the place.

"I have tea in the kitchen," Juanita said, "and some fresh cookies."

"That sounds wonderful," Maddie answered as she took off her hat and gloves. She sent the girls to find the valise that held the secret new dolls from Hamleys on Madison Avenue and followed their mother into the kitchen at the back of the house. The low-ceilinged space, with its long, polished table and benches, its brand-new sink and refrigerator, was spotless with Juanita's care and smelled of sugary fresh cookies and the stew that bubbled on the stove.

It should be a cozy place, as it usually was, but Juanita's expression was still tight, weary, and she wouldn't quite meet Maddie's gaze.

"Is everything okay, Juanita?" she asked as the housekeeper laid out a plate of the bizcochito cookies and a pot of tea. Maddie bit into the fresh, crumbly pastry, tasting the cinnamon and anise on her tongue.

Juanita flashed her a strained smile and turned away to stir at the stewpot on the stove. "What makes you ask, Señora Maddie? Is there something wrong with the house?"

"Of course not. The house looks beautiful, as usual, thanks to you. It's just that Eddie said—"

"Oh, that boy! He is going to be the death of me yet," Juanita snapped. The pot lid clattered to the floor, and she pressed her hand to her mouth. "He won't listen to me! I'm only trying to do what's best for him. He has to learn to get along in the world, and making trouble will get him nowhere. Nowhere but jail or an early grave."

Maddie nodded sadly. The trouble between the Indians, the Anglos, and the old Spanish settler families was the canker at the heart of her desert paradise, one she could never get used to. "He says that you want to send the girls to Loretto, that Tomas hasn't been around much."

"Tomas. When he *is* here, he doesn't say much," Juanita muttered. She reached for a bowl of carrots and started chopping viciously. "I should have listened when my brothers told me not to marry him, that we would never see eye to eye once the romance wore off. But I was only fifteen, no idea of the world. I had never even been away from the pueblo. What did I know?"

Maddie took a sip of her tea. At least her own family had liked Peter. Marrying an Alwin was the only thing she did right. "Your family didn't like Tomas?"

"Still don't. But it was good for a while, with us both working and then the children. And this place. Best job I've ever had, Señora Maddie, and that's the truth. I thought we could settle down again."

"Where has he been going lately?"

Juanita sat down in the chair across the table from Maddie, her shoulders slumped. "Who knows? I hear whispers—maybe a place on lower San Francisco Street."

"Really?" Maddie said sharply. She had never been down in that part of town herself. No lady, not even a bohemian artist like herself, had been. That was the territory of the brothels and the rougher sorts of speakeasies, not the bars where regular people went to dance and sneak a cocktail. Tomas had never seemed like that sort to her, but then again he was awfully quiet. Secretive. Not every man was like her Pete, sunny and open as a summer day.

She shook her head, feeling the familiar pang of sadness that was always there when she thought of Pete. "I'm sure he isn't going down there," she said, but she was afraid she didn't sound convincing, even to herself.

Juanita laughed. "He's done things like that before, when we were younger, but he always came back. This time feels—different."

"Different how?"

"I don't know." Juanita reached for the teapot and absently polished it with her cloth. "He's angry, even with the children. It's actually a relief when he's not around. He scares the girls."

Maddie propped her chin in her hand, her thoughts racing. "Is that why you want to send them to school?"

Juanita reached up to touch the small silver cross pendant around her neck. "They'll be safer with the sisters. They'll learn how to be ladies. Father Malone says he can help me find a place for them there."

But they could never learn to be *white* ladies. That truth hung between them, unspoken. Maddie had met some of the sisters, despite her own New York Episcopalian upbringing, and found them fair and kind, if strict. Their school was a good one, teaching math and science as well as literature, history, and ladylike things such as needlework and music. Pearl and Ruby would receive a fine education there. But how would they really fare? Would they feel as strange and awkward as Maddie herself always had as a girl at Miss Spence's School for Young Ladies? Except in art class. She had never felt strange there.

In art class, she could be entirely herself, could see people and nature and life in a way beyond the canvas. Maybe it would be the same for the twins.

"I can help you with the girls, if that's what you want, Juanita," Maddie said. "But are you sending them to school to protect them from their father? The bruise on Eddie's cheek . . ."

"I'm sure that wasn't from Tomas. I told you—Eddie has been running with the wrong friends," Juanita snapped. She jumped up and stirred furiously at the stew. "Tomas just isn't happy that Eddie's been getting into trouble."

Maybe getting into trouble with the same sort of people Tomas himself met on San Francisco Street? Maddie remembered Oscar's warnings on the train, that the bootleggers had been getting more out of control lately. "Could Eddie go to the boys' school if the girls go to Loretto? He might be a bit older than the average student, but I'm sure he would catch up fast."

Juanita shook her head. "Tomas would never let that happen. He never cared so much about the girls, but his *son* . . ."

"Eddie says he misses his relatives at the pueblo. Maybe if your brothers are still there, they could help too?"

"No, no," Juanita said vehemently. "That's in the past. There's nothing there for Eddie. Education, the church, the new ways—he has to find his way in *this* world."

Maddie felt the cold touch of sadness. They all had to find their way in a new, strange, often ugly world after the war, but Eddie and the girls seemed so young for such a burden. "If I can help . . ."

Juanita's expression softened, and she nodded. "You help plenty, Señora Maddie."

"You help me too. More than you can know." Maddie remembered when she first arrived in Santa Fe, sunk in her grief, hoping a journey across the country would heal her. Juanita had helped her make this house a true home, been a friend to her when she most needed it. "You're like my family, and if you have troubles . . ."

Juanita smiled. "Our troubles always pass, one way or another. Eddie will settle down, and Tomas will—well, do as Tomas does. Men are just like that."

"Men are like that," Maddie murmured. She thought of Pete, of his uncomplicated humor and easy presence. Somehow the memory of his smile changed into the doctor she had met on the train, the shadows in his beautiful blue eyes.

The girls came running into the kitchen with Maddie's trunk lugged between them, clamoring to open their presents, Buttercup barking at their heels. Maddie gave them the long white boxes, tied with elaborate pink bows, that she had carefully guarded on the journey. Pearl and Ruby squealed as they opened them to reveal two dolls, one with chestnut curls and one with blonde braids, each dressed in the height of New York fashion in drop-waisted, beaded silk gowns. A whole wardrobe came with them: fur-trimmed coats and feathered hats, chiffon tea frocks and satin ball gowns, velvet opera cloaks, with tiny shoes and parasols and handbags.

The colorful array looked odd scattered on the old flag-stone floor, but the girls shrieked with excitement. "We can put on plays!" Pearl cried.

"Oh, Señora Maddie, this is too much," Juanita protested.

"I had a doll like this when I was their age, and I adored her. When I saw them in the toy store window, I couldn't resist. They're as much for me as for them, I promise," Maddie said. She remembered her doll, Princess Clarissa, with so much fondness. She had been her only friend for a long time. "I got Eddie a new suit too, tailor-made on Madison Avenue, and ties and handkerchiefs." And a new hat and fur-trimmed coat for Juanita, but that would have to be carefully finessed to get her to accept.

She owed the Anayas more than she could repay.

"I can also talk to Eddie, if you like," she said. "Maybe an Eastern school would work, as a last resort?"

Juanita wiped at her eyes. "I'll think about it all. You won't say anything about this to Tomas?"

"Of course not." Maddie popped another cookie into her mouth. "I think I'll have a bath and change, then go out to the studio for a while."

Juanita nodded. "I expect you'll be glad to get back to work."

"Indeed, I will." Maddie had been itching to paint for days and days, images flooding her mind. There was only time for a few quick sketches in New York and for buying up art supplies to send back to Santa Fe. They were hard to come by in New Mexico.

"Dinner will be ready when you're done," Juanita said briskly, trying to dry her eyes and get back to a normal day. Maddie had the feeling Juanita would much rather be alone for a while, so she made her way to her bedroom at the back of the house. It was a small space, but pretty, with an old Spanish bed hand-painted with roses and ribbons, crowned with a pink-and-white-striped canopy. The same silk draped the windows, blocking out the afternoon sun, and covered her dressing table.

Behind that was a rare luxury on Canyon Road—a bathroom, with a real tub and water closet with hot and cold running water, laid with blue-and-white tile. Maddie had installed it when she moved in, attracting much curiosity among the locals.

She turned on the taps and dropped in some lavender salts before she went back to the bedroom, taking off her jacket and silk blouse and unfastening her skirt. It felt so good to get out of the dusty travel suit. Still wearing the shocking satin bralette and tap panties she'd bought at Madame Fleurie's (along with silk stockings and new satin nightgowns), she dug in her armoire for a plain cotton frock.

As she laid it out on her bed, a glint of light drifted between the slats of the shutters and shimmered on her diamond wedding ring. She studied it as if she had never seen it before, thinking of the doctor on the train. She had quite forgotten what it was like to think a man was handsome. And to wonder if he thought she was attractive too.

After Pete died, she had felt cast down into a deep, dark hole for so long. She had lain in bed, not dreaming, not thinking, just hurting. Until the healing light of New Mexico, she had thought she would never feel a spark of hope again. But through work and friends, she was slowly, slowly climbing up out of that abyss, clutching at that light.

In New York, the darkness had closed in on her again. But no more. Not now.

Maddie turned to her dressing table. Her reflection, backed by the sun through the shutters, caught her attention. She usually just glanced in the mirror to be sure her hair was tidy or to slick on a bit of pink lipstick before going out. Now she pulled the pins from her dark, heavy hair and let it tumble down to her shoulders. She wondered if she should get one of those shingled bobs worn by so many of the chic ladies she had seen while having tea at the Plaza. Her mother would be so scandalized, just as she had been when Maddie cast aside her corset for the satin bra!

The table was cluttered with perfume bottles and silver brushes, with lipsticks and ribbons. At its center was a silver-framed photo of Pete in his uniform, his blond hair shimmering, his funny, crooked smile fading as the photo grew older. How young he looked.

She turned away from his smile, the smile that had always made her feel so warm and happy and safe. That safety was only an illusion in the end, and she ended up alone, cast out into the ice and snow without that smile. Art was all she could rely on. Art and herself. It had been a hard lesson, but a valuable one.

Surely Juanita had learned that lesson too, that a woman could only rely on herself in the end.

Maddie dropped her pearl earrings and turquoise bracelets into her jewelry box, but she kept on her ring. She couldn't take it off, not quite yet. She shed her fancy new lingerie and went to slide deep into the warm bath, so deep her head went under and she floated.

How strange the world was from under there, she thought. The hammered tin ceiling above the tub was distorted, stretched into strange creatures, the painted blue trim shifting color like the sea. Yet maybe it was the world above the waves that was really upside down and crazy.

CHAPTER 3

An hour later, freshly bathed and dressed in her simple cotton frock and a pair of old cowboy boots a man on the plaza had once given her, Maddie made her way across the garden to her studio. Like her bath, the garden was a haven of beauty, created of towering old horse chestnut trees and one ancient salt cedar and laid out with flower beds and winding paths. Soon, it would burst into color and scent with honeysuckle climbing the walls, along with white and yellow roses, white daisies, pink peonies as large as dinner plates, and bushes of fragrant lavender and rosemary.

Tomas had helped her create it, working alongside her, digging into the dirt and sketching out pathways. She wondered what had happened to him now, where that man she knew then had gone.

She slicked back the still-damp strands of her hair into her hairpins, determined to get that bob soon, and wrapped a silk scarf around her forehead. Just behind the house was the guesthouse where the Anayas lived. In the back corner

of the garden was her studio, a small, separate adobe building with tall windows and skylights. She pulled open the
creaking door and slipped inside.

After the brilliance of the blue-and-gold afternoon light,
the shuttered dimness of the studio blinded her. She blinked
until finally she could see again, to find the one place she
missed most of all when she was gone.

It was a small space that had once been a toolshed, but
she had enlarged it a bit, adding the skylight and more windows, shelves for supplies and a sliding cabinet to store finished canvases. Her easel sat at the far end, with a table for
her palette and paint box, and a dais in front for models.
Photos and postcards were tucked on corkboards for inspiration. The air was warm and dusty, heavy with the scents
of oil paints and linseed.

The most delicious perfume in the world.

Maddie drew back all the window shutters, letting in a flood
of light. This was the one place where Juanita never cleaned, so
the shelves were dusty and the old blue rug on the floor needed
a beating. A few half-finished paintings were propped along
the walls, and sketchbooks were piled everywhere.

She smiled and felt herself settling down once again. She
took a deep breath and pulled away the cloth over the work
in progress on her easel. After weeks away, she realized it
was not half-bad. When she was in the middle of a painting,
it always drove her mad, as if the scene was never going to
come out right, never match the perfect vision in her head.

It never did, of course. Nothing could. Paintings took
on a life of their own, just like the breathing, living desert

and mountains around her, and she had to flow with them. Sometimes, something even better than what she had imagined emerged. And sometimes they ended up on the bonfire.

She didn't think this one was fodder for the flames, though. It was a portrait of Pearl and Ruby, just begun before she left. They sat on the dais, dressed in their white frocks and pink hair ribbons like proper young ladies, their arms linked, but there was the glint of mischief in their eyes. There was the sense that they would leap up and run away at any moment. Behind them were banks of flowers, just barely sketched in. The brilliant colors would offset the white dresses and dark hair so wonderfully.

She would have to get them to sit again soon, and that would be a challenge. Perhaps she should have held off on the dolls, she wondered, like a bribe? At least she could keep them in her studio and give Juanita a little rest.

She flipped through a pile of sketchbooks and found the very first one she used in New Mexico. She hadn't been meant to stop there at all. Gwendolen Astor, a cousin, had been going to visit friends in California and asked Maddie to join her on the journey. Everyone hoped it would help bring her out of her grief, and so it had, but not in the way they thought. When they arrived in Santa Fe, Gwen just hoped to see a few "real Indians" and buy some of their jewelry, but something in Maddie had stood up and paid attention again, after so long in that darkness. When Gwen left, Maddie stayed on. She stayed in the hotel at La Fonda while her new house was finished and then moved in.

Thank the sky gods of Santa Fe for that two-day stop, she thought as she studied those first tentative sketches of mountains and the curves of adobe buildings. She found a scene she thought might be a good start for a new landscape, a small, old cottage set amid the willows near a river, backed by reddish-brown cliffs.

She turned back to study the twins' portrait, considering the colors she needed to find in the new supplies she had brought back. Some rose madder for their cheeks, certainly. A bit of blue to catch the highlights of their hair. Plenty of flake white for the dresses, and a hint of pale blue and pink.

"Maddie! Yoo-hoo, my darling, are you in there? No use pretending you aren't; I can see that awful schmatta you're wearing. How many times have I told you to burn it? No more hiding your light under a bushel."

Maddie laughed and ran outside to find her neighbor and friend, Gunther Ryder, hanging over the picket fence that separated their property. He *never* hid his light under a bushel but was always immaculately dressed in stylish suits and brightly colored cravats, a straw hat on his curling red hair. But then he was a writer, not an artist, and the only mess he made was a bit of ink on his manicured fingers.

"Gunther, how I've missed you!" she cried, dashing over to hug him.

"Dearest, be careful or you'll spill!" he said, holding up two cocktail glasses. He kissed her on her cheek, laughing, and left a trail of his lily-of-the-valley cologne behind. "I have missed you too. It's much too quiet at this end of the road with you gone. You must never go away again."

"I think I can safely promise that."

"New York as ghastly as you feared?"

"Worse! But I did get some new clothes, you will be happy to hear."

"Thank God, darling. I could never bear to go out with you in that old black gown again."

Maddie laughed and drew back to look at him better. He was not much older than her, but his green, catlike eyes always seemed full of a hidden sadness, a life she couldn't imagine. He had traveled all over the world, especially to the Middle East, before settling in Santa Fe and always told wild, fascinating tales of his adventures. But Maddie was sure there was even more he did *not* tell. Maybe one day he would confide in her, but for the moment she was glad of his steady friendship and his amusing stories. Her mother would have hated the fact that he was her best friend now—Gunther (whose real name was Geoffrey) was a Jew *and* a man who liked other men. He was perfect in Maddie's eyes.

"Come, sit down, let me have that cocktail," she said, opening the gate between their gardens. "I want to hear everything that's been happening."

"Oh, my dearest, it would take all night to tell you. Here, let me add a bit more orange juice to that drink."

Maddie had already taken a sip, and she choked on the potent, searing liquid sliding down her throat. "Pojoaque Lightning?"

"Only the best, darling. There's a new man in town, you know, with a bar over on Palace Street. He brings it in for ten dollars a barrel, so no more driving out to Pojoaque. He's quite fabulous."

"Hmm." Maddie took a careful sip after he added more juice and found it palatable. It was doing its warming, delicious work, spreading to her fingers and toes like the sunshine. "What happened to Bertie?"

Gunther sighed and took out his silver cigarette case. He lit up a Gauloise and exhaled a stream of silvery smoke into the air. "Oh, dearest, he left for California, as they always do. And I'm afraid the new gorgeous bootlegger likes the ladies too much. But never fear—my true love will come along."

Maddie laughed. "I hope so." And maybe one for her too? That seemed like too much to hope for.

He took another drag on his cigarette and gave her a narrow-eyed look. "How was New York really, darling?"

"Oh, you know. The usual sort of stuff. Tea at the Plaza with Mother's friends, a dance at the Ritz. I did see the funniest play, *Madame Says Maybe*. It just opened there from London. Mother thought it was horrid, so I loved it, of course. I met a gallery owner or two, and they liked my sketches, so it wasn't all wasted time."

Gunther sighed. "I do miss it sometimes. The lights of Broadway and all that. But it's no place for black sheep like us, dearest, not with our horrid families breathing down our necks. Though if I'm black, you're surely only a mild shade of silver."

Maddie laughed. "Not according to my mother. She even wrote to me after I left, telling me how I have failed my duty as a Vaughn. I *am* glad to be home. I have so much work to do, and painting just doesn't go for me in New York. Do tell me all the gossip."

Gunther lit another cigarette and told her whose marriages were on the rocks, who was romancing whom, which artist was vying for a new gallery show, who had run off to Taos with whom. "All the usual; you haven't missed a thing. But what of you, my love? Any hot romances in the city?"

Maddie sipped at her cocktail and smiled. "My mother did try to set me up at that dance with her friend Mrs. Schuyler's son. He tripped on the dance floor and tore the hem of my new green silk robe dansant. And there was a very pretty actor in that play. I got his autograph after."

Gunther snorted. "All weak tea, darling."

Maddie hesitated, staring down into the orange, swirling depths of her drink. She thought of Dr. Cole, his blue eyes and that English accent. "Well. There was . . ."

"Oh, a tale, darling! I can tell. Spill all to your Uncle Gunther."

"It wasn't anything interesting. I just met someone on the train. A doctor. From England."

Gunther gave a happy sigh. "Oh, I do love an accent! Handsome too, I suppose."

"Very. Such blue eyes, and a beard."

"Delicious!"

Maddie finished her cocktail. "I'm a bit worried about something, though."

"Worried, dearest?"

"Yes. I've heard odd things about Tomas Anaya."

"Your gardener? That tall, broody fellow with the broken nose? He always seemed quiet, but how can he help it with such noisy daughters? It must be the only way to cope, to pretend you're not there."

"His wife says he has been acting strangely lately."

Gunther frowned at his cigarette. "You know, I think I may have seen your Tomas recently. I only noticed him because he seemed so out of place. It was a few weeks ago; I'd quite forgotten until now."

"Not at the Golden Rooster!" Maddie cried. She knew Gunther often went to the Golden Rooster Club just outside town, a place for gatherings of men of a certain persuasion.

"I am sorry, darling, but it was. It was rather late, and I was a bit tiddly, but I remember that nose. He didn't seem to be at all interested in it all, if that helps. Most unusual."

"Then why was he there?"

Gunther shrugged. "He seemed to have an errand or something like that. Really, that's all I remember. He did say something about that new place on Palace Street too. Maybe he runs rum for them or something."

"Most odd," Maddie murmured. She had never seen Tomas drinking, but some people were quite secretive about it. And a lot of bootleggers didn't drink much themselves, since it would drain away their profits.

"La Fonda tonight, dearest? The Hendersons are back in town, and Olive is still talking about a new exhibit at the museum for the summer. They should all have some lovely new gossip for us."

Maddie shrugged away the puzzle of Tomas at the Golden Rooster, resolved to come back to it later. "Oh, that reminds me! I did get you something in New York. You might like it for tonight. I'll just go fetch it."

"I do hope it's a new cravat!" he called after her as she hurried into the house, a bit unsteady on her feet after the Pojoaque Lightning. "Mine are all absolutely worn to shreds."

As Maddie made her way down the corridor toward her bedroom, she could hear Juanita and Eddie arguing in the kitchen, Juanita's voice growing higher as Eddie replied sullenly. Not wanting to embarrass them, she tiptoed into her room to fetch the tissue-wrapped parcel and tried to sneak back into the garden without being seen.

As she passed the kitchen door, she heard a sudden louder shout.

". . . my own life, Ma!" Eddie cried after a crash, as if something slammed into the wooden table. "I'm old enough to do what I want with it!"

"You're just a child," Juanita answered, her voice thick. "Everything I do is for you and the girls. You're all I have."

"That's not true. You can always leave, go back to the pueblo."

"You know I can't! Thanks to your father. It's all ruined."

"Just because he's such a shit—"

"Eduardo," Juanita shouted. "Never use that word! Where have you learned such language?"

"Where do you think?" Eddie muttered. "It's not like I have a choice now."

Juanita let out a choked sob, and Maddie started to go to her. She knew it would embarrass Juanita to be seen like that, but she couldn't just pass by. She took a step toward the kitchen when suddenly the front door behind her opened, sending light and a windy swirl of dust into the dark coolness of the house. Startled, Maddie whirled around, thinking it was Gunther, or maybe the girls, who would have to be kept away from the quarrel. But it was Tomas Anaya who stood there.

Tomas was a tall man and a powerfully built one, his shoulders broad under his worn tweed jacket. His gray-streaked black hair fell over his brow, hiding the expression in his deep-set dark eyes and setting off his crooked nose. His skin had the faint sheen of sweat, and he seemed almost pale, yellowish, as if he was ill in some way. Even his eyes had a yellow tinge to the whites of them. He scowled when he saw Maddie there and swiped his wrist over his forehead.

"Didn't know you were back, Mrs. Alwin," he said tonelessly. His swung the door shut behind him.

Maddie unconsciously took a step back. "This morning. Eddie fetched me from the train station."

"He's a hard worker when he wants to be."

Maddie nodded, studying Tomas carefully. He did seem ill, swaying on his feet, but he had been well enough to bully his son and wife lately. And what had he been doing at the Golden Rooster, or the new club on Palace? "Indeed, he is. I don't know what I'd do without him, or Juanita and the girls."

"They know their place; I'll say that for them," he muttered.

Juanita appeared in the kitchen doorway, her face blotched red with tears, her hair straggling from its pins. There was no sign of Eddie.

"There you are, Tomas," she said, tidying her hair and swiping at her eyes. "It's a good thing you're here. Eddie had to fetch Señora Maddie from the station this morning, and now he's gone to bring in the firewood. He's too young to be working so hard all the time."

Tomas scowled. "He's plenty old enough to do it, and more. He's almost a man. You coddle him too much, Juanita. If he worked harder, he wouldn't have time to get into trouble."

Juanita's hands curled into fists. "And I hear you make him do things he has no business at!" She glanced at Maddie, who was afraid her own shock showed too well on her face. Juanita took a deep breath, getting herself under control again. "Well, you're back now; that's all that matters. You can bring in the wood and get a fire started in here."

"No time for that. I just came to fetch some tools. I have a new job to do." He brushed past Juanita into the kitchen, his boots heavy and loud on the wooden floor.

Juanita frowned. "Are you at least staying for supper? I made stew, with some fresh roasted chilies."

"Not tonight, I told you!" Tomas shouted back. "You never listen to me."

"I—I'm just going to find the girls," Juanita muttered and hurried to the back of the house after her husband. There was a crashing noise but no more shouting.

Completely baffled, Maddie returned to the garden, glad of the sunlight and fresh air. Was there something strange in that cocktail? Maybe she had hallucinated the whole odd scene. What had been happening in her house while she was gone?

She dropped onto the bench next to Gunther, feeling as if she had just run a mile.

"Something wrong, darling?" he asked, lighting a new cigarette.

"I'm not really sure," Maddie murmured.

"Nothing a fresh cocktail and a good gossip won't fix," he said cheerfully. "Are those my new cravats then?"

Maddie looked down at her hands. She had forgotten why she even went into the house in the first place. "Oh—yes. Green silk with white dots, and a very pretty crimson I'm told is all the rage now in Paris."

"Darling, you *are* a muffin!" Gunther cried, unfurling the length of emerald silk. "I shan't look so shabby now; it's really been quite shameful. Now, my love, do tell me more about your lovely new doctor friend . . ."

Chapter 4

"Baby, baby blue eyes, stay with me by my side, 'til the mornin', through the night, can't get you out of my mind . . ."

"Is that really how the tune goes, darling?" Gunther cried as he led Maddie down the winding street, past the Loretto Academy toward La Fonda, the two of them hurrying arm in arm as they sang. "It's simply the bee's knees!"

"It's the most popular song in New York right now," Maddie said, a bit breathless from trying to keep up with his long strides. The path to the town plaza from Canyon Road was not a long one, but it was bumpy and rutted, and a person had to take great care walking it to avoid tripping in a pothole. It was especially perilous on the way home, after a cocktail or two.

"It sounds like a foxtrot to me." Gunther hummed the rest of "Baby Blue Eyes" as he grabbed Maddie in his arms and danced with her down the flagstone walkway, past astonished pedestrians on their way to promenade the plaza on the warm spring night. The bells from the cathedral tolled the hour, and she could glimpse their honey-colored stone towers against the sunset sky.

Maddie laughed as they twirled and spun, and Gunther whirled her right through the carved doors of La Fonda. "Gunther, stop, stop! I have to change my shoes before anyone sees me."

"Of course, dearest. We must always be at our sartorial best." Still humming, Gunther took off his hat and glanced in a nearby mirror, making sure his pomaded hair was still patent leather–smooth. "I have to say, I do miss dancing."

"We dance here," Maddie said. She took off the rubber rain boots she wore on the dusty streets and exchanged them for her new red-and-gold T-straps. She smoothed the skirt of her red ruffled dress, embroidered with gold flowers down the hip and falling to the knee in the newest style. There really was something to be said for new clothes; they were like putting on a disguising suit of armor.

"Not *proper* dances, like a *thé dansant* at the Ritz," Gunther said with a sigh. "We should organize something."

"There's Mrs. Nussbaum's tea room on the plaza," Maddie said. "Lovely cinnamon toast."

"Oh, no, darling! We couldn't do it there. We need a palm court or a rooftop garden."

Maddie envisioned a rooftop terrace, lined with green palms and ferns, the town spread out below them as they sipped their cocktails and an orchestra played. "You must organize it then. It sounds lovely. But I have so much work to catch up on, especially if there's to be a new exhibit at the museum." She thought of the Pueblo Revival–style fine arts museum, practically brand new as it had only opened in 1919 but already filled to the brim with the best art of the town and crowded with tourists and buyers. To show something there would be splendid, if she was ready for it.

"So I shall! It will be my new pet project. It has been rather dull here lately."

"What about your current novel?" Maddie asked. Gunther had already published two books to good reviews back in the East and said he was in the middle of a new one, a love story about an Indian maiden and a rancher.

Gunther frowned. "That isn't going so well at the moment. Maybe a party is just what I need to restart those creative juices." He straightened his new green cravat, studying it closely in the mirror. "By the way, dearest, I did remember something else about your fearsome Tomas."

Maddie remembered the quarrel she had overheard in the kitchen. She hoped there was indeed an answer to Tomas's strange behavior, one that might help set Juanita's mind at ease again. "Oh, yes?"

"I stopped in that wonderful new little club over on Palace. The one where the owner manages to get some lovely bottles from Mexico, not the usual local Lightning. I told you about it. I saw your Tomas going into the back room just as I got there. I thought he looked familiar, but it was too crowded to see anything else, and I forgot until now. He does get around, doesn't he?"

Before Maddie could answer, she heard a voice call, "Mrs. Alwin!"

She resolved to ask Gunther more about this new bar later. She turned to smile at Anton, the Swiss concierge of La Fonda, who oversaw everything that happened at the busy hotel and always kept her table open at the restaurant. He hurried toward her, an image of fashion in his well-cut black suit and shining golden hair, his signature monocle in his eye.

"Anton," she said, hurrying to shake hands with him. "How very lovely to see you again."

"We're glad to see you here again, returned safely to Santa Fe. Mr. Ryder has been moping without you."

Maddie laughed. "I doubt that. But perhaps you can help Mr. Ryder with a new scheme he has for a *thé dansant*. Guests here would surely love it."

She left Gunther and Anton talking avidly about dances, thinking she really needed to visit the bar before she faced everyone. As she moved through the lobby, she felt truly at home again at last.

La Fonda was the largest gathering place in town and the most elegant, though not in the stuffy New York way of her mother's favorite haunts. It was built in the style of a Spanish hacienda, surrounding an open courtyard with a large tiled fountain at its center. Maddie glimpsed the fountain and the ghostly shapes of metal tables and chairs in the twilight beyond the tall doors made of painted glass panes. In the summer when nights were hot, everyone liked to sit out there, but in the winter the south portal with its covered ceiling and massive adobe fireplace had to suffice.

The corridors around the courtyard were filled with fine painted furniture cushioned with sheepskin and bright Navajo rugs on the tiled floors. The reception desk was busy checking in a touring group that had just arrived, a quarrelsome knot of people still in their dusty travel clothes, demanding the best rooms. They would relax soon enough, Maddie thought, once the New Mexico light played its magic on them.

She skirted around them, heading toward the bar, but she never made it that far. "Maddie, is it really you?" someone called. She saw Olive Rush, the local organizer of all things artistic, marching across the lobby, several of their friends towed in her wake. Olive was an Eastern heiress, but one who, like Maddie, had never quite fit in there. She was an intellectual bluestocking, a Quaker, interested in art and architecture and native cultures, and she was superb at organizing exhibitions and tours of local art. Her velvet Navajo skirts twirled around her as she hurried toward Maddie.

"It is me, Olive, happy to be back again," Maddie said with a laugh. "I hear there is something new brewing at the museum?"

"Of course there is, and I must tell you all about it. But come and have a drink first. Everyone is dying to see you and hear what's going on in New York! Did you get to Stieglitz's gallery while you were there?"

Maddie followed Olive toward the portal at the back of the courtyard. There was already a crowd there, and someone had wound up a gramophone. Two waiters hurried past with trays of glasses, cocktails poorly disguised as "lemonade." Suddenly, Maddie felt a bit dizzy, overwhelmed by the noise and the happiness of seeing her friends again, and she swayed unsteadily on her new, high-heeled shoes.

"Maddie, are you quite well?" Olive asked. "You look pale suddenly."

"Just the long trip, I think. I just got back today," she answered with a smile. "I'll be in the ladies' necessary."

"Don't be long! We'll order you a drink."

As they turned toward the portal, Maddie went the opposite direction, toward the ladies' room that lay along a back hallway. It was quiet in that part of the hotel, the noise from the lobby just an echo. But when she pushed open the door, she found she wasn't alone there.

Elizabeth Grover, a young lady who was another refugee from the East, but not one who seemed to have any artistic aspirations beyond associating with artists, stood at the tiled counter in front of the tall mirror framed in hammered tin. She wore a gown almost as new as Maddie's, a green-and-gold creation embroidered in an Egyptian pattern with a matching headband on her short blonde hair. Elizabeth was bent over the counter, and when she jumped up at the sound of the door opening, Maddie glimpsed a bit of white powder around her nose.

Maddie carefully closed the door behind her. "Are you all right, Elizabeth?" she asked cautiously. Cocaine was certainly becoming a trend in New York, but she hadn't seen it before in Santa Fe. Pojoaque Lightning was more the local poison.

Elizabeth flashed a bright smile and quickly swiped whatever it was on the counter into her beaded handbag. "Never better, Maddie. I didn't know you were back in town yet."

"Just today." Maddie stepped up to the mirror and dug around in her own bag for her lipstick. "It looks like I've missed a lot of excitement since I've been gone."

Elizabeth laughed, a high-pitched, strained sound. "Not at all. When is it ever exciting here? That's why it's so nice."

"Something looks new here." Maddie gestured to the bit of powder on Elizabeth's nose, which was quickly wiped away.

"Oh, well, I did make a new friend, over at that new place on Palace. Have to keep things fresh somehow. Would you like a bit? They can get you some, very cheap."

"No, not at that moment, thanks," Maddie said, blotting at her lipstick. The new bar on Palace . . . Could it be the same place Gunther saw Tomas? Were they dealing in cocaine now, as well as bootleg liquor?

"Well, come on, the others will miss us," Elizabeth said.

Maddie nodded, still deep in concerned thought, and followed her out of the ladies' room. As they stepped out the door, a sudden piercing scream broke the pleasant hum of the hotel corridors. Panic flashed cold through Maddie; she remembered all too well the sobs of her mother-in-law when the telegram came about Pete. She ran toward the sound, which was only growing louder into a steady wail, Elizabeth on her heels. A boy with bright-blond hair brushed past them as he ran by, but everyone else was at the end of the hall.

Maddie followed the clamor past the first-floor rooms to a service hallway where a doorway led out to an alley-way behind the hotel. The door was open, and waiters and chambermaids, as well as a few guests, clustered around it, peering out at the night. Anton was also there, his arm around a sobbing chambermaid, his face grayish-white in the lamplight.

"Anton, whatever is going on?" Maddie asked.

"It's horrible!" the maid wailed. "I'll never forget it, never ever."

Maddie pushed her way through the crowd. "No, Mrs. Alwin, don't go out there!" Anton shouted after her, but it was too late.

In the narrow alleyway, piled with rubbish cans and faintly lit by the glow from the windows above, slumped a body. For an instant, Maddie thought it must be a discarded carcass from the hotel's kitchen, it was so dark with blood. Shocked, her stomach tightening, she made herself peer closer and saw to her horror it was a person, a man. His clothes were torn beneath the dark stickiness of the blood, his head twisted at a strange angle on the dirt of the alley. His face was covered in an odd, bright-red froth of blood. A man, discarded like a bit of trash.

A hot rush of bile surged in her throat, and she pressed her hand hard to her mouth to keep from being sick. "Oh, dear heavens," she gasped. "It's Tomas Anaya."

CHAPTER 5

"I can't bear it! It's too gruesome, like something in a detective novel," Elizabeth Grover sobbed. Her fashionable makeup had smeared, mascara and rouge making a positively Picassoesque pattern on her cheeks. Her blonde hair straggled from her beaded headband. Maddie feared they all looked quite so worse for wear, huddled like shocked refugees in the sitting room Anton had hastily arranged for them as they waited for the police to arrive.

"How could someone get chilled off like that? Here, in our own hotel?" Elizabeth cried and blew her nose into a lace-trimmed hankie. She seemed to be coming down hard from whatever high she had achieved in the ladies' room. Her eyes were red-rimmed, her hands shaking.

Maddie sighed as she gestured for one of the chambermaids to bring Elizabeth some coffee. That *was* the question, wasn't it? Who on earth would "chill off" Tomas Anaya and then dump his body near the busiest spot in town in such a gruesome way? What could it mean?

She felt that wave of bitter sickness rise up in her throat again and pressed her hand to her mouth. Gunther, who sat on her other side on the leather settee, seemed to sense that she felt all at sea and pressed a glass of water into her hand.

She gave him a weak smile, as if to pretend it was all in an evening's work, but even he looked solemn and worried. They all did, packed into that little sitting room to wait: Olive Rush and her artist friends, the sniffling maid who had been so unfortunate as to find the body, Gunther who now held her hand, and the bartender who Maddie had glimpsed hastily hiding the booze under the patio flagstones. They all looked pale and shocked and deeply, deeply nervous.

Santa Fe was usually a peaceful enough town, at least compared to her old home in New York. Besides the bootlegging, there wasn't much going on that would interest a crime novelist. Certainly not murder. Everyone knew everyone else, and if one person did indeed "chill off" another, in Elizabeth's words, everyone would have suspicions of who it was right away.

But now—now Maddie was stumped, and everyone else seemed to be too. In the silence, the seemingly endless waiting for who knew what, she wanted to scream. The walls seemed to be pressing in on them, and she longed for nothing more than to jump up and flee into the night.

She knew she couldn't. She owed it to Juanita, Eddie, and the girls to stay, to tell the police what little she knew, and to tell Juanita what happened when she got home. It was the least she could do for them now.

"Oh, no," she whispered. Juanita and the children. How would they bear this? She remembered all too well how it felt when they told her Pete was dead, the horrible, blank, yawning emptiness. Yet she had known what happened to her husband, why he died. Who knew what had really happened to Tomas? What would she tell Juanita?

Maddie buried her face in her hands, trying to black out the terrible glimpse she'd had of the—the thing that had once been a man. Tomas Anaya. He had been at her house only hours ago, arguing with his wife, larger than life. And now he had become nothing in some horrible way she didn't understand.

She took a gulp of the water Gunther had given her and made herself take a deep breath. She couldn't think about that part of it now, couldn't let it invade her nightmares, as Pete had for so long. She had to find a way to help Juanita now. But where to start? It all seemed so senseless.

Gunther patted her hand, and she glanced up to see him smiling at her gently. She smiled back and clutched at his hand, glad of its warm solidity. Whatever had just happened, she was still there among friends, and it gave her strength.

She remembered what Gunther told her earlier, about Tomas Anaya being seen in some rather disreputable places around town lately. He had also been arguing with his family, worrying his wife and making Eddie angry. But over what? Did it have to do with whatever activities he was involved with at those clubs?

And what had really happened to drive the Anayas away from the pueblo in the first place? To estrange them from their families? Maddie felt foolish for not asking them more about such things earlier, maybe even when Juanita first came seeking employment. But the Anayas, like almost all pueblo people, were deeply private about family matters. Maddie herself had come to New Mexico hoping to forget, and she certainly hadn't wanted to pry into other people's business. She wasn't her mother, who ruled her New York and Newport staffs with an iron fist.

But now she wished she did know more. It was obvious Tomas had been carrying some dark secrets. Dark enough to get him killed, and perhaps even to put the rest of his family in danger. And Maddie had only questions, no answers at all.

"Why can't we just go home now?" Elizabeth cried. "We don't know anything. It's so unfair to keep us here. Such a bore." Her foot in its high-heeled silver shoe was tapping frantically on the tile floor, and Maddie worried she would soon crash hard from the cocaine.

"A man has been killed, rest his soul," Olive said calmly. She was a Quaker, and Maddie had never seen her lose her composure at anything—except when she thought a painting had been badly hung at the museum. "I'm sure the police will just take our names and send us on our way, but if we can be of help we need to try."

"But I don't want to be involved at all!" Elizabeth wailed. "None of us should be. He wasn't even one of us, was he? What does it matter?"

Not one of us—just some Indian. Maddie's hand curled into a fist, and Gunther took it tightly between his fingers.

"A vicious murder in our town affects us all," Gunther said, his voice slow and serious, as if he tried to talk down a toddler having a tantrum. "We can't let such a scandal happen."

"What if a murdering maniac is on the loose?" someone said. "Something like Jack the Ripper? None of us are safe!"

"Jack the Ripper was over fifty years ago, and in England," Olive said with a sigh.

"That doesn't matter," Elizabeth said. "He's right. There are always fiends out there, just waiting to copy such things. I remember reading about it. They happen all the time!"

"Perhaps Anton could send in some sandwiches," Gunther suggested in a most reasonable tone. "None of us can think on an empty stomach."

"I'd rather have an orange blossom," someone muttered.

In any event, there was no time for either food or cocktails. The door opened, and Anton, who looked rather paler and more flustered than Maddie had ever seen him, led in a tall, portly man in a slightly worn suit and a uniformed policeman. Everyone went perfectly silent and still at the sight of them—even though Maddie was sure she had seen the young policeman before, out of uniform and enjoying an orange blossom or two himself.

"Everyone, this is Inspector Sadler," Anton said, discreetly wiping at his damp brow. "He is newly arrived from

El Paso, appointed by Mayor Winter himself, and will be looking into this—this most unfortunate matter. I am sure he will have it cleared up very shortly."

The inspector scowled as he studied their little gathering. "I'll take as long as I need to, er, clear things up, Mr., hm, Anton. I always do my job thoroughly. Considering who this was, he was probably only drunk and had a fight with some bootlegger. That's usually the way of it, both here and in El Paso."

Maddie felt her cheeks turn hot with anger all over again. Gunther's hand tightened on hers, and he leaned close to whisper, "My darling, who could *ever* trust a man with a mustache like that? It's positively Victorian. Prince Albert come among us again. I'm sure the inspector is under the delusion that it's 1860."

Maddie bit her lip to keep from giggling hysterically. It was indeed a very *un*–au courant bit of facial hair, swooping walrus-like in the middle of the inspector's round, red face. When he took off his hat, it appeared all his hair had quite migrated to that mustache. But it was his eyes she didn't much like. Narrow, dark, beady-bright—and far shrewder than his dismissive words made him seem. Those eyes swept over all of them, seeming to miss nothing and disapprove of everything.

He rather reminded Maddie of her mother, and she automatically sat up straighter.

It seemed her caution was entirely warranted. Inspector Sadler glanced down at a notebook in his hand, scowling. "Now which of you would be Mrs. Alwin?"

Maddie slowly raised her hand. "That would be me, Inspector Sadler."

He narrowed his eyes at her. "And you knew the deceased? You called out his name when he was found."

She straightened her back even further and folded her hands in her lap, smiling at him calmly as she remembered her old etiquette lessons. Her nanny had once said manners were a protection in uncomfortable situations, and she was right. "Yes. He is—was married to my housekeeper."

"Perhaps we could have a quick word then, Mrs. Alwin? It shouldn't take too long. Tony here will take statements from the rest of you." The inspector gestured to the uniformed policeman, who looked rather young and quite disgruntled to be given such a dull task.

"You can use my office, Mrs. Alwin," Anton said. "I will have some tea sent in."

"Thank you, Anton." Maddie rose slowly to her feet, smoothing the skirt of her now rather crumpled red-and-gold gown. It had seemed so pretty and cheerful earlier. Now it just seemed terribly frivolous.

Gunther gave her hand one last squeeze, one more reassuring smile, and she followed the inspector down the hallway to Anton's office off the lobby. Usually no one was allowed in there at all; Anton was the ruler of La Fonda, and this was his inner sanctum. Maddie was a bit disappointed to find it was just an office, with a desk cluttered with paperwork, filing cabinets, and a couple of chairs.

But she had no time to indulge any curiosity. The inspector waved her to one of the straight-backed chairs and took a seat behind the desk. After a maid left a tea tray and closed the door behind her, Inspector Sadler leaned closer and gave Maddie a wide smile. She didn't trust it at all.

She was an artist, she reminded herself. Her job was to be observant, to remember things so they could be brought back to life later. She had to do that now; it seemed more important than ever. She couldn't let herself be intimidated.

"Mrs. Alwin," he said slowly, as if she was a child. Just like Gunther had spoken to Elizabeth earlier. His accent was flat, the vowels bit off, as if he was from somewhere in the East. Maine, maybe? "I'm very sorry a lady like yourself should be in such an unpleasant situation."

Maddie took a sip of the tea. It was dark and strong and sugary, just what she needed to fortify her wits. "My husband died in the war, Inspector, so I'm not totally unacquainted with—unpleasantness. Not usually quite so close up, though."

"I would imagine not. You say the victim worked for you?"

"His wife is my housekeeper."

"And would you know of anyone who disliked the man? Enemies?"

Maddie remembered the way Tomas quarreled with Juanita and Eddie and the bruise on Eddie's cheek. Gunther's gossip about the unsavory nightclubs. But she couldn't prove the cause of any of those things. "I am from New

York, Inspector. My mother taught me how to make servants do their tasks correctly, but I know nothing of their private lives. Nor do I want to." That was not entirely true. She and Juanita often sat up late laughing over movie mags or talking about what their dreams had been when they were young, hopes for the girls, plans for the house. But she didn't know much about their private lives before they came to Santa Fe. That was their business.

Until now.

"The Anayas are good workers," she said. "I seldom saw Tomas. He took care of the garden."

Inspector Sadler scribbled something in his notebook. Maddie tilted her head to try to catch a glimpse, but the man's handwriting was atrocious. "So you don't know what he did in his off hours?"

"I have no idea." That, at least, was totally true. Maddie wasn't sure at all what Tomas did in places like the new speakeasy on Palace Street.

"No family problems?"

"Like I said, Inspector Sadler, such things are not my affair. They do their work well."

"But they don't live wherever it was they came from?"

Maddie took another sip of tea. "I believe they are from the pueblo at San Ildefonso. But no, they live here in Santa Fe, in a guesthouse on my property. It would be a rather long drive for work every day, don't you think?"

Inspector Sadler studied her for a long moment, but Maddie had enough practice in not giving away all her thoughts, thanks to her mother. She merely looked back with a calm smile.

Inspector Sadler shuffled his papers. "There will probably be an inquest, Mrs. Alwin, and you might be called to testify."

"I'm happy to assist in any way I can, Inspector. Mrs. Anaya is a most excellent housekeeper."

"Be that as it may . . ." He snapped the notebook shut. "Seems a waste of time, if you ask me. Probably just some drunken brawl. You know what people can be like when they drink. I'm here to help clean up this town, and that will serve to make sure this doesn't spill over to others as well."

Maddie pressed her lips together hard. "Quite," she said shortly. "If that's all . . ."

"For now, Mrs. Alwin. I'll have to send Tony to tell the widow what happened."

Maddie shuddered to think of Juanita hearing what happened from a policeman. "I can tell her myself, if that is quite up to protocol."

The inspector waved it away as if it was no matter to him how Juanita found out her husband was dead. "Sure, whatever you'd like."

Maddie escaped the office as quickly as she could. She saw that the uniformed policeman was still talking to the others, and she decided to wait for Gunther before she left. As much as she wanted to be safe at home by her own fire, she also dreaded telling Juanita what happened. And she didn't relish the thought of being by herself in the darkened, narrow streets either. *Jack the Ripper, indeed.*

She went back to the ladies' room, thinking she could at least tidy her hair and fix her lipstick, small actions she had some control over. But as she turned down the corridor, she saw she had made a mistake, for two more policemen were in the process of removing the body.

It was on a stretcher, covered with a stained blanket. Maddie pressed herself tight against the wall. She didn't *want* to look; everything in her urged her to turn away. But she remembered what she had decided about observation and made herself watch as they went past her.

Tomas's hand had escaped the cover, flopping and so pale it looked blue-white. Old scratches stood out dark red against the paper-whiteness. Yet the fingernails were the oddest color, almost blood purple, stark next to the old sheet. Then one of the policemen yanked the cover up, and they were gone. Maddie could hear the maidservant who found the body sobbing softly, and she was led past by a tall, thin boy with a hat pulled low over his brow, muttering softly to her. The boy looked strangely familiar, but they were gone before she could get a second look.

Maddie spun around and raced to the ladies' room before she could finally let herself be sick.

CHAPTER 6

"A re you sure you don't want to come home with me for a while, Maddie dearest? I could mix us up some Pink Ladies, help you gather your thoughts," Gunther said as they drew near Maddie's house.

Light gleamed in the windows, amber gold and welcoming. Juanita would have kept them burning for when Maddie got home, even as Juanita herself tucked the twins up in their bed and retired to read her evening prayers. Juanita always worried about Maddie when she went out at night, which made Maddie feel even worse now, knowing Juanita would welcome her home without knowing the terrible news Maddie carried.

She shivered at the thought of what she had to do and at the exhaustion that seemed to pull her down and down until she was sure she would sink into the dusty earth. Her eyes itched with tiredness and she rubbed at them hard, but she couldn't erase the images of what she had seen that night.

But surely her Pete had seen even worse in France, and he had faced it. She could too. Juanita was going to need her help.

"No, Gunther darling, but you are a love for asking," she said, forcing herself to smile. "If I drank one of your concoctions, I would go straight to sleep. While that would be lovely, I have to tell Juanita what happened. She can't hear it from that inspector." She shivered again, remembering that man's all-seeing little eyes.

Gunther nodded, frowning. "He was a chilly one, wasn't he? I wonder why they brought him onto the police here. Seems too perceptive and suspicious by half."

Maddie bit her lip as she thought of Inspector Sadler and his Eastern accent, his stoic demeanor that gave away nothing but seemed to see everything. The police department in town was a small one, and rather notoriously lackadaisical. Bootlegging was widespread and seldom caused the purveyors any trouble unless they failed to grease the right palms, and public violence was rare. Why *was* the inspector there, and right as a murder happened too?

Then again, she thought with a pang, the murder might not have attracted attention at all if it hadn't happened at *the* social hub in town, the place where everyone with money and influence tended to congregate. It would just be thought of, like the inspector himself said, as a drunken fool getting into trouble. In his own words, he was there to "clean up the town" and make sure such things didn't happen to other people. Important people.

And that made Maddie very angry indeed. She could feel it in the pulsing of her heart in her ears, the tightening of her stomach. Juanita had said Tomas was involved in something mysterious lately, something that worried her. Surely whatever it was might have caused his murder? Juanita deserved some answers, and Maddie very much feared no one would really begin to search for them.

She hated the helpless feeling that realization gave her, the same feeling she often had with her parents—that there was no way to *make* someone do what was right.

But there was one thing she could do. Had to do.

"At least let me come inside with you," Gunther said. "I know I'm quite the silly flibbertigibbet, but I can help you with this."

Maddie reached out and squeezed his hand. "You are certainly *not* a flibbertigibbet." And he wasn't. He wanted people to think so, but she knew that he was very serious inside, thinking too much about everything, just as she did. It was one of the reasons they were such good friends. "But I have to do this myself. I owe it to Mrs. Anaya, for all she's done for me."

Gunther nodded. "You do what you must, my darling. But do come over for lunch as soon as you can. Tomorrow, maybe. We can talk it all over."

"I will." She watched as Gunther made his way through their connecting gate into his own garden. He lit a cigarette, and the tiny red flame was like a beacon in the night, quickly vanishing. And Maddie was alone.

She glanced up at the stars, so bright and glittering, like silver sequins scattered across a rich black velvet gown. Before she came to New Mexico, she had never seen such stars. In New York, they were hidden by streetlights and skyscrapers. Here the sky seemed so close she could reach up and touch it or jump up and lose herself flying through the galaxy. Sometimes she even let herself fancy that one of those stars was Pete, that he beamed down at her and her new home.

Tonight, though, that vastness made her feel very alone and deeply sad. How fast life could change, could shatter into a thousand shards, just like all those stars. How hard it was to put it all together again.

She turned away from the impersonal glow of the stars and hurried into her house. Just as always, Juanita had left two of the lamps on in the sitting room. The soft glow undulated over the carpets and cushions and paintings she had collected so carefully and loved so much, but now it all looked strange. Almost like a place she had never even seen before. Shadows moved around the vigas of the ceiling, and all she could think of was ghosts.

"Don't be silly," she told herself sternly. She had to be strong now. She knew she could do it. She'd done it when Pete died, when she volunteered at the hospital, when she moved alone to Santa Fe. She could dig deep now and do it again.

The house was silent, but she could see a bar of light peeking under the kitchen door. She took off her dusty boots and tiptoed over to push the door open.

Juanita usually went to bed after tucking in the girls, but she was still awake, almost as if she sensed it would be no ordinary evening. She sat at the table in her pink quilted dressing gown, her long braid of black hair snaking over her shoulder. A cup of tea was in front of her, the steam rising like a gray plume, and she just stared at it intently, as if her thoughts were far away.

"Juanita," Maddie said softly.

Juanita visibly startled, her shoulders twitching as her head swiveled toward the door, her eyes wide. "Oh, Señora Maddie," she said, her voice hoarse. "I didn't hear you come in."

Maddie sat down across from her, trying to organize her thoughts, to know what to say. What had her mother-in-law told her when that telegram came? She couldn't remember at all. "I'm sorry I startled you. I didn't think anyone would still be awake."

"I was waiting for Eddie. He still hasn't come home after that silly quarrel this afternoon. Foolish boy." Juanita pushed her chair back from the table. "Let me get you some tea."

"No, thank you, Juanita. I . . ." Maddie swallowed hard past the sudden hard lump that formed in her throat and plunged ahead. "I'm afraid I have some bad news."

Juanita sat back down in her chair, heavy and fast, as if she could no longer stay upright. "About Eddie?"

Maddie shook her head. "I haven't seen Eddie since this afternoon either. No, it's—it's Tomas. I'm afraid he's dead."

Juanita's face went ashen, and her hand froze as she was reaching for her teacup. Other than that, she didn't move at all. Maddie remembered that feeling very well, as if time turned to ice. "How? How do you know this?"

"His body was found at La Fonda, not long after I arrived there."

A frown flickered across Juanita's face. "What was he doing there?"

"It was in the alleyway behind the hotel," Maddie said, dreading the explanation she had to make. She knew she had to say it fast. "He had been, well—killed. A maid found him. I—I'm so very sorry, Juanita."

Juanita blinked twice and shook her head. "That fool."

Maddie was surprised at the words, the sudden, sharp vehemence of them. She remembered that Juanita said her husband had been acting strangely lately. But foolish? "Do you have any idea who could have done this?"

"He wouldn't tell me what he was doing lately. He was so angry all the time, he . . ." At last, the ice cracked, and she let out a sob. She buried her face in her hands. "I didn't think it would come to something like this! How could it? My poor babies. What will I tell them?"

Maddie quickly got up to pour Juanita another cup of tea, adding plenty of sugar as they had for her at La Fonda. She pressed it into Juanita's shaking hand and urged her to drink deeply. "I'll help you any way I can. I'll help you tell the children. It can wait until morning."

Juanita nodded and sipped at her tea in silence for a long moment. "Tell me what happened, Señora Maddie. What you saw there."

Maddie told her about the maid's screams, the way the police came and the inspector asked questions of everyone who was there. She didn't mention the state of the body or the way she saw it hauled away.

"Inspector Sadler took my address, so he might call here with some questions," she finished.

Juanita's eyes widened, and she clutched at the collar of her robe. "Ask questions *here*? Why would he do that? I won't be able to tell him anything more than you did."

Maddie was surprised at Juanita's sudden fear. "I'm sure it's just routine when a murder is committed. Nothing to worry about. We'll stay together the whole time."

"But—the children . . ."

"I'm sure he won't bother the children," Maddie said, though she really didn't know. She couldn't read the inspector at all.

"They won't know anything, just like I don't," Juanita murmured. "Tomas didn't talk to me at all anymore. He wouldn't listen to anything."

"Juanita, you told me earlier that Tomas had been behaving—oddly lately. That he and Eddie were arguing about Eddie's friends . . ."

"Eddie had nothing to do with all that!" Juanita cried. She slammed the teacup down on the table, sloshing liquid on the polished wood surface. Maddie was startled at the sudden movement from the usually gentle and mild Juanita. "Whatever Tomas was doing, it was nothing to do with them."

"I know." Maddie reached out to press her hand. Juanita's fingers were cold and shaking. "And that's all you have to tell the inspector, if he even comes around here at all. I'm sure he has a lot to occupy his time."

But she had a sneaking suspicion Inspector Sadler *would* come around. Surely there was some reason a sleepy town like Santa Fe would bring in a man like that. She had the feeling he was some kind of Prohibition agent, sent from El Paso to "clean up."

Did Tomas figure into that somehow? And what did Juanita really know? For Maddie was quite sure her friend knew more than she was saying.

Maddie feared she was too tired to try to fathom it all yet. The shock was fading away, drowning her energy until she felt quite boneless and worn-out. She couldn't even imagine how Juanita was feeling.

"You should go to bed," Maddie said. "I can give you some of the sleeping powder the doctor in New York gave me, if you like."

"No, thank you, Señora Maddie," Juanita said. She sat up straighter, visibly gathering her tattered strength. "I'll just look in on the girls first. It will be time to start breakfast in a few hours."

"Oh, never mind about breakfast! In fact, if you want to take some time off, take the children to visit your family . . ."

Juanita shook her head. "I'd rather just keep on with my work for now. Thank you for telling me, Señora Maddie. I'm glad it was you, and not some strange policeman."

"Of course." Maddie watched Juanita make her way out the kitchen door, toward the guesthouse.

Maddie tiptoed to her own bedroom at the end of the house. She went through the motions of changing into her nightgown, rubbing cold cream on her cheeks, brushing her hair, hardly realizing what she was doing.

She fell into her bed and pulled the fluffy silk blankets close around her, as if they could be a protective cocoon. She was so achingly exhausted, she was sure she would fall right asleep. Yet oblivion wouldn't come. Her mind insisted on running back and forth over every second of the evening, like a film reel endlessly unspooling.

She heard the maid's screams, saw Elizabeth leaning over the counter with her white powder, smelled the sourness of the alley. Remembered the sight of Tomas's gray hand flopping from under the sheet. Surely that meant he had not been dead long, if rigor mortis hadn't yet set in? She knew that much from the detective novels she liked to read. And the dark color under his nails. It was strange, and she tried to remember if she had seen anything like that in her hospital volunteer days.

Finally, she gave up and turned on her bedside lamp. She reached for the sketchbook and charcoal pencils she kept in the nightstand drawer and started to draw everything she remembered. The way the body was left in the alley, who was there. The pale hand.

Only once she had recorded it all on paper did she take one of her sleeping powders and fall into blessedly dreamless sleep.

CHAPTER 7

Something bright and insistent pierced through Maddie's gritty eyelids, and she groaned and rolled over in her bed. She reluctantly opened her eyes to see that she had forgotten to close the shutters before she fell asleep, and now the bedroom was flooded with the pure white-yellow morning sunlight. She blinked, still half-caught in the darkness that had enveloped her all night.

Then she remembered everything that happened. Tomas dead. The inspector's questions. The horrible, horrible night.

She bolted straight up off her pillows, and pain shattered her brain. She felt as if she had drunk far too much, but there hadn't been time for even one cocktail last night, and she had turned down Gunther's divine Pink Ladies. She shook off the fuzzy feeling in her head. There was no time for that today if she was going to be of any help to Juanita, no matter how much she really wanted to pull the covers back over her head.

She climbed out of bed and padded into the bathroom to bathe and find some lipstick. The chalky-gray visage and tangled hair that greeted her in the mirror was sure to scare anyone who took one look at her.

When she made her way to the kitchen, she found a covered breakfast tray on the table and a kettle of tea on the stove. The back door to the garden was open, letting in the cool morning breeze, and she glimpsed the twins sitting there on the steps with their new dolls. Buttercup lay at their feet. Juanita was nowhere to be seen, but Maddie could smell the acrid tinge of dye coming from the small laundry room off the kitchen.

She poured herself a strong cup of tea, snatched a piece of toast off the tray, and peeked into the laundry room. It was filled with tubs and drying racks, the air steamy, and Juanita was stirring a tangle of dresses in a vat of inky dye, making mourning clothes.

Maddie remembered all too well how her maid did that as soon as the telegram about Pete came to the door, and the toast turned to ashes in her mouth.

Juanita's eyes were red-rimmed but dry, her cheeks pink from the work, her hair straggling from its usually tidy braided bun. She went about her work in silence, her face expressionless.

"How are you this morning, Juanita?" Maddie asked softly.

Juanita glanced back over her shoulder. She didn't look surprised to see Maddie there. She didn't look like anything at all. Maddie remembered that numb feeling too. It had been a blessing of sorts, for a while. Better than the sharp, stabbing pain that came after.

Juanita tucked a lock of hair behind her ear. "I'm well enough. There's eggs and oatmeal on the table too, if you want them, Señora Maddie."

"I'll heat it up later. Did you and the girls eat? Have you told them what happened?"

Juanita shrugged. "I told them, but they don't seem to have understood quite what it means yet, poor things. I got them to take some toast by letting them have some of that marmalade of yours they love so much. I'm afraid they ate a whole jar. They'll have bellyaches later."

"They can eat all the marmalade I can find down at Kaune's Grocery later, if they like. Did *you* eat? You'll need your strength." Maddie thought she should say that, since everyone said it after a death. Her own mother had insisted on plying Maddie with steak and chops after Pete died, declaring she needed the iron, but Maddie doubted it had helped much.

"A bit. But . . ." Juanita frowned, and Maddie could tell she was debating whether to say something. Finally, she nodded. "I'm afraid Eddie hasn't come home."

"Not at all?" Maddie cried.

"His bed hasn't been slept in. I—" Juanita's voice cracked, and she stirred harder at the clothes. "That boy will give me the ague! I haven't seen him since yesterday. He doesn't even know about his pa, and I have no idea where he could be. He could—he could be dead too!"

She suddenly dropped the wooden paddle and buried her face in her hands. Maddie hurriedly put down her half-empty cup and went to put her arm around Juanita's shoulders. She didn't, couldn't, say the words that hovered all around them, that Eddie had been fighting with his father, had been furious with him. What if—what if something terrible happened between them?

"I'm sure he will be home at any moment," Maddie said. "You said he's been running with some new friends. They were probably just out and about being silly boys. Should I go look for him?"

Juanita swiped at her eyes. "I wouldn't know where to start. I'm sure you're right, Señora Maddie. He'll be home soon; he never stays gone too long. He always comes back to help with the day's work. He's a good boy, really."

Maddie could hear the strain in her voice, the desperation to believe. "Of course he is."

"I just wish—wish . . ." Juanita's voice broke on a sob.

"Mama?" a tiny voice whispered from the doorway. "What's wrong?"

Maddie glanced back to find little Pearl standing there, clutching at her doll. The girl's dark eyes were wide and frightened.

"The dye is making my eyes water, that's all," Juanita said. She turned away as if to hide her tears, her own fears, from her daughters. "You must go and play with your sister."

"Maybe I could persuade the girls to help me in my studio," Maddie said, giving Pearl a bright smile. "I'm terribly behind on the portrait, and it would be lovely to have it in the next museum exhibition."

Juanita nodded, and Maddie took Pearl's hand to lead her outside. The girls always loved to be in the studio, to look at the colorful paints and pastels, and to help Maddie prepare canvases and mix new pigments. The challenge was usually to get them to sit still long enough to get some work done on their portrait.

Not today, though. Today they were quiet and subdued, holding hands as they took their poses on the draped dais. Maddie busied herself organizing her supplies, making a note that she needed to order some more new tubes of paint, and adjusted their chairs so the light from the window was just right. She asked the girls questions about their new dolls, what their names were and where they came from, the parties where they would wear their pretty clothes, and gradually the girls started talking again. They even smiled a bit.

"Mine is named Phoebe," Ruby said, holding up the doll with blonde braids. Phoebe wore a filmy pale-green chiffon tea dress, much too early in the day, but like an eccentric duchess, Phoebe didn't seem to care. "And Pearl's is Alexandra, like that pretty English queen in your book."

Maddie smiled. The girls loved the books about British royalty she had brought back from her own European tour so long ago and always begged to look at them, to hear about her court presentation all over again. A more different world than their Santa Fe life was hard to imagine. Yet Juanita seemed sure school would widen that world for them.

But maybe now she just wanted to keep them safe?

"And what would Alexandra wear to meet her name-sake?" Maddie asked, drawing the soft line of their hair, the two dark heads bent close together.

"She would need a tiara," Pearl said. "And feathers. I would wear pink. Pink's my favorite." She went quiet, studying her doll's blonde curls. "But Mama says we have to wear black for a while now, since we won't see Pa again."

Maddie put down her pencil and studied the girls' faces in concern. They looked solemn, but their eyes were dry. Mostly they just seemed rather puzzled. "I know how sad you must be, my dears. I've had to wear black for people I loved too, and I felt terribly lonely and worried. But I promise you're never really alone."

"Was it for your husband, Señora Maddie?" Ruby asked. "The one who died in the war?"

Maddie swallowed hard before answering. "Yes, among others. And I still miss him, but being here with you has helped me."

The girls glanced at each other, talking to each other without words as they so often did. "Was it because Pa yelled at Mama and Eddie that he was struck down?" Pearl asked. "Sister Angelica at church says mal—mal . . ."

"Malice," Ruby supplied.

"Malice in our hearts means we don't trust God to make things right, and we'll be struck down," Pearl said. "Is that what happened?"

"I bet it was the way Pa smelled like drink and smoke whenever he came home that did it," Ruby said, solemn beyond her years. "That's when he argued with Mama."

Maddie wiped her hands on a rag, feeling the slight, cold touch of panic. She was surely the last person equipped to tell seven-year-olds about mortality and sin! She barely ever went to church. "I am sure that was not it. I think . . ."

She was saved from answering by a frantic knock at the studio door. It swung open to reveal Juanita standing on the steps, her eyes wide with fear.

"Señora Maddie, you must come at once!" she cried. "That man named Inspector Sadler is here. He says they're looking for Eddie!"

★   ★   ★

Maddie quickly tidied her hair and removed her paint-stained work apron, smoothing her sailor-style pale-blue day dress. She had to admit her stomach fluttered a bit nervously at the thought of facing the inspector again, and she wished she had some sense of her mother's imperious hauteur to carry her through. Her mother's daily armor of Edwardian satins, corsets, and pearls wouldn't hurt either.

But there was no time to change into more formal clothes or do anything at all. The fear in Juanita's eyes, the way the girls instinctively ran to cling to their mother, told her she had to stay calm.

"Did he say why they were looking for Eddie?" she asked as she pushed the pins tighter into her twist of hair.

Juanita shook her head. "But he has a policeman in uniform with him. That can't be so good."

Maddie had to agree, remembering the young man hovering with the inspector last night. He was polite enough with the ladies at the hotel, but the police weren't always noted for their fair treatment of the Indians. "And you still haven't seen or heard from Eddie yet?"

"Not a word. It's not like him." Juanita's lips tightened, and she clutched at her girls as she whispered in Maddie's ear, "Do you think he *could* have been with Tomas last night?"

With him and shared his fate? Maddie shuddered at the thought. "I am sure he wasn't. Didn't you say Eddie had been avoiding his father lately? I didn't see anything at all that would indicate Eddie was there last night."

She had only glimpsed the body in the alleyway and that blond boy darting away. Suddenly, she realized where she had seen him before. Talking to Eddie on the train platform the day she came home. And then he was walking with the sobbing maid later at La Fonda, a cap pulled over his hair. Who was he? One of Eddie's recent "bad" friends?

"I know he wasn't there," she murmured, but a bit unsure now. "I don't think he would be strong enough to beat up a large man like Tomas." Alone, yes. But with friends?

Juanita nodded, yet Maddie could tell she wasn't convinced, that she was still out of her mind with worry. Was this how her own mother had felt when she saw Maddie grieving? Was this why she worried about her being so far away? Not control, but—concern?

It was a dizzying thought, and one she didn't have time for yet. She watched as Juanita knelt down to quickly kiss the girls.

"Pearl, Ruby, I want you to stay here in Señora Maddie's studio until I come for you, just for a little while."

The girls stared at each other. "Alone?" they chorused. Usually they were forbidden to sneak into the studio.

"Yes," Maddie said as she took a box down from the shelf. "In fact, why don't you use my colored pencils and this sketchbook to draw some scenes for your dolls? Your mother and I will be back very soon."

Maddie and Juanita left the girls to their new task and hurried into the house. Inspector Sadler was in the main drawing room, and he looked even larger and more intimidating in the light of day, his girth and old tweed suit strange against her delicate furniture and colorful paintings and cushions. He was examining her shelf crowded with books, his hands behind his back as they clutched at his bowler hat. The dark-haired policeman—Tony?—still so young he had spots on his chin, shifted on his feet nervously in the corner.

Maddie could understand his nervousness. The police force in town was a small one, close-knit, mostly related to each other, and acquainted with all the usual troublemakers in the little streets. Bribes were common for the run-of-the-mill stuff like bootlegging, but brutal murders were few. Now here was a new, tough inspector from the outside and a murder right on the doorstep of the most crowded social spot in town.

But Maddie refused to be intimidated in her own home. She had already had enough of that with her parents and her in-laws. This was *her* house, and Juanita stood solidly at her side.

"Inspector Sadler, how delightful to see you again," Maddie said with a determined smile. "Have you come about the inquest?"

"Mrs. Alwin. No, the inquest has not yet been set. A few matters to tidy up first. I see you like Keats," he said, gesturing to her bookshelf. "'Beauty is truth, truth beauty,'— that is all Ye know on earth, and all ye need to know.'"

"I'm impressed, Inspector," she said in surprise, not sure if his love of poetry made him more or less scary. "Yes, Keats is one of my favorites. I often think of his imagery when I'm painting. Can I offer you some tea?"

He scowled, as if angry that poetry had distracted him. "I'm sure your housekeeper told you this isn't a social call," he said.

Maddie reached for Juanita's arm. "She did. I understand you're looking for Eddie Anaya."

"So we are. We have a few questions about what happened to his father last night. I'm sure you remember *that*, Mrs. Alwin."

As if she could ever forget. The memory of the scene in that alley would haunt her nightmares forever. "Of course. But Eddie had nothing to do with that."

"Maybe, maybe not," Inspector Sadler said. "We have someone who says the boy was seen on the plaza with his father earlier that evening and the two were arguing. Quite loudly."

"That's not true," Juanita interjected fiercely. "Eddie couldn't have been with Tomas at all."

"Oh?" Inspector Sadler said, raising his eyebrows. "So he was here all night, was he?"

"Eddie is a young man, Inspector," Maddie said. "I'm sure you remember what that was like." Back when Victoria was queen of England, she thought, but bit her tongue. "He doesn't like to hang about the house with a bunch of women. He probably was with his young friends, looking at pretty girls on the plaza or something."

"It's one of those young friends who told us they say the boy with his father," the inspector said.

Maddie thought again of the boy with the blond hair at the station. "Who is this friend?"

"My cousin Harry," the young policeman said, speaking for the first time. "He works as a busboy at La Fonda sometimes. He was there when the body—err, when Mr. Anaya was discovered and thought he should tell me what he saw."

Maddie nodded, thinking of the glimpse she had of the boy in the alley, the way he walked with the sobbing maid. Why would the kid cheese on Eddie now?

"I take it your son isn't at home, Mrs. Anaya?" the inspector said.

"Not at the moment," Juanita said, all quiet dignity, though Maddie could see the fear in her eyes.

"He often runs errands for me, Inspector," Maddie added.

"Well then, I would appreciate it if he came in to talk to us when his 'errands' are finished," Inspector Sadler said. "I take it you're on the telephone?"

Maddie nodded, and the inspector and the policeman turned toward the door. "Wait!" Juanita suddenly cried.

Inspector Sadler stopped, his bowler halfway to his head. "Yes?"

"Where is my husband's body?" Juanita asked.

"At the morgue, of course," Inspector Sadler said. "At St. Vincent's Hospital. In cases like this, there has to be an autopsy. The coroner, Dr. McKee, is on a case in Las Cruces right now, so we'll have to wait until he gets back. Then it will be released to you."

"But that can't be," Juanita insisted. "Tomas has to be buried quickly as possible, and with all the rites! I have to take him home or his spirit will wander."

The young policeman looked sympathetic, but the inspector had a face of stone. "Regulations are regulations. Things have been too lax around here until now. But I'm going to set them right. And if you want us to find who did this to your husband, Mrs. Anaya, you won't make a fuss."

The two men left, and Maddie slammed the door behind them. Juanita collapsed onto one of the chairs.

"How can he move on if I can't do what's proper?" she whispered. "I owe him that, at least."

Maddie knelt down beside her and took her hands. They were trembling. "Juanita, are you sure you have no idea where Eddie could be? Or who this Harry is? This is terribly important. I have the feeling Inspector Sadler is a man who would never let any detail go." And he was obviously set on making an example of his new "law and order."

Juanita shook her head and blinked hard, as if to clear her mind. "I do know some of his friends, though I've never heard of one called Harry. Eddie also likes to help out at the livery stable sometimes; he's so good with the horses. I can get the girls at the dairy down the street to look after the twins while I go look there for him. But Tomas—his spirit . . ."

Maddie nodded. She knew a little of what they believed at the pueblo. A body had to be buried quickly, facing north since that was the direction of origin for all people, and with their belongings. Then there would be a vigil and a releasing rite. She hadn't been able to properly bury Pete. Surely Tomas deserved that now.

She suddenly remembered the handsome English doctor from the train, Dr. Cole. He'd said he was going to work at Sunmount and also that he had a friend who was a coroner and was going to help him out. "Juanita, you go look for Eddie. I think I might know someone who can help us with Tomas."

Now if she could only persuade Gunther to let her borrow his wonderful little Duesenberg . . .

CHAPTER 8

"Whee!" Maddie cried, quite unable to help her burst of exuberance as the car flew down the winding road at the top of Canyon Road and up again, turning toward the foothills. Despite the seriousness of her mission, she had to admit she did love it when Gunther loaned her his car, which wasn't very often.

Not that she could blame him. The Duesenberg Model A was a thing of beauty, cream-colored with gold trim and a wine-red upholstery, low and trim and fast, even on Santa Fe's questionable roads. It seemed to skim along even when the pavement ran out and she was driving on dusty trails. The scarf she had tied around her hair threatened to blow away, and her gloved hands clutched the padded steering wheel as she swerved around a pothole.

It was a glorious day, one she relished even more after the dark events of the night. Even through her tinted glasses, the sky was a cloudless, pure turquoise blue, stretching endlessly overhead, so close she was sure she could reach up and touch it. The air had a particularly crisp, dry bite to it as the sun warmed the breeze around her, bringing with it the green smell of pine that overtook the smoky scent of the car and the new leather of the seat. Summer was coming; she could feel its softness all around her.

Sunmount was outside of town, built in the foothills where the patients could receive maximum advantage of the fresh air and sunshine and take pleasure in the sublime beauty of the views. Maddie remembered reading that the doctors there believed having a positive outlook on life, that patients enjoying their time and absorbing all the peace and beauty of the mountains, helped with their recovery.

Maddie had to agree with them. This place had raised her spirits, her hopes, when she had been sure she would never enjoy anything again. After Pete died, she'd felt like an old woman—worn-out, numb. Now she felt alive.

But Tomas Anaya was not, and his family, her dear friends, were suffering for that, just as she had once suffered. She had to help them if she could.

She slowed down to turn along the paved track that led to the sanatorium. Sunmount had been built in the early part of the century and had only grown in popularity due to its success rate at curing patients, so the road leading to its enlarged campus was well-kept. The Duesy planed along as if on silk as the hills rose around her, purple in the shadows, smelling ever stronger of pine and juniper.

Several of the artists Maddie had made friends with had started out as patients at Sunmount and stayed on after the cure, caught by the land just as she was. The poet Alice Henderson and her painter-architect husband, William, the de facto leaders of the local art group, had come when Alice was ill, and they sometimes returned to Sunmount to give salon talks. Maddie had last been there to hear them speak, but that was months ago, before she went back to New York.

She'd forgotten how pretty it was until she shifted down into the shallow valley. Far from a place of illness and fear, it looked like a cozy mountain village, nestled in the beautiful rolling hills. Maddie drove past rows of little bungalows, painted white with steeply shingled roofs and screened-in porches where the patients could take the air.

She rolled around a lawn where a croquet game was in progress and waved at the players. At the end of the path was the main hospital and administration building, a two-story structure also painted white, with gleaming windows thrown open to the fine day. It looked more like an old Spanish mission church, all soft-edged walls and dark wood trim, than a medical facility.

She parked the car in the graveled drive and suddenly realized she was about to see Dr. Cole again. The ridiculously handsome Dr. Cole, of the sky-blue eyes and yummy English accent. And she had been driving through the wind and dust.

She reached for her handbag and dug out her silver Cartier compact, quickly powdering her nose and checking her lipstick. She looked presentable enough, and her blue-and-white-striped driving dress and dark-blue coat weren't creased. She took off her headscarf and put on her blue-and-white cloche hat.

She *was* on a serious mission, true, but her mother had always said it was easier to get a "yes" answer when a lady looked presentable. It always worked for her mother and her charities, so there must be something to it.

But Maddie didn't want to think too much about any other reason she might be concerned about her appearance. She slid out of the car and made her way up the steps to the heavily carved front doors.

Inside it was shadowed and cool, smelling of fresh air and a faint medicinal tang. The beauty of the outside was reflected in the carved handrails of the staircase, the murals on the whitewashed walls depicting the sky and the mountains. Maddie was sure they must be new, as she hadn't seen them before, but there was no time to indulge her curiosity about them. She nodded to strolling patients in their white robes and slippers and hurried past a billiards room, where a noisy game was in progress, and the elegant salon where the lectures and plays were held, past bright Navajo textiles and pottery on shelves to the main desk.

The receptionist glanced up at her with a smile. "I'm afraid visiting hours aren't until later this afternoon, Miss . . ."

"Mrs. Alwin."

"Oh, yes, I do remember you! You were here for Mr. Henderson's excellent talk on local architecture a few months ago."

"And you have an excellent memory! I was here; it was quite fascinating. But I'm not here to visit a patient. I'm looking for a Dr. Cole."

She frowned. "Are you ill, Mrs. Alwin?"

"Oh, no. I met Dr. Cole on the train, and I was hoping he could help me with a—a small problem." "Small problem" felt like a silly thing to call it all, but Maddie didn't want too much gossip to spread, not yet.

The receptionist looked rather curious, but she was too professional to say anything. She just smiled and rose from the desk. "I think Dr. Cole is on rounds in the ward, but I'll just go check. If you'd care to wait a moment?"

"Thank you," Maddie answered. "Please tell him I won't take up much of his time."

As the receptionist hurried up the stairs, Maddie strolled over to examine the murals. The background was a wide blue sky with flat, pueblo-style rooftops standing out in pale-tans and whites—not complicated, but very alluring. It made her want to look closer, to be in that place.

"They're quite nice, aren't they?" an English-accented voice said behind her. "They were done by a former patient here, an architect named Meem."

Maddie spun around to find Dr. Cole smiling at her. *Oh, hotsy-totsy*, she thought. He *was* as handsome as she remembered, maybe even more now that he was smiling. Those shadows of sadness in his eyes that she thought she saw on the train seemed gone now, and his eyes were as clear as the turquoise sky outside.

"Hello, Dr. Cole," she said.

"Mrs. Alwin." He took his hand from the pocket of his white coat and held it out to shake hers. It was warm and firm, a few calluses along the base of his long fingers. "I was hoping to see you again one of these days. I'm glad it was so soon."

He was glad to see her too? A warm glow seemed to spread over her cheeks at the thought. She reminded herself why she was really there and pushed away that tiny touch of heat. Surely, maybe, there would be time for that later?

"I thought you would call me Maddie," she said.

He laughed. "You said only your friends call you Maddie."

"I do hope we'll be friends," she said. "I could certainly use one right now."

His expression changed, became serious, like the sun vanishing behind the mountains. "Are you ill? Is that why you're here?"

"No, no, I'm very well. But I could use your professional opinion on a matter."

He glanced around at the bustle of nurses and patients around them. "Shall we walk outside? You can tell me all about it."

"I don't want to take you from your work too long."

"It's time for my lunch anyway." He offered her his arm and led her outside, back into the bright sunshine.

They strolled along the gravel pathways that wound around the croquet lawn and a patch of grass where a group of ladies in fluttering white gowns did stretching exercises. It all seemed so peaceful, so far away from what had happened. Dr. Cole's presence, quiet and steady, made her feel calmer as well, able to think a bit more clearly.

"I have to say I'm intrigued to hear what brought you out here, Maddie," he said. They sat down on a bench under a large cottonwood tree with a gorgeous view of the mountains, all purple and gray and blue in the distance. "I was rather hoping you'd invite me to one of your parties at La Fonda. Your friends sound like a fascinating bunch."

Maddie thought of people like Gunther and Olive and laughed. Yes, they were a riot. "They are that, certainly. And of course, you are welcome, at any time at all. But today I—well, I need to ask a favor, Dr. Cole."

"Only if you call me David. That's only fair if I call you Maddie."

She smiled. "Yes, David."

"Now what's your favor?"

"I'm afraid it's a bit complicated." She quickly told him all about the Anayas, of her friend Juanita and what had happened to Tomas, the fact that now the police were looking for Eddie.

He listened to it all with a thoughtful frown, nodding, never interrupting as men so often seemed to do when a woman was speaking. "I'm sorry for Mrs. Anaya then. I was a medic in the war, you know, and met too many ladies in just such a terrible situation, losing their menfolk unexpectedly. What can I do to help?"

"I remembered you said you had a friend who sometimes worked as coroner here. Is it a man called Dr. McKee?" she asked.

"Yes, that's him. We met in the war. I only saw him briefly when I arrived here."

"The inspector says he's gone to Las Cruces and the autopsy can't be done until he gets back, so of course the body can't be released for burial. Juanita is quite upset she can't take him back to the pueblo in time for the correct rituals. It would be one less thing for her to worry about since Eddie is still missing. I was wondering—could you possibly do it?"

He seemed to think this over in silence for a moment. "If the police agree, of course I'll do it. I've done such things in England before."

"Oh, thank you!" Maddie cried. "I know she will feel a tiny bit easier once the funeral rites are properly over."

"You may have to be patient for a couple more days, Maddie. Some of those tests take a bit of time, even with recent medical advances." He rubbed at his beard. "Tell me, did you see the body yourself?"

Maddie shivered as she remembered that terrible, still figure in the alleyway. "Only for a minute. It was very dark, and I—well, I'm afraid I felt a bit ill."

"Perfectly understandable." He briefly pressed her hand. "I sometimes feel sick myself, even now after the war."

"I do remember there seemed to be a great deal of blood in the alley. Not so strange, I guess, if the police think it was a beating."

"A beating? Not a stabbing or shooting?"

"They didn't say anything about that. I didn't see a single wound, though like I said, I didn't look too closely."

David frowned. "So much blood. He probably wasn't just dumped there then. But the hotel was busy that night?"

"Oh, yes. There were loads of people in the lobby and the restaurant."

"And no one heard anything?"

"I had only just arrived. I was in the ladies' necessary when I heard the maid scream. I'm afraid most people were already a bit tiddly and noisy. No one goes back to that part of the hotel much." Maddie thought of the maid's screams and the boy who walked her past later.

"And there's nothing on the other side of the alley?"

She shook her head. "Not for a few blocks. Across the street in the other direction is the chapel and the school of the sisters. It was all dark when I walked past on my way to La Fonda."

"Strange. It must have been an awfully noisy and messy affair."

"Oh, yes," Maddie said, feeling rather dim she hadn't thought of that herself. She had to find a way to talk to some of the staff, the only people with reason to be near the alley. Or maybe a guest with a window facing that direction or something. Surely the inspector should be looking there instead of at innocent boys?

"Is there anything else you remember?" David asked.

Maddie closed her eyes and forced herself to remember that night, details she might have missed. It had all happened so fast, in such a blur. But there was one thing . . . "When they were carrying the body away, his hand fell from under the sheet. It was an odd color."

"Odd?"

"Yes. I don't have even a bit of your medical experience, but I did do some Red Cross volunteering when soldiers were shipped back from the war, and then during the flu epidemic. I saw a few bodies. His skin looked grayish already, but the nails were almost purple. Rigor mortis hadn't set in either."

"Fascinating," David said quietly. He had a faraway look in his blue eyes, and Maddie knew it was same look she got sometimes when she was painting. Thoughts whirling away in another world. "When can we get started then?"

"Your patients . . . ?"

"I'll ask one of the other doctors to cover them for a couple of days. It sounds as if there might be something going on with your murder case, Maddie."

"*My* murder case?"

"Well, ours now, I suppose. We'll have to figure it out together. Can you give me a ride back into town?"

Maddie rather liked the sound of that word—ours. *We.* She hadn't been a "we" in so long. "Of course. My car is out in the front drive."

"I'll meet you there."

Maddie watched him hurry back into the hospital, and she went to wait for him by the Duesenberg. She was very curious about what he might be thinking about Tomas's murder, what clues he might find. Between his medical knowledge and her social contacts in town, maybe they could figure something out. It seemed like the police might look no further than poor Eddie.

David met her at the car within half an hour, a tweed jacket replacing the white coat and a valise and medical case in his hands. "Is this beauty yours?" he asked, running an admiring hand over the Duesy's cream-colored hood.

Maddie laughed. She had never thought she could be jealous of a car! "I wish it was. It's my friend Gunther's car, though he seldom drives it."

"Now that is a pity."

"It is indeed. Want to see how fast it goes?"

He needed no more urging. He tossed his bags into the back and jumped into the passenger seat. Maddie slid her dark glasses back onto her nose, started the car, and sent them flying back down the road into Santa Fe.

It was an exhilarating ride, with them talking about New York and London over the purr of the engine. She left David at the hospital behind the cathedral, but before going home and having to give up the Duesy, she decided to stop at the post office to see if any mail had yet to be delivered that day. She was expecting a parcel of art supplies ordered from New York and maybe another scolding letter from her mother.

There were no boxes waiting behind the counter, just two letters. One was from her cousin Gwen in California, no doubt full of movie star gossip and weather reports of endless sun, as Gwen's letters usually were. Maddie tucked it into her handbag to read and savor later, a bit of vicarious glamour. The other letter looked unfamiliar.

Maddie carefully studied the block letters that formed her name and address. They were dark and plain, the paper cheap, and there was no return address. She tore open the envelope and read the short message in growing horror.

You don't know what you're doing. Better leave it alone and stay in your art studio or you'll get hurt, just like your friends. Don't talk to the police or go searching anymore.

Maddie felt her cheeks turn hot, and she stuffed the paper into her bag. To her surprise, the post office looked just the same as it had a moment before. The shuffling, bored people in line, the rows of mailboxes. Yet she felt horribly as if a hundred eyes were watching her. Seeing everything she did.

She hurried out into the bright light of day. The town around her—the adobe buildings, the dusty lanes, and the people hurrying past on their errands—also seemed like an odd, new place. She decided suddenly to go by the police station, see if they had any ideas on the letter-sender. Even if the inspector was careless, someone there would surely know something.

She didn't have to go all the way to the jail to run into Inspector Sadler, though. He was on the corner of the plaza, munching on a sandwich from one of the vendor's carts, his bowler hat pulled low over his brow.

Maddie pulled the car over and called out to him. "Inspector," she said. "I have something I must show you."

He lowered his sandwich with a frown. "Mrs. Alwin," he said unenthusiastically. "How did you know so quickly?"

"Know?" Maddie said, puzzled.

"I—never mind. I guess you'll find out soon enough. What is it you need to show me then?"

"I just received this." She took out the note and thrust it under his nose. He looked at it as if she held out a day-old sardine, which she thought it might as well be.

"What is it?" he asked again.

"Read it yourself. It's a threat," she answered. "It seems someone has been watching me."

He looked it over, his eyes narrowing. "Looks like a prank to me."

"A prank!" Maddie cried. "No one I know would pull a prank like that."

He handed it back. "I see things like that all the time. It's usually silly kids. But it wouldn't hurt to be more careful, Mrs. Alwin. Stay inside for a while. Mind your own business."

"My own business?" What on earth could be more important business than trying to help her friends?

He gave her a smile that was dripping with phony sweetness. He reached out as if to pat her hand, and Maddie drew back. "You paint pictures, right? Better stay with that. My job is to catch criminals, and rest assured, we're doing just that. You definitely might want to stay in after dark, as well, just to be on the cautious side." He tipped his hat and strolled away, taking out his sandwich again.

"The cautious side," Maddie hissed. Men. They always thought the "little ladies" needed to stay out of real life, stay on the sidelines waving handkerchiefs and simpering, like maidens in *Ivanhoe* or something. Well, nuts to that. If he wouldn't help her, she had to help herself. She stuffed the horrid note back into her bag and turned toward home. Much to her surprise, Juanita was already back from her own errand of asking Eddie's friends about his whereabouts. She paced the walkway outside Maddie's gate and waved frantically as Maddie turned off the car.

"What is it?" she called. "Did you find Eddie?"

"Oh, Señora Maddie . . . Eddie is in jail!"

CHAPTER 9

As Maddie drove Juanita to the jail where Eddie was being held, she told her about Dr. Cole and his promise to do all he could to see that Tomas could be buried as soon as possible. She wasn't sure what to say about the blood, the strange little details she had almost forgotten about the scene of the crime, not until David could tell them more. And she said nothing about the strange note she had received. She would have to take a closer look at it later.

"He sounds like a kind man," Juanita said, her face solemn under the brim of her black straw hat. It had once been trimmed with yellow ribbons and a white silk flower, but it was now plain to match her newly dyed black dress. She watched the houses and shops flying past, still looking as if she was far away in her own world. Usually she was a bit nervous when Maddie borrowed the car; now she didn't even clutch at the black handbag on her lap. "There aren't enough of those in the world."

Maddie had to agree. Dr. Cole *did* seem like a good man. "He wants to do what he can. He said he saw too many bad things in the war. What did you hear from Eddie's friends?"

Juanita shook her head. "These boys today. They do as they like, never listening to their elders. We wouldn't have done such things in my day."

Maddie nodded. Juanita sounded much like her own mother. Cornelia Astor Vaughn always bemoaned her daughter's lack of duty and proper etiquette. She knew proper behavior and respect for authority and elders ran just as deep in Juanita's world as in New York society.

Yet Juanita and Tomas had left their home for some reason. Something Eddie seemed to resent. But enough to do harm to his own father?

Maddie doubted it, due to what she knew about Eddie. He had a rebellious streak, as most teenagers seemed to, but he was kind and loving to his mother and sisters. Yet she also had a feeling the boy knew more than he said to her. It wasn't in the Anayas' nature to confide in anyone, quite natural when they came from a world where so much had been betrayed. Maddie hadn't even known they couldn't go back to the pueblo until that conversation in the kitchen.

"Eddie's friends said they haven't seen him since they were playing dice outside Kaune's Grocery that afternoon, after he brought you home from the station. He told them he had to leave early for some reason," said Juanita.

"And no one saw him after that at all?"

"I asked all over town. No one at all. He wasn't at his usual places, like the livery stable."

No alibi. Even Maddie—who knew little beyond what her attorney cousin, Gwen's brother, would talk about at dinner parties and information she'd picked up from reading the G. K. Chesterton novels she and Gunther passed back and forth—thought that sounded dangerous. She knew she had to find Eddie a good lawyer, but who?

They pulled up in front of the police station, where she had left David not so long before. It was an unprepossessing stucco and brick-fronted building that had replaced the old, small stone structure on Canyon Road, which had resembled a medieval dungeon of sorts. This one, as plain and modern as it was, was no less intimidating.

Maddie parked the car on the dusty street outside the iron-bound front doors that held Eddie inside. In contrast to the brilliant, blue-gold light outside, the building was dark inside, but not the comfortable, serene shadows of Sunmount. There was a thickness, a stickiness, to the air, the smell of stale fried food and sweat. A policeman stood behind a counter piled high with papers in haphazard stacks.

His gaze took in Juanita, with her dark hair and skin, her plain coat and hat, and he turned away without a word. Now even angrier, Maddie peeled off her gloves and marched forward, deliberately flashing her large diamond wedding ring and her mother's pearls that she had impulsively looped around her neck before they left the house.

She slapped her palm hard on the counter, making a loud cracking sound, and he looked up. His expression slowly changed to wary politeness.

Maddie felt her face turn hot, but she made herself keep staring back.

"How can I help you, Mrs. . . . ?"

"Mrs. Vaughn-Alwin," Maddie said, using her mother's haughty opera-committee voice. "And Mrs. Anaya. We have come to see Mrs. Anaya's son, Eduardo Anaya, who I believe you are holding here without the proper due process of an attorney's advice."

He appeared most uncertain. He looked every bit as young as the uniformed officer who had been at La Fonda, and she wondered if they were related. In any case, she was glad he seemed new at his job. An older lawman, seasoned in Western ways, would have been much harder to crack with snooty New York society manners. She hoped she could bluff her way through and get Eddie out of there before the police knew what was what.

"The inspector says . . ." he began.

"We want to see him *now*," Maddie insisted. "He is just a boy and has been locked up alone for hours. I am sure people like Senator Jones would be most interested to hear such treatment goes on here. New Mexico has only been a state for ten years. We have a reputation to build as a place of American justice, don't we?"

"Señora Maddie, do you really know Senator Jones?" Juanita whispered.

Of course she didn't. Her only friends were artists and writers. She avoided politics, except for voting after women's suffrage passed; there was enough of that name-dropping business among her relatives. "Just go with it," she whispered back. She glanced at the bewildered young policeman. Yes—he definitely had to be related to the one at La Fonda.

He scowled. "Okay, but only for ten minutes."

"Thank you." Maddie and Juanita followed him down a dark, narrow hallway, past a series of locked doors that only had tiny grilled windows where guards could peer in at inmates and slide in trays of food. It smelled even worse here, of urine and bleach, and Maddie couldn't stand thinking about poor Eddie locked inside.

She could hear rhythmic banging on the doors, the patter of pacing feet. "Mostly we just get drunks here, and thieves. Hardly ever murderers." The policeman sounded hideously excited at the prospect.

"He is *not* a murderer!" Juanita snapped.

"He's just a child," Maddie added. No one with any sense could think a skinny teenager could deliver such a fatal beating to a large grown man single-handedly, let alone one's own father. The policeman just shrugged and opened a door at the end of the hall. It slid back with a rusty scrape. "Ten minutes," he said and practically shoved them inside. The door slammed behind them, and a key turned in the lock.

For an instant, Maddie had to ignore the hard, bitter knot of panic that rose up inside of her. Ever since Pete had died, ever since she'd started having nightmares of him trapped in a mud-infested trench, she had hated closed spaces. But she was there for Eddie, the poor kid who had been there for much longer than ten minutes.

There was only one small, barred window near the low ceiling, lighting a narrow bed, a chair, and a covered bucket in the corner. And Eddie, huddled on the bed, his knees drawn up to his chin, his face pale under the fading bruises.

"Mama!" he cried when he saw them and burst into tears. He looked scared and overwhelmed and alone, more like a four-year-old than fourteen. Maddie's heart ached at the sight.

Juanita ran to him and took him in her arms, rocking him as she murmured soft Tewa words.

"Have you come to take me home?" he asked hoarsely.

"Not yet," Juanita said, "but Señora Maddie has a plan."

A plan would be overstating the matter, Maddie thought. She felt just as helpless and frightened as Eddie did. But she would never show him that.

"I'm finding you an attorney," she said, sitting down on the other side of him. "Surely he can have bail set when we sort this out. In the meantime . . ." She took a bag of his favorite lemon drops from her handbag and passed it to him. "Tell us what happened. They say one of your friends saw you at the hotel that night."

"It had to be Harry, that rat," Eddie said around a piece of the hard candy. "He works there at La Fonda. We used to be friends, but not since he started trying to get me to help him with—with some stuff."

Stuff? "Bootlegging, you mean? Does this Harry help smuggle hooch to the clubs in town?"

"Eduardo!" Juanita cried. "You know that's against the rules. Your uncles . . ."

"I told you I didn't do that stuff, Ma," Eddie protested. "I know we could use the money, but I wouldn't do that. Not after Uncle Diego talked to me last time we saw him. I just play dice sometimes with Harry and the others. Pa had been following me that night; that's when I decided to turn around and follow *him*. That's only fair, right?"

"What did you see when you followed him?" Maddie asked. "Did you see who did this?"

Eddie swallowed hard and shook his head. "I didn't see him get—that. Killed, I mean. I swear it! The police keep saying I must have, but I would have helped him, stopped it. He wasn't always the best dad, maybe, but he was mine."

"I know you wouldn't have, Eddie," Juanita said, holding his hand tightly. "But we need to know what you *did* see."

"I saw him talking to someone there on the corner, by the side of the cathedral where it's dark. It was someone I thought I had seen before. I don't know his name, but he *is* a bootlegger. They say sometimes he can find other stuff for people too."

Maddie thought of Elizabeth Grover in the ladies' room. "Cocaine," she murmured.

"That's right. Snow, the boys call it. From Mexico," Eddie said. "Harry says you can make a lot more money there, more than on Pojoaque hooch. And Dad was talking to him." His face screwed up, and he kicked out in sudden anger that seemed to drown out the fear. "After the way he treated *me*, when he thought I was running the gin! It was him doing it, all along. He was mixed up with guys like that, and it got him killed. He must have had snow money, and he let the girls go without new dresses."

Juanita looked absolutely appalled. "It can't be," she whispered.

"We don't know what really happened," Maddie said. But it sure sounded like it. Bootlegging was usually a harmless enough thing in Santa Fe. They were too isolated for Prohibition agents to bother them much, and everyone knew where to get it, whether you wanted cheap Lightning or French champagne. Hard drugs, on the other hand . . .

"What's important is that *you* didn't do it," Maddie said. "We'll have you out of here as fast as we can. In the meantime, I'll get some blankets and some proper food sent over. Don't say anything to anyone until a lawyer gets here."

The policeman pounded on the door. "Time's up!"

Juanita gave her son a quick, firm hug. "Do what she said. I love you, my son, and this will be over very soon."

"I'm the man of the family now. I'll take care of you and the girls as soon as I'm out of here," Eddie answered, wiping at his eyes. "I'll get a job and everything. If Dad's spirit . . ."

Juanita shivered. "Don't worry about that. Your uncles will do it all."

"We can go back there now, can't we?" Eddie said. "To the pueblo."

There was no time to answer. The door opened, and it was Inspector Sadler who stood there, scowling at them. Maddie remembered how he had dismissed that note she received, and she scowled back at him. There would be no help from any official quarter on anything. "Time to leave, ladies. *Now*."

Maddie took Juanita's arm and led her past the glowering inspector. They had one more glimpse of Eddie, looking red-eyed and forlorn on his bunk, clutching at the bag of lemon drops.

"His attorney will be here soon, Inspector," she said. "I'm sure you will do what's proper and legal and leave the boy alone until then."

She didn't wait for him to answer, but she could feel his glare burning into the back of her neck as she and Juanita left the police station. Outside, the sun momentarily blinded her after the gloom, and she took a deep breath of the fresh, clear air tinged with piñon smoke from last night's fireplaces. People hurried by on their usual errands like it was a normal day, like the world hadn't tilted awry.

Juanita was silent beside her, her face like marble. They made their way back to the car and climbed in, sitting for a moment as if to get their bearings.

"It couldn't have been that way," Juanita murmured.

"What couldn't?"

"Tomas being involved with things like that. Bootleg-ging. In fact, he . . ." Her words faded.

"In fact, what?" Maddie urged.

Juanita shook her head. "Tomas had his faults, I have to admit that. But drink wasn't one of them, not now. What-ever killed him—it wasn't bootlegging." She bit her lip.

Maddie started the car and shot out onto the road, turn-ing toward home. She knew Juanita would only tell her what she wanted to know if Maddie gave her time. The Anayas were private about their family matters, even with friends like Maddie. But Maddie did believe that Juanita thought Tomas wouldn't have been selling drugs to people like Elizabeth.

But she wasn't at all sure that his death had nothing to do with bootlegging. Everything seemed to keep com-ing back to that. Maybe he had tried to keep Eddie from becoming involved, or maybe he had gotten in someone's way? Booze, and now cocaine, made some people around town big money, and Tomas wasn't a man to be unobtrusive when he disapproved of something.

Maddie tried to make her whirling mind settle down, to think who might have done such a thing to Tomas. She was sure it wasn't Eddie, but what about the rest of the Anaya family, or Juanita's relatives? Maddie didn't know enough about them yet, except that for some reason the family never went back to the pueblo. Surely that must mean something had gone wrong, and no one knew how to hurt a person like family. Or maybe Tomas really had been involved in nefarious bootlegging operations or angered someone high up on the criminal chain. Maybe he had friends or enemies even his wife knew nothing about, and it was now up to Maddie to find out about them.

The most important thing at the moment, though, was to get Eddie out of that awful place.

She dropped off Juanita at the house and drove around to leave the Duesy with Gunther. She found him sitting in the shade of his front portal, his typewriter set out in front of him but no manuscript papers in evidence. He put out the cigarette he was smoking and waved to her as she stopped the car in its pine-plank shelter.

"It doesn't look as if you did *too* much damage, my darling," he said as she hurried up the steps to join him. "But it is horribly dusty. What on earth have you been up to? You look positively knackered."

"I feel rather knackered." She sank into one of his cushioned wicker chairs and took off her blue cloche hat to let the cool breeze ruffle her hair. She thought again of cutting it off, especially if she was going to rush around town like she was in a *Perils of Pauline* film.

"Well, here. Have some iced tea, and tell your Uncle Gunther all about it."

Maddie gestured toward the typewriter. "Aren't you working? I don't want to interrupt."

Gunther waved her words away and poured out a drink from the pottery pitcher on his desk. "Plenty of time for that later. I would much rather hear about what you and my car were up to today."

Maddie sipped at the wonderfully cool drink and told him about her trip to Sunmount to see if Dr. Cole could help with the problem of Tomas's funeral rites.

"Not that man with the lovely English accent you met on the train?" Gunther exclaimed.

"The very one." Maddie sighed at the thought of the doctor's blue, sad eyes.

"My dear, how clever of you to go see him again so soon!"

Maddie laughed wryly. "Yes. So romantic to ask him such a gruesome favor. He was quite nice about it, though, and agreed to help me right away."

Gunther sighed. "That's the English for you. So civilized."

"But then I had to tend to something not so civilized. I had to go to the jail."

"Darling! Were you speeding in my car that much?"

"I only wish that was it." She told him about Eddie's arrest. "So I need to find out if you know any good lawyers. We need to get the poor kid out of there."

"Poor young Eddie. He always seems like a nice one—for a temperamental teenager that is." Gunther lit another ciga-rette and frowned thoughtfully into the plume of smoke. "I can't think of anyone right now, but I know who would."

"Oh, yes!" Maddie cried. "Olive, of course. She knows positively everyone in town."

"Exactly. I saw her heading to the museum this morning, getting ready for that new exhibit. You should take a couple of your paintings down there. She's been after you to contribute something for ages, and a little bribe never hurts. I'm sure she could find you someone top-notch."

Maddie finished her drink with a sigh. It looked like a long day would be even longer. But Gunther was right. Olive did know everyone.

Chapter 10

Maddie walked to the art museum across the street from the old Palace of the Governors and near the shady plaza. When she and her cousin Gwen had been making their way across the country toward California, poring over guidebooks at every stop along the way, they'd become quite excited at the mention of a "palace." She'd expected something like the castles she'd seen as a girl, touring Europe with her parents, all brocade corridors and crenelated towers.

But this old Spanish palace was nothing like that. It was a long, one-story adobe structure built around a large shady courtyard, with a pillared portal in the front where artisans sold their jewelry and pottery to eager tourists. The Victorian wrought-iron railing along the flat roof, which had been added to make the style more "modern," was in the process of being removed to take it back to its older, more unique appearance. A few people milled about in the shade of the portal, but it was quiet at that hour.

The small warren of rooms inside had once held exhibitions by local artists, but the number of artists had outgrown the old, drop-ceilinged space and made a new museum a necessity. It had only been finished in 1919, yet it looked much older, as if it had always been there on that corner, with its pueblo-like rounded walls and towers.

Maddie hurried across the plaza, which was also quiet at that hour, with only a few old men gossiping on the iron benches around the obelisk of the war memorial and dogs sleeping in the shade. In the evening, it would be filled with young men and girls, eyeing each other as they promenaded, maybe even flirting a bit under the close watch of stern chaperones. Just as she had once danced with awkward young swains at cotillions and tea dances as her mother looked on from the gilded chairs along the walls.

Maddie was sure the plaza was a much more fun social setting than the ballroom at Sherry's Restaurant, but she had no time to linger. She hurried up the steps into the museum, her portfolio tucked up under her arm.

Compared to the quiet afternoon outside, the museum was all aflutter. Workmen hurried past with ladders and buckets of paint, getting the walls ready for the new exhibit. Like the exterior, the interior had been made to look like an old pueblo, all cool stone floors and adobe walls. But there was still the scent of newness about it, from the pine wood planks of the floor and the dark ceiling vigas to the sharpness of the fresh paint.

Olive Rush stood in the midst of it all, directing the workmen and the young apprentices who were hanging the new paintings in the galleries. The artists all got studio space at the back of the museum in exchange for the work and hurried about their tasks to get to back to their canvases sooner.

Olive was quite unmistakable, a tall, spare, thin woman with a paint-splashed smock over her pleated Navajo velvet skirt and tunic, her plain face surmounted by the wrapped folds of a scarlet turban.

"No, no, not there!" she was saying to a young man who perched high on a ladder, hanging a scene of pueblo natives gathered around a bonfire on a starry night, the sky streaked with lavender and velvety black behind them, a girl on a turquoise horse in the background. It was definitely one of Olive's own, Maddie thought; no one else had a modernist style quite like that. It hung next to a few images of adobe interiors and shimmering aspen trees by a man named Berninghaus from Taos. "It's too big to hang there; it will overwhelm the smaller ones. I meant it for over the fireplace."

She suddenly spun around and dropped her gesturing hands when she saw Maddie standing there in the doorway. "Madeline! I see you've taken my advice and brought some of your work to display at last. And just in time too, as the next show opens in just a few weeks."

"I did bring a couple of things to show you," Maddie answered. "But I mostly came to ask your advice."

"Of course, of course, but first things first. Let's take a look at what you have there." She snatched the portfolio from Maddie and led her into a smaller gallery, one where light poured from the tall windows and gleamed on the works already hung there. A painting by Olive that Maddie had seen before, an oil portrait of the San Ildefonso pottery-making couple Maria and Julian Martinez, hung on the wall next to a case of their glossy, distinctive black-on-black pottery. It shimmered like the most polished jet.

"What do you think of them?" Olive asked, gesturing to the display. She had always been a great advocate for the local native art, organizing exhibits at the museum and sending it to galleries in the East where they often gained much acclaim. "I just went out to San Ildefonso last week. The Hendersons loaned me their car. This batch has only recently been fired. Glorious, aren't they?"

Maddie studied the collection of pottery closer, the etched designs of serpents and circles within circles. The black was perfectly dark, shimmering like the night sky. "They are stunning."

"Mrs. Martinez is quite a wonder," Olive answered. "Did you know she can fire dozens of pots and plates at a time, and none will crack? Everyone else is afraid to fire more than two or three. The beauty of her work should be known *everywhere*."

Maddie completely agreed. She glanced up at the portrait of the woman wrapped in her shawl, a baby on her lap. The Martinez family was from San Ildefonso, just like the Anayas. She wondered if they knew each other or even if Olive, who so often traveled around to the different pueblos collecting such objects for the museum, might have heard something there.

Olive unwrapped Madeline's package and held the canvases up to the light. Madeline had only brought two small pieces. One was of the mountains in the distance at sunset, the purple shadows of them outlined in shimmering pinks, corals, and golds. The other was of Buttercup sitting in Maddie's own garden, surrounded by the riot of colorful flowers, the tan adobe wall of the house behind them. Olive studied them with a silence that made Maddie nervous, a small frown on her face as she turned them one way then another.

"I know they are quite simple compared to Mr. Parsons or Mr. Baumann," Maddie said, fidgeting a bit. Sometimes her parents' comments still ate at her confidence. Ladies were only meant to be amateur artists, doing little sketches in their spare time, never putting themselves forward.

"Nonsense! Your sense of color and light is most extraordinary, Madeline," Olive said stoutly. "They will be perfect to hang in the first alcove. You're sure to sell them immediately. Are you certain you don't have more ready? Something larger?"

Maddie thought of the half-finished portrait of the twins, which reminded her of poor Eddie's plight and the questions she meant to ask Olive. "No, not yet."

"Oh, well, it's a start. At least I can see that your confidence is growing, just as mine did when I was young and finally went to Paris. Before that, my parents were sure I shouldn't live on my own, let alone try to make a living with art." She propped the paintings up with another group waiting to be hung in the display. "Now you said you have a favor to ask?"

Maddie glanced at the glow of the shining black pottery. "It actually has something to do with San Ildefonso. The family who works for me, the Anayas, they're from the pueblo, and—well . . ."

"Oh, yes," Olive said with a frown. "That nasty business at La Fonda. It sounds quite complicated. Let's go have a chat over tea, shall we? I can't think at all with all this hammering and shouting."

Maddie and Olive left the chaos of the museum and made their way to Mrs. Nussbaum's tearoom on the east side of the plaza in a two-story, balconied building with the bank on one side, the grocer on the other, and offices upstairs. Tucked between the bustle of the bank and the grocery, it was a little oasis of wicker chairs and potted plants, smelling of sugar and cinnamon and the yeasty goodness of fresh bread. It was usually quite popular, but like the plaza outside the windows, it was quiet at that hour. They found a table tucked away in the corner and ordered cinnamon toast and tea. As with anywhere else in town, gin or rum could be had in a teapot, but that day Maddie just needed plain old Darjeeling.

"So tell me what's amiss," Olive said, biting into the buttery toast once they'd been served.

Maddie quickly told her of Eddie's arrest and Juanita's fears for him and their search for a good lawyer.

"I see," Olive said briskly. "Yes, indeed, it is all about who one knows around here. I do know a lawyer, one who does some work for Governor Mechem's office. A Mr. Springer. He fancies himself a bit of an artist and archaeologist too. I'm sure between us we can persuade him to look into things for this poor child. Especially if it gives him a chance to help the governor look all law and order. It's almost election time, of course." She took out a sketchbook from her capacious handbag and jotted down a name and address. "I'll give him a phone later and hint there might be a blank space in the gallery for some of his drawings soon."

Maddie took the paper with some relief. She did still have a lot to learn about her new home, a lot of people to meet. "Thanks, Olive. I certainly owe you."

"Just paint faster to sell more for the museum!" Olive poured out more tea. "Now tell me more about the Anayas. Have they been living in town long?"

"Longer than I've been here," Maddie answered. "Juanita is quite wonderful. I couldn't do without her. She helped me so much when I got here and missed my husband so much I couldn't stand it. Her children are lovely too. Tomas—I just don't know much about him, except that he was quarreling with his family lately, especially Eddie. But Eddie swears he didn't even see his father that night, and I believe him. He's not the sort to be a killer."

Olive shook her head. "Madeline, we could *all* be killers, given the right circumstances." She took another thoughtful sip of tea. "I do remember there being some gossip at

San Ildefonso a few years ago, some families that had broken away for some reason, but I was so new there then and not trusted. I know they were hit hard by the flu in 1918, and there was a lot of upheaval and division in its wake. I'll see what I hear next time I'm out there."

Maddie nodded. She knew if anyone could find out anything, it was Olive. She was well known for finding the best native artists and bringing their work to the attention of the art world, as well as helping anyone who ever needed it, despite her own straitened finances.

"For now, let's just join forces and get Mr. Springer to help," Olive said. "And send me more paintings! But I must get back to the museum; things always go wrong when I'm not there to supervise every second."

They left the tearoom, Olive to go back to the museum and Maddie toward home. The sun was starting to set, turning the adobe walls of La Fonda a pale gold and streaking the sky a rosy pink. She could hear the slow tolling of the bells from the cathedral, and a few people were emerging to stroll through the plaza. She dodged past kids with hoops and nodded to the elderly men gossiping on the benches.

On the corner, she glimpsed Inspector Sadler taking a brown paper package that seemed to contain sandwiches from one of the uniformed officers. Maddie thought of Eddie all alone in that cold jail, of the note she had received telling her to stay home and mind her own business, and she marched across the grass to confront the man.

"Inspector Sadler," she called. "Hard at work catching a murderer, I see."

He scowled at her. "The police here have their proper procedures now that I'm in charge, Mrs. Alwin, and it's safer not to share their activities with civilians," he said, tucking his parcel under his arm with an impatient grimace. "The killer has already been safely locked up. I know it's hard for you to accept that it was a mere domestic matter, you being friends with the boy like that . . ."

"Because it's not true," she insisted, wishing she could just punch the man and be done with it. "Which you would know if you looked past the end of your nose."

His face turned red. "I told you before, Mrs. Alwin. It's safer here to mind your own business. Have you received any more notes?"

Maddie remembered that terrible little message, the way it had made her feel as if a hundred eyes were watching her every move, and she shifted her handbag on her arm as she tried not to feel that way again. She wouldn't let anyone keep her from doing what she had to do. "No."

"Surely that's because the writer is locked away. You should be careful who you hire in your own house. Now if you'll excuse me, there's a lot of work to be done to keep this town safe."

He tipped his hat and strolled away, and Maddie watched him go in anger. She reminded herself that Eddie would have a lawyer soon and the boy would be out of that wretched place. She turned toward home and tried not to feel like everyone on the plaza was watching her, wishing she would stay home and mind her own business. A curtain twitched in an upstairs office above the grocery store, a pale face peering out, making that feeling even stronger.

She pushed those feelings away and marched on. There was no time for stuff like that yet, not with so many things to worry about.

Her thoughts on finding a lawyer for Eddie, Maddie turned the corner at Kaune's Grocery to start the walk home and suddenly stopped as she glimpsed a familiar face. It was the boy she'd seen that night at La Fonda, the one with bright-blond hair, Eddie's so-called friend.

He seemed to be in a hurry, ducking through the gathering crowds on the sidewalk, and Maddie impulsively decided to follow him. Glad she'd worn flat shoes, she dashed after him down San Francisco Street, past shops, keeping his blond head in sight. He seemed to be wary, glancing behind him, stopping sometimes in doorways, and Maddie was careful to stay out of his sight.

He turned down a narrow lane called Burro Alley, and she plunged in after him. The walls of the buildings were close on either side, mostly windowless as they were the backs of shops. At the end of the alley, he turned right onto Palace Street. Maddie followed, until he stopped at one of the windowless buildings. He gave a strange knock at the door, two long raps and one short, and the door opened. He slipped inside, and she heard a bolt shoot into place behind him.

She studied the building carefully. Once, long ago, it had been a saloon, but it had been empty for years, used for storage by other businesses. But she remembered what Gunther had said about some new club on Palace, one where both Gunther and Elizabeth Grover said you could get anything you might want in the way of booze or snow. Was this it?

She only knew she couldn't get in now by herself, no matter what kind of joint it was. Surely neither the boy, Harry, or anyone else would tell her anything.

She noticed the sunset was deepening, turning purple and magenta overhead. She had to get home before dark. As she skirted her way back around the plaza, she saw that the evening crowd was out in full, young men and ladies eyeing each other and giggling under the stern gaze of their parents seated on the iron benches, enjoying the warm spring evening.

She didn't go straight home, though. Instead she went to knock on Gunther's door. She was assured by the lights glowing in his windows that it was still too early for him to be out.

He opened the door, his eyes widening with surprise at seeing her. He still wore his velvet smoking jacket, a cravat in his hands, his hair curly and unruly without its pomade. "Maddie, my darling, it's utterly peachy to see you, but if you're asking to borrow my car again, I must ungallantly say no. You are much too reckless, my love, and the chassis was nearly snapped in two."

"No car tonight, Gunther dear, I promise," she said. "I need you to escort me out someplace. Someplace I can't go alone."

"Oh, that does sound intriguing! You know I've been trying to lure you to the darker fun side for ages. Now where do you want to go?"

"That new club on Palace. The one where you said you once saw Tomas Anaya."

Gunther pursed his lips. "Your wish is my command, dearest. As long as you don't wear that dreadful black satin again. I've warned you against it too many times."

Maddie laughed and kissed his cheek. "I promise, no black. I told you, I brought back oodles of things from New York."

"I'll call for you in a couple of hours then. I have to finish my toilette."

Maddie went back to her house through the garden gate. But it wasn't as quiet there as she expected. Juanita sat in the front sitting room talking with a man. He was older, tall, and elegant in a dark suit adorned with a gold watch chain, his silvering hair and impressive mustache reminding Maddie somewhat of her own father.

"Señora Maddie," Juanita said with a hopeful smile. "This man says he is a lawyer, Mr. Frank Springer. He says he's here to help Eduardo."

Mr. Springer immediately rose to his feet and gave Maddie's hand a firm shake. "Always happy to meet a friend of Olive's!" he said. "You have to come to one of my wife's parties soon; she does love to meet new people, especially artists. But what can I do to help you now?"

Oh, golly, Maddie thought. Olive certainly didn't let any grass grow under her feet.

CHAPTER 11

Mr. Springer sat down on the portal with Maddie as Juanita hurried to make him some tea, and he brought out a very official-looking portmanteau of papers as she told him what she knew of Eddie's case so far and the fact that the inspector wouldn't allow her to post bail even to bring Eddie home while they waited.

"It sounds as if that Sadler fellow has no idea of procedure around here, which is no surprise," Mr. Springer said with a disdainful frown. "This isn't the Wild West anymore, and I should know. I've been out here for decades. Even a boy like young Mr. Anaya is subject to due process."

"So what do we need to do next?" Maddie asked.

"He'll have to have a preliminary hearing as soon as the circuit judge returns, and it must be within ten days," he answered. "He should have been advised of his rights immediately and conditions imposed for his bail or release. He has no criminal history, I assume?"

"Just silly things boys do sometimes," Maddie said. "No arrests or anything of the sort. And he is quite young."

Mr. Springer shook his head. "Sadly, even young men can be sent to prison or a juvenile center away from his family. I will go the jail right away and see if I can arrange for bail or at least find a magistrate to hold a quick hearing. I will let you know as soon as I have some news."

"Thank you so much, Mr. Springer," Maddie said, shaking his hand after he packed up his valise and stood to leave. "It means a great deal to me."

"And to me," Juanita said as she returned with the refreshments. She insisted he take a freshly made cake with him, which he accepted with alacrity.

He smiled, and she saw it quite transformed him from a fearsome old gentleman to an only somewhat intimidating one. "It is my pleasure to help, Mrs. Anaya. And I look forward to seeing some of your art, Mrs. Alwin. I'll be in touch soon."

After he left, Maddie sat down again on her wicker chair and stared up at the sky as it started to darken and turn sunset pink at the edges. She remembered her own childhood, the pranks she and her brother and cousins would sometimes play, the trouble they would get in with Nanny and, worst of all, their parents. How easy it was to ruin everything in one's life, when a person was too young to know any better.

"Eddie will be home soon," she whispered to herself. She had to believe that. And she had to make Juanita believe it too. She pushed herself up from her chair and went into the house to go over with Juanita what might happen next with her son.

★   ★   ★

When Gunther called on her to depart for the night's adventure on the town, Maddie was very glad she had left her old black satin hanging forlornly at the back of her wardrobe. Gunther was dressed in one of his sharply tailored suits and the green-and-white polka-dotted cravat she'd brought him from New York, his red hair so slicked back with lemon-scented pomade, it looked dark.

"What do you think?" she said, giving a little spin. She had picked out one of her new dresses, a pink silk overlaid with paler-pink chiffon and embroidered with an intricate pattern of flowers and vines in silver beads. The flounced skirt below a beaded silver band was shorter than she had ever worn before, revealing more of her new sheer, French stockings and silver strapped shoes than she ever would have in her mother's drawing room. Here, she felt light and free. As if she could run and twirl and do anything at all.

She could even help Eddie, if she gave it all she had. And she intended to. The memory of Juanita's face as she listened to Mr. Springer, so hopeful and frightened all at once, drove Maddie onward.

"Darling, you are absolutely the elephant's elbow," Gunther said, helping her into her matching pink satin coat.

"We'll be just like Fred and Adele Astaire on the dance floor."

"If I had only paid more attention in cotillion," Maddie said with a sigh.

"They never taught us anything useful in cotillion anyway," Gunther said. "No Charleston, no shimmy."

"True." Maddie had learned all of the most important things only after her life turned upside down, once she lost Pete and found a new home. She had learned to look out for herself. To sometimes leap before she looked and sometimes to be cautious. Speaking of which, she tucked Pete's old service revolver and some ammunition into her handbag before they left the house.

Instead of walking as they usually did, they took the Duesy. As they jolted over the narrow roads, Maddie told Gunther about the lawyer Olive had sent and what he'd told them about Eddie's situation.

Gunther frowned. "And you think you can find something to help the kid? Are you sleuthing tonight?"

"Like Father Brown?" She and Gunther were both quite devoted to Chesterton's detective priest. She thought about it for a moment. "Maybe. I just need to learn to be observant and clever like the good padre."

"Darling, you *are* clever. You went to Spence, didn't you? And that art school. Artists often see details other people don't. That's your job."

She supposed it was. When she looked at people, she saw not just their appearance, their clothes, their faces, but the expression in their eyes, the way they watched the world around them. "It's the job of a writer too."

"So you think I can help?" he said eagerly, downshifting as they bounced through a pothole. "Do tell. I've been so hideously bored lately."

Maddie told him about the boy, Harry, who she had seen at La Fonda and then again that afternoon, how he had been Eddie's supposed friend, the one who peached him to the police.

"You think we'll find him there tonight?" Gunther asked.

"It's a long shot, I know. But if he's working at La Fonda and at this place too, maybe rum-running or even getting snow for people, surely he must work other places. Know how it's all connected."

Gunther looked intrigued, as she'd known he would. He liked a good detective story as much as she did. But he shook his head. "No one knows how it's all connected, Maddie, you know that. We all know our own scenes, and we don't ask too many questions."

Maddie nodded. She *did* know that. Yet she also knew she had to prove that Eddie had nothing to do with the bootlegging operation, at least not on that night, and he certainly hadn't done in his father. But how was Tomas involved in it all? He certainly seemed like a man who angered easily and drove others to anger too. If he was the one doing the rum-running, anyone could have killed him.

Gunther parked along the street next to the museum where Maddie had met Olive, and they hurried up the walkway arm in arm. She could hear guitar music from the plaza, the hum of laughter, but just a block away all was silent. The building looked just as nondescript and deserted as it had been in the afternoon.

Gunther gave three quick knocks at the door, waited, then two more. Not the same pattern as the boy earlier but just as strange. The door slid open an inch and a man peered out. Obviously Gunther was familiar, for the door opened and they were quickly ushered past. The door shut and locked behind them.

Inside, it was a completely different world. The walls were papered in dark red, lined with leather banquettes and small tables that surrounded a mirrored dance floor. Along the other end was a polished bar manned by bartenders in crisp white dinner jackets, shelves of bottles glittering like jewels. There was the red of grenadine, the acid green of absinthe, the diamond clearness of vodka. No cheap bathtub gin there. There were even waiters hurrying past with trays of food: fine steaks, caviar, chocolate mousse parfaits.

At the far end of the room, there was a small stage where a band played "I'll Build a Stairway to Paradise." A few couples circled the dance floor, flowing in and out of the rhythm as the people at the tables watched. Everyone wore suits and stylish dresses, beads flashing, skirts swirling. Maddie was even gladder she had worn one of her new frocks and patted at her grandmother's pearl-tipped combs tucked into her chignon.

132 of Amanda Allen

As her eyes adjusted to the dim light, she recognized a few people, artists she had met at parties and the museum and Elizabeth Grover dancing with an older gentleman Maddie knew was a state senator with ambitions to be governor. Elizabeth wore another expensive gown, dark purple with lavender and blue beads, a blue bandeau binding her blonde bob. She was laughing, her pupils dark and large in her blue eyes, so Maddie thought she must have already taken the little packet from her satin handbag in the ladies' necessary again.

"I've never seen anything like it here," Maddie whispered to Gunther. "I could almost be in New York again."

"Rather splendiferous, isn't it? Come along, darling, let's get a drink and then have a little spin around the floor. Maybe you can sneak behind the scenes later and look for your bootlegging boy."

A young woman in a flounced version of a black-and-white maid's outfit took away Maddie's coat, and Gunther found them a table near the dance floor where a waiter hurried to take their order. As they waited, Maddie studied the crowd around them a little closer. It was an interesting group indeed, a mix of local politicians and well-known artists. People it wouldn't be a good idea to cross. Had Tomas ran afoul of one of them?

When the cocktails arrived, they were a lovely pink shade, almost as if to complement her dress. She took a sip, and her eyes widened at the taste. "You're right. No ordinary hooch here."

"Only the best, my love," Gunther said as he gulped down his own drink. "Hope you brought your checkbook."

Once the drinks were finished, he took her hand and led her onto the dance floor. The band played a foxtrot, and Gunther was a skillful leader, turning and spinning her so she could see every bit of the room. Waiters came and went from an old-style green baize door all the time, but none of them was the blond boy. Not that she expected a young kid like that would be let out in front at a joint like this. She would have to find a way to do a little exploring.

"Mind if I cut in?" a voice said from behind her.

She glanced back to see a man she was sure she had never met before. If she had, she would have completely remembered. He was what her cousin Gwen, who was addicted to movie mags, would have called a "stunner."

And she wouldn't be wrong. He was tall and lean, with dark hair and eyes and cheekbones that could have cut glass. He was also perfectly dressed in a tailored black suit with white tie, pearl cufflinks gleaming at his wrists. It was as if Rudolph Valentino had suddenly landed in their little desert town.

"Of course not," Gunther said. "You *are* the boss here, after all. Maddie, meet Robert Bennett. Mr. Bennett, my friend Mrs. Madeline Alwin."

"I certainly know who the lovely Mrs. Alwin is," Robert Bennett said with a dazzling smile. "I'm glad you decided to grace my little establishment tonight."

Gunther smoothly spun her into Mr. Bennett's arms and gave her a little wave as he headed back to their table. More people had crowded in since they arrived, and he soon vanished from her sight.

For just a moment, Maddie let herself enjoy the music, the movement. She had forgotten what it was like to be in a handsome man's arms on an elegant dance floor, and it was rather—pleasant.

"I would hardly call it a 'little' establishment, Mr. Bennett," she said as he twirled her out and in again, making her laugh. She looked over his shoulder, fearing if she looked at him too long, she might become more than a little dazzled and forget her real errand that night. "It's a beauty."

"I'm glad you like it. It's a great compliment coming from someone with your artistry."

"You know I'm an artist?" Maddie said, surprised.

"I don't open businesses just anywhere. That would be foolish. I have to know there's an elegant clientele around first. An artist, daughter of the Vaughns of New York, granddaughter of an Astor. I know this is nothing like what you could find on the Upper East Side, but I do my best."

"Your best is swell indeed," Maddie answered, very disconcerted by his extensive knowledge. "But I don't think it's fair you know about me and I know nothing about you. You must have quite a story, Mr. Bennett."

"Please, call me Rob. And my story is a boring one, especially to a lady from New York. My father owned a grocery in Minneapolis, wanted me to take it over, but I knew I wanted more. *Needed* more, to see the world, meet new people."

"I certainly know the feeling," she answered. She thought for a moment of her parents' house, so dark, so filled with the past, with expectations and pressures. Of the threatened "rest cures" at asylums if she didn't meet those expectations. "Why a nightclub, though? Surely you could have gone into the films or something like that."

He laughed. "I'm flattered you think so. The problem is, I can't act worth a nickel. What I like is seeing people enjoy themselves and have a good time." He gestured around the room, which had grown louder as the booze flowed freely.

"And pay for the privilege."

He twirled her around again. "Of course. We all have to find a way to eat somehow, Mrs. Alwin."

"But why Santa Fe? We're such a sleepy little place."

"Little but mighty." He spun her out and in, a spiral as smooth as his voice, his smile. "Believe me, Mrs. Alwin, this town is going places. Look what's happened in only a few years. New Mexico is a state now; you have art museums, poetry readings, famous people. It's a beautiful spot too, which I'm sure you know very well."

"Of course. It's why I came here." She thought of her house, her sanctuary on her quiet road, dogs sleeping under trees, the same people at the same places. It was a wonderful world, but she wasn't sure about expansion.

"You see? Not to mention all the health seekers and your famous sunshine." He drew her in closer as another couple bumped into them, and she could smell his expensive cologne. "I've opened businesses in a lot of places. I know when a town is ripe for it."

"You've certainly attracted a large clientele in a short period of time."

"Word of mouth. Best advertisement there is. I hope you'll be a regular here too."

Maddie laughed. She had become so early to bed, early to rise in her widowhood. But . . . "I'll admit, your cocktails are quite delicious."

"Better than at La Fonda?" His tone was as affable as before, but she sensed a new current beneath, a sort of tension.

Maddie gave him a sharp glance. His eyes had narrowed, yet he still smiled at her, that Valentino gleam. "Maybe just a bit."

"I know everyone in town is a regular there. I like to know my competition. But we're different from them in a few ways, I hope." He drew her closer to speak more quietly near her ear. "I hear something a bit unpleasant happened there recently. Something to do with your own household."

Maddie felt her shoulders tense, and she studied him carefully. She knew perfectly well Santa Fe was a small place where gossip spread like wildfire down the mountains, but she felt a small, cold touch of disquiet that this man knew so much.

But then again, she *had* come to the club seeking information. And Rob Bennett seemed to have it in spades.

"My housekeeper's husband was killed there, it's true," she answered. "Mrs. Anaya is very upset about it, of course."

Rob nodded. The music ended, and he said, "Sit with me for a while, Mrs. Alwin?"

Maddie glanced at her table, but Gunther wasn't there. She nodded and followed Rob to a banquette in the corner that had a view of the whole room. He waved his hand, and two more cocktails quickly appeared.

"You should forget about your Mr. Anaya," he said quietly, his handsome face serious. "He was troubled, and you and his wife are well rid of him."

Maddie could barely breathe at his words. "What do you mean by trouble?"

Rob took a gold cigarette case from his inside jacket pocket and offered her one. She shook her head, and he lit one before answering, exhaling a silvery curl of smoke.

"I'm no saint, Mrs. Alwin. I freely admit that," he said. "I've done things I'm not proud of. A man has to in this world if he wants to get ahead. We're not all Astors."

Maddie gave a wary smile and took a sip of her drink. It was just as delicious as the last one and seemed to go straight to her head. She had to be so careful of so many things. She studied Rob Bennett's unearthly handsome face in the soft light of the shaded lamp on their table. It cast shadows around him, as if he was really in a movie.

"None of us are saints, Mr. Bennett—Rob," she said. "But what did Tomas Anaya do? What *could* he have done to deserve what happened?" She shivered at the memory of that body in the alley.

"Having a drink or two is one thing," Rob said. "People have always done that. It's not a party without a tipple, and until this ridiculous law is repealed someone might as well help people out."

"And make a little living out of it?" Maddie said, eyeing his fine suit, his pearl cufflinks.

He laughed. "I told you—I'm no saint. But I don't smuggle hard drugs, nor do I deal in the brothel business. Booze, a bit of gambling maybe—that makes enough for me."

Maddie was shocked. She had wondered about it, of course, but to hear it stated out loud was something else. "Tomas Anaya was involved in drugs? In prostitution?" She remembered that the Anayas had had to leave their pueblo home for some mysterious reason. Was it because Tomas was a criminal? One who dragged his own wife and children into such terrible things?

Rob shrugged. "It's easy enough here, close to the Mexican border. It's not in my line, but some get caught up in it all and can't get out. There's a young woman who comes here some nights to dance. She works at an establishment on San Francisco Street, the lower side at the edge of town. Mavis. She was friends with your Mr. Anaya. They say he liked to spend money on her."

"You mean they were . . . friends?" Maddie said tightly, thinking of Juanita. She *had* said Tomas used to be involved in such things, but had he been still?

"None of my business. But if you want to know more, she might be able to tell you something."

"But you would advise me against knowing—something?"

"It's best to stay out of certain matters, especially for a lady like yourself. Safer that way."

"I learned a long time ago that you can't live life just staying safe at home," Maddie said. You couldn't help the people you cared about that way either. She couldn't have done anything to help Pete. She had to try to help Eddie now. The kid had his whole life ahead of him, a mother and sisters who needed him.

She took another sip of her drink. "I'm a widow, Rob, the black sheep of my family, an artist. I'm not quite as shockable as all that."

He studied her for a long moment, a bemused smile on his face. "I suppose you're not at that."

"I love my home here, but I know there are more unpleasant things under the surface. Just like it was in New York." She watched the dancers on the floor, a flashy Charleston now, garters sparkling, feet flying, spirits high as a kite. "Is this Mavis here now?"

Rob stubbed out his cigarette. "I haven't seen her in a few days. She works at a place called Mrs. Holmes's, but she comes here once or twice a week." He gave her a cheeky little grin. "I wouldn't mind if you wanted to come back again to check."

Maddie laughed. "I just might, if the drinks are always this good. This is absolutely scrummy."

"We do aim to please," he said.

Elizabeth Grover suddenly stumbled out of the crowd to their table. She had lost her beaded bandeau and her hair was tousled, her cheeks red, her eyes dark and wide. "Robbie, darling," she slurred. "You promised me a dance."

Rob gave Maddie a half smile, half grimace. "So I did, Liz. If you'll excuse me, Mrs. Alwin?"

"Of course. It's been most—enlightening."

Maddie watched as he took Elizabeth's hand and led her onto the crowded floor. He seemed to be holding her up more than dancing with her, her arms looped tightly around his neck as she whispered into his ear. They vanished into the whirl.

As Maddie finished her drink, she studied everyone around her. They all seemed to be having a very good time, laughing, talking loudly, the music blaring. No one watched her at all. The green baize door opened and closed to a steady stream of waiters carrying trays of drinks, plates of food. It was all quite splashy, very New York–ish. Surely all quite expensive and complicated. Yet Rob Bennett seemed so easy with it all.

The door was propped open for a moment to let in a man with a large platter, and Maddie glimpsed the inner workings of a bustling, steamy kitchen.

A figure, smaller than the others, darted through the steam just for a second. Something about him, maybe the bright hair or that quick darting movement, was familiar to her. It was him, the boy.

She left her table, and as the door swung closed again, she slipped past it into the noise of the kitchen. It was even louder than the dining room, filled with shouted orders and the strong smell of food cooking, confusing and chaotic. She got a few odd glances, but everyone was too busy to confront her or kick her out.

She darted behind a rack of glasses and saw the flash of that blond head down a narrow corridor, just as she had on the street earlier that day. The boy dropped a crate of more glasses down on a table and dashed out.

"Hey!" one of the cooks shouted after him. "There better not be any missing from that delivery like last time."

He didn't answer, just kept running away. Maddie dashed after him, but by the time she got there, he was gone. There was only a door, half-open to the night outside.

She peeked past it and saw a narrow, dark lane, much like the one where Tomas had been found. It was quieter and cleaner, filled with stacks of crates and rubbish bins shared between Rob Bennett's place and the bakery behind it. It was suddenly quite silent after the roar of the crowd, and she shivered at the emptiness, the chilly wind. Her shoes weren't up to the dust and gravel, and the boy was gone. Rob's warnings about minding her own business rang in her head.

Disappointed, she made her way back into the club to look for Gunther. She found him standing near the bar, smoking one of his Gauloises, sipping a martini, and chatting with a handsome waiter.

"Maddie, there you are, my darling," he said. "This is Mike. He works here. He's actually read one of my books, can you imagine?"

"I thought *The Savage Sunset* was the bee's knees, Mr. Ryder," Mike said, his tone full of awe. "I hope to write a novel myself one day."

"No better place than here to do it," Gunther said. "So much lovely inspiration."

"I just have to save up my pay here to take a little time off."

"Maybe Maddie here could paint your portrait," Gunther said with a tip of his cocktail glass toward her. "She's an artist, you know."

"I'm always looking for models," Maddie said. She dug a card from her handbag, pushing aside the pistol she fortunately hadn't needed, and gave it to Mike. He *was* interesting-looking, and it couldn't hurt to know someone who worked at the club for the mysterious Mr. Bennett. "I just saw someone I thought I knew—my friend's son. Blond, quick?"

Mike laughed. "The one like a chimney sweep in some Dickens novel, you mean? He's just one of the delivery kids who run errands around here. I don't know his name, though."

Mike went back to his work, and Maddie leaned on the bar next to Gunther. She saw Elizabeth at a table with her senator, but Rob was nowhere to be seen. "Bertie's replacement?" she said, gesturing to Mike as he dashed between tables.

"Who can say, dearest?" Gunther answered vaguely. "He seems nice enough, doesn't he? Have you found any clues in your own search?"

Maddie sighed. "I did think I saw that boy who was at La Fonda, the one Eddie knows, but he vanished out the back door after he dropped off a delivery. He was totally gone when I got to the door, the whole street empty."

"He probably ducked into the tunnels."

"Tunnels?" Maddie asked, curious.

"If he's a delivery boy, he'll have to make his way around to all the bars and speakeasies, won't he? They run under the whole plaza, though I'm not sure why they were originally built."

"Fascinating," Maddie murmured. She hadn't heard of such a thing. It seemed like something in a romantic Gothic novel, awfully eerie. Who knew *what* could be there, hiding right below their feet?

"Now don't even think about going down there alone, Maddie," Gunther said sternly. "I get the chills just thinking about you getting lost."

"I would find a guide, I promise." She smiled at a waiter as he set out another pretty pink drink in front of her. "Thank you, but I don't think I'm the one who ordered this."

"On the house," he said. "Mr. Bennett's orders."

She glanced across the room to see Rob watching her. He held up his own glass in a toast, and she nodded.

"You seem to have made a friend," Gunther said.

"He seems nice enough," she echoed Gunther's own earlier words. "He's certainly a looker and full of information. He told me Tomas has been splashing money about on a woman named Mavis. What do you hear about Mr. Bennett?"

"Nothing at all. That's one of the fascinating things about him. A man of mystery."

Maddie took a drink, but she found she was suddenly quite tired. It felt like it had been a long night. "Gunther, dear, would you mind escorting me home now?"

"Not at all." He put out his cigarette in one of the crystal ashtrays. "It's gotten rather dull here now."

One of the girls in the flouncy dresses brought Maddie her coat, and she set off into the night with Gunther. The cold, clear air seemed delicious after the smoke and perfume of the club, and it was so quiet it made her ears hum. There were still a few people on the plaza, couples lingering under the new streetlamps, shadows flickering. She hadn't learned much, except that Tomas seemed to have even more secrets than she had realized. That everyone had more secrets than she wanted to know.

*   *   *

Despite the late hour, Juanita was up and waiting when Maddie stepped into the house. She sat at the kitchen table in her quilted dressing gown, a steaming mug in front of her along with a glossy fashion magazine of Maddie's. It looked as if she had been cleaning out some of Tomas's belongings, for a crate sat on the floor, filled with shirts and bandanas and bottles. The bottles made her think of booze and the trouble Tomas might have been in that led to his death. There was a jar of hair pomade, a faceted bottle of something like cologne, and a couple other bottles. They looked a bit like the ones in the crate the boy had dropped off in the club kitchen before he vanished.

Juanita saw her looking at the box, and she kicked it away. "It looks like he was keeping hooch hidden, doesn't it?" she said, her voice low, toneless. "Hypocrite."

Maddie longed to ask her what she meant by that, but Juanita shook her head and tried to smile. "Some cocoa, Señora Maddie?" she said, pushing herself back from the table.

"Oh, Juanita, that sounds perfect just now." Maddie sank gratefully into a chair and kicked off her heeled shoes. Buttercup scampered up onto her lap, and the sweet smell of chocolate filled the kitchen. She was glad she wasn't in New York; she was too old for so many late nights.

She took a long drink of the cocoa once it was ready, thick and sweet and slightly spicy, as only Juanita could make it. It drove out the lingering bitter tang of cocktails.

"I'm afraid I didn't find out much tonight, Juanita," she said. "I thought I saw that boy, Harry, the one you said was Eddie's friend. But he vanished."

"He'll come back around, unless he's already run away from town," Juanita said. "It's not a big place here; there are only so many spots he can go. Mr. Springer called and said I can take Eddie some more of his things first thing in the morning. He's already been moved to another cell, a bigger one, until the judge gets back. Mr. Springer said it won't be long."

Juanita was trying to sound hopeful, but Maddie could see the sadness in her eyes. She reached out to squeeze her hand. "You, me, Mr. Springer—we're all working just as fast as we can to find out what really happened. I'm sure that between us we'll be done in no time, and Eddie will be back here where he belongs."

Maddie tried to sound hopeful too, to project a confidence she was far from feeling.

She glanced over the table at Juanita's reading material, a film mag open on a glossy photo of Norma Talmadge. The cropped waves of the actress's shiny, dark hair framed her smiling face, a fur collar of an evening cloak drawn up around her neck. *Love finds our favorite sweetheart!* gushed the headline.

"She does look pretty, doesn't she?" Maddie said wistfully. "I do wonder sometimes what my hair would look like in a bob."

Juanita looked shocked. "Are you a—a *flapper* now, Señora Maddie? I read that term all over the place; it sounds terribly naughty."

Maddie laughed. "Never. I'm an old widow with dull clothes; no one would call me a flapper. I also can't do the Charleston, I don't carry a flask in my garter, and I would be exhausted if I tried to stay up clubbing until three every night. I don't know how those bright young things do it."

She thought of Elizabeth Grover with her cropped hair and beaded gown, her handbag full of contraband and her many dance partners. Now *there* was a flapper.

Juanita frowned down at Norma's smiling face. "Well, I hope Pearl and Ruby never decide to become flappers then."

Maddie sighed. "Me neither, Juanita."

"Oh, I almost forgot. Dr. Cole called while you were out," Juanita said. She took a slip of paper from her dressing gown pocket and passed it over the table.

Dr. Cole. *David*. Maddie felt a sudden excited flutter deep inside at the thought of him, a new energy, but she pushed it away. It was surely no time for schoolgirl giggles over handsome blue eyes! She scanned the penciled words: *Found something interesting. Meet me at hospital at ten tomorrow morning?* There was also a telephone number.

Maddie glanced at the clock. Ten was really only a few hours away. She sighed at the thought of a hospital first thing in the morning. She had hated the place ever since her volunteer work when the men came home from war and during the 'flu.

Yet she had to admit she was also intrigued. She had the feeling that David was not the sort to use the word "interesting" lightly.

CHAPTER 12

The next morning, Maddie was up bright and early despite her late night and walked toward St. Vincent's Hospital in the sharp, clear sunshine of midmorning. A few fluffy, cotton-like white clouds drifted through the sky, which shifted between turquoise and an almost violet-blue with no sign of rain. She hurried past dairy wagons on their way to make deliveries, artists selling pottery and jewelry on the plaza, and workers lugging buckets of paint to houses.

She smoothed her beige kid gloves and pushed her oval sunglasses back up her nose. She didn't want to think too hard about what had made her dress in one of her new stylish outfits, a fashionable suit of lightweight pale-green tweed and a brimmed hat of beige straw with green trim. It certainly couldn't be because she was seeing Dr. David Cole again.

Surely not.

She paused on the corner where the large French Gothic cathedral sat across from La Fonda. The square towers of honey-colored stone glowed almost rosy in the morning light. Once, when she was caught in the sticky, dark web of grief, someone had told her that one day she would notice beauty again. Feel that spark of life, art, and joy again. She hadn't believed them back then.

But now, as she looked up at the jewel-like stained glass catching the pure, clear light, she saw what they meant. She wanted to help Juanita find that one day too.

She cut through the garden between the cathedral and the hospital, which was run by the Sisters of Charity and had been for over fifty years. It was a three-story, white brick Victorian structure, clear windows blinking down at the passers-by. Maddie hurried up the steps and into the foyer.

The familiar old smell of a hospital—disinfectant, stale air, the tang of medicine, and the faint tinge of fried food—brought back a flood of memories from that time after the war when she had volunteered with the Red Cross.

Nursing nuns rushed past her, bustling efficiently in their starched white wimples and aprons over their black wool habits. An orderly pushed a trolley carrying a groaning patient under a blanket. One of the sisters said she would fetch Dr. Cole for her right away.

Maddie fought the urge to fidget and pace as she waited, keeping herself from checking her hair and lipstick. She was there on an errand. That was all.

"Mrs. Alwin—Maddie," he called, and her self-deception of not looking forward to seeing him personally crumbled. He hurried over to take her hand with a smile. "I'm so glad you could make it."

"Of course," she answered. "I'm so grateful you're doing us this favor."

A frown flickered over his face, and she saw something she recognized very well in his blue eyes, a sadness overlaid with curiosity. She had felt that way much too often herself. "I found something—well, rather interesting."

"Interesting?"

"Yes. I wasn't sure if such information would upset Mrs. Anaya too much, so I thought I would get your opinion first."

"I'll be happy to tell her whatever she should know," Maddie said. "She is a very strong woman. But I admit, I'm intrigued."

"Come with me. I'll show you what I've found." He led her toward the lifts. "Are you particularly squeamish, Madeline? I should have asked before."

Maddie laughed. "Not very. My mother thinks I'm quite unladylike."

He laughed too, and she almost hoped she heard a note of admiration in it. "I didn't think so."

"I wasn't allowed to take real anatomy classes at art school," she said as they stepped into the lift and he pulled the iron grate into place. "I did work at a hospital as a Red Cross volunteer at the end of the war, when—well, when I knew my husband wasn't coming back. I stayed on to help during the influenza. Just changing dressings, pushing a tea cart around, things like that. But I did see some things."

The doors clanged closed, and she found herself in the small space all alone with him. She wanted to break free, to run away—and for the lift ride to never end.

"I can imagine."

"Nothing like you saw in Europe, of course," she said, staring hard at the lit-up buttons marking off the floors.

That small frown flickered over his brow again and then was gone. "And you never caught the 'flu yourself?"

Maddie shook her head. "Back in the 1890s, when I was very tiny, my mother and I had a similar illness. Fevers, chills, congestion. We never got sick in '18, but my father did. Fortunately, he survived. I was able to help out in the New York hospital." She shuddered to remember what she had seen there, the rows and rows of sick people and not enough beds for them, all of them coughing their lives away.

David nodded seriously. He stroked his silver-flecked beard in thoughtful reflection. "I saw that sometimes myself. If people had been ill back then, twenty or so years ago, they didn't catch the Spanish 'flu. Intriguing. My wife . . ." He paused. "My wife was not so lucky. She died before I returned from France."

Maddie was shocked. That would certainly explain the deep sadness she often sensed in him, the sadness that echoed her own. That faraway look in his eyes. Her heart ached for him. "Oh!" she cried. "I am so terribly sorry. I didn't . . ." She swallowed hard, not sure what she should say.

"It was a long time ago," he said. The lift doors opened, and he took her arm to help her out. "I'm afraid I didn't warn you this was the morgue. I promise you won't see anything untoward, though. Nothing your mother would object to."

She had to smile. "I told you, David, I'm not squeamish. Not too much, anyway. I'll do whatever I can to help Eddie. And I am very interested. I do like a good detective novel from time to time."

"I thought so." He led her through the bare cement basement. The air felt cold, clammy, and the smell of disinfectant was even stronger, overlaying something sharp and metallic, like blood. She was glad she had worn a suit with a warm jacket, even if she had really chosen it because it was pretty.

He took her into a small room, windowless, lined with stainless steel counters and cabinets with a drain in the middle of the sloped stone floor. A body covered in a white sheet lay on a concrete slab, and Maddie realized it must be Tomas. She could see a glimpse of a hand under the hem of the sheet.

She swallowed down a sudden bitter tang of sickness and hoped she had meant it when she told David she wasn't squeamish. She didn't want him to think she wasn't brave, even as she felt like a terrible coward.

He picked up a notebook from the counter and flicked through the densely written pages. "I thought the amount of blood, the pattern of bruising, was a bit odd. It looked like he was surely beaten to death."

"Yes," Maddie agreed, remembering the scene at La Fonda. She wished she had paid more attention, taken note of more details. It all seemed to have happened in a flash. "That's what I thought, or maybe that he was stabbed. I didn't hear or see any gunshot."

"No. I thought so too, yet once I looked closer that just didn't seem right." He folded back a corner of the sheet and held up the hand. It was the palest gray but with those quite dark fingernails she remembered. "I've ordered some toxicology tests, but I think maybe Mr. Anaya here was being poisoned before his death."

"Poisoned?" Maddie cried. She stared down at the hand, so horribly pale, and ran through her mind everything in her own kitchen, her own garden. Surely that couldn't be. None of the rest of them were sick. Unless . . . "Why do you think that?"

"I saw such things in medical school. Most of my own work as a medic on the battlefield was much more straightforward. Yet I remember studying the signs very well. Skin discolored, blood turning to a strange foamy consistency. Mr. Anaya has such signs, here and here. See? I also noticed it in the autopsy itself. If he was beaten in this way, the way he was the night he died, it would have been painful but not fatal."

"Someone trying to make a point, maybe?" Maddie said, thinking of Tomas's strange activities around town and how many people seemed to dislike him.

David gave a wry smile. "I like to read detective novels too. The internal bleeding was extensive, and there is also quite a lot of bruising here and here."

Maddie frowned. "What sort of poison? Something quick, something he would have taken that day?"

He shook his head. "I think it was something slower acting. An arsenic, perhaps. That can be found in any rat poison at the corner store or even cleaning agents. Or an herb. I don't know much about the local flora, I admit. It could have been disguised in food or drink. It might have made him feel ill beforehand. Had he been complaining of such things?"

"I don't know," Maddie answered, feeling foolish she hadn't asked such things herself. "I had just gotten back from New York. I can ask Juanita, though. He did seem a bit feverish when I last saw him, his eyes a bit yellowish."

"I think someone really didn't like your Mr. Anaya."

"I think a lot of people didn't," she said, thinking about what Mr. Bennett had told her, the woman from the brothel, the possible bootlegging, the mysterious way he and Juanita had had to leave their home. The quarrels between him and his family. There was so much she didn't know, so much the private people in Santa Fe kept hidden.

"Of course it would be his wife who had the most access to him in that way," David said carefully.

"Oh, no," Maddie protested. "I know Juanita. She wouldn't do this, nor would Eddie. And whoever beat him—would they have known it would hasten his death?"

He glanced down at the body, his eyes narrowed. "So maybe we're looking for at least two people? Or maybe one who wanted to be rid of him, one that wanted to, as you say, teach him a lesson."

Maddie did like the sound of that word—*we're*. It made her feel not so alone for the first time in ages. That she had a partner in something. This wasn't a puzzle she had to solve herself. She had lots of people helping her.

She looked down at that pitiful gray hand. In life, Tomas Anaya had been a large man, a bit intimidating. Now he was shrunken, sad, like all those poor boys who had come back from war only to be struck down by septicemia or the 'flu. It wasn't fair, wasn't right. His family deserved answers.

She suddenly noticed a slightly yellow tinge beneath the gray of death. It made her think of some of the soldiers who had been gassed in the war, a sickly yellow-green color to their nails and their skin. She *had* noticed Tomas seemed unwell when she saw him at her house. Maybe David really was right. Maybe Tomas had been poisoned before he died, eaten from the inside out like those soldiers. But who would do that, and how?

She frowned as she tried to remember something that seemed stuck in the depths of her brain, something just beyond her grasp.

Then she remembered—that box of Tomas's belongings that Juanita had been packing the night before. There were a few bottles, hair pomade, maybe breath freshener, and a strange, faceted bottle with a little bit of amber-colored liquid in it. She had thought it was cologne. Juanita had hinted it was hooch, which somehow made him a hypocrite. That would make sense if it was like the bottles the boy Harry delivered to the speakeasy. What if it was something else entirely?

And where had he gotten it?

"I think I might have an idea," she said.

"I would be very interested to hear it," Dr. Cole answered. He tucked Tomas's hand under the sheet again, carefully, respectfully. She liked his calm, dignified attitude. "But I can't ask you to stay in such a place any longer or your mother might hear of it and be angry with me. Maybe you would join me for a meal sometime soon?"

"Oh, yes, thank you," Maddie said gratefully. She felt like she could do with a drop of a drink herself after so much strange information, and she wanted to hear what David might think about the bottles she had seen at Mr. Bennett's club. "That would be lovely. Lunch at La Fonda? I have a favorite table in the dining room. And maybe we could look for a clue or two while we're there?"

He smiled ruefully. "I would love nothing better, Mrs. Alwin—Madeline. But I fear duty calls at the moment. Sister Adams, the duty nurse, is very strict, and I'll be in a lot of trouble if I don't review all the new information on the patients' charts after her rounds."

Maddie laughed despite a little pang of disappointment that there wouldn't be just a little more time with him that afternoon. Time *not* spent in a morgue. "I quite understand. I'm sure I met many Sister Adams types when I was a volunteer. I do hope you are visiting *living* patients this afternoon?"

"I promise all of them are still with us."

"Thank you so much for taking the time to help me. It's very kind of you."

"Not at all. It's all very intriguing." He glanced away, a sadness flickering through his eyes once more. "And no man should ever go without justice. There's too much wrongdoing in the world that goes unanswered."

"Indeed there is." She wondered again what sadness it was he carried. The terrible things he must have seen in the war? The loss of his wife? He fought against the injustices that made her angry and helplessly sad, as well, and he saw darkness that lingered in people's hearts. Whatever had led him to pursue a healing profession, to try to right at least some wrongs? If only she could get to know him better. It was a feeling she hadn't had in a long time, that flicker of excited interest, that feeling of knowing someone that she had only just barely met.

They walked together back to the lift, and Maddie was glad to be leaving behind the dank, dim small rooms of the basement morgue. Dr. Cole was quite right. There was too much sadness in the world as it was without any poor soul being taken out of his life, away from his family, too early and in such a terrible way.

"If you don't have to work too late, maybe you'd care to have dinner at my house tomorrow?" she said, trying to sound casual, offhanded. How did a girl do that? She had known Pete since childhood and never had to learn any sort of dating games with him. She felt terribly silly and unmodern now. "You can tell Mrs. Anaya more about what you've found."

He smiled, and suddenly she didn't feel quite so silly or unsure anymore. "Thank you. I'd like that. Maybe I could also be privileged to get a little glimpse of your work too? As a man who can't draw a stick figure himself, I'm always in awe of artists."

Maddie smiled back at him, trying not to blush like a schoolgirl. "I think that could be arranged."

*   *   *

Maddie left David at the gates to the hospital garden. He turned to wave at her from the steps, and she waved back, afraid she was grinning like a fool. Despite everything that was happening, she had to admit she did rather enjoy the doctor's company, his intelligent conversation. The way his hand felt when he took her arm. She hadn't felt that way in a long time.

She turned to head home and heard the bells of the cathedral toll the hour, as they had when she'd first arrived to meet David that morning. She glanced up at the bell towers, half-shadowed now, and she remembered that Juanita had said Father Malone there was helping her with the girls and the school. She wondered if he knew about Tomas too, even though Eddie had said his father wasn't one for church. On impulse, she hurried up the wide stone steps and through the heavy bronze front doors.

Inside, all was a cool, calm hush. It was a pretty church, all soaring, airy vaulted ceilings and gilded pillars just like the cathedrals she had seen as a girl in France. The inlaid mosaics of angels and the rich glow of the stained glass windows made her think of Pete and how he would talk about the beautiful places they would see after the war: Westminster Abbey, Notre Dame, St. Mark's.

A woman in a calico apron was scrubbing at the black-and-white marble floor of the foyer and told her Father Malone was near the altar. "Cleaning out the candle holders," she grumbled. "Even though it's not his job."

Maddie thanked her and made her way down the aisle, past the marble baptismal font. It was mostly deserted at that hour, with only a few people at silent prayer in the pews. The cool air was scented with lemon polish and candle smoke, and her shoe heels clicked on the stone floor. She could see why Juanita liked to take refuge here.

She found a stout figure in a black cassock at the foot of the altar screen, scrubbing out the wrought-iron candlestand just as the cleaning lady said. Maddie wondered what the archbishop, who was rumored to be rather grand, thought of that. The priest peered up at her through thick spectacles, a friendly smile on his round lined face.

"Father Malone?" Maddie said.

"Yes, that's me. How can I help you, young lady?"

"My name is Madeline Alwin. My housekeeper, Juanita Anaya, says you're her friend."

"Oh, yes, the good Mrs. Anaya! I just heard about Eduardo today. Tell her I will call on her this evening and go with her to the jail if she likes. She must be so worried."

"Yes, indeed. We all are."

"Of course. The lad can't have done such a thing, I'm sure of it."

"That's what I think too," Maddie said, feeling a rather friendly glow toward the man. "I'm trying to help her however I can. Juanita and her girls—well, they're like my family in a way."

"And how can *I* help you then, Mrs. Alwin?"

Maddie glanced up at the altar, painted with bright scenes of saints and angels, glowing with giltwork from the windows above. "I know that you must see so many people here in town. Juanita has seemed worried about something lately, something to do with her husband. I just thought . . ." Her words faded away. She wasn't sure *what* she thought, really. Only that she was worried about Juanita and so was Father Malone.

"Are you a churchgoer, Mrs. Alwin?" he asked.

"I sometimes go to Holy Faith, up the street. Though not as often as my mother back at St. Thomas on Fifth Avenue would like."

He smiled. "Ah, a fellow Easterner! I'm from Boston myself, though that was a long time ago. As an Anglican, I'm sure you know the seal of the confessional."

"I do, and I wouldn't want you to tell me anything Juanita told you in confidence," Maddie said quickly. She wanted Juanita to tell her such things on her own. "But if you know of any general concerns . . ."

He gestured for her to sit down with him on the front pew. "It's true there is something that has been worrying her and is a general concern to myself and also the archbishop."

"Really?" Maddie asked, intrigued. "What is that, Father?"

He looked at the altar, the angels reflected in his spectacles. "I've been out here a long time, since I was a young man in the missions. A lot here has changed in the last few years, but some things have stayed the same." He gave her a sharp glance. "What brought *you* to New Mexico, Mrs. Alwin?"

"My husband died in the war, and I was a bit lost for a while. I was on a cross-country trip with my cousin, who wanted to see the film stars in California. There was just something in the air here, the light, that—it comforted me, I suppose."

Father Malone nodded. "A spiritual feeling. It's everywhere here. This land is a great gift from God. But sometimes it can also be, shall we say, misleading."

Maddie was puzzled. "What do you mean? Is Mrs. Anaya . . . ?"

"No, not her. But she feared her husband was involved in something quite odd." He studied Maddie closely for a moment, and she tried not to fidget, as she had at St. Thomas as a child. "You're a war widow, Mrs. Alwin. You know that a certain sort of person, mediums, have been growing in popularity."

"Yes, I did see such places in New York. Séances, card readings, things like that."

"Have you been to a séance?"

Maddie shook her head. "I think if my husband wants to talk to me, he will. I don't need to pay someone to reach him."

"Quite right."

"But I don't think I've seen such things here."

"A woman has set herself up in a small shop over Kaune's Grocery on the plaza. A Madame Genet. Mrs. Anaya feared her husband was going to see her."

"I wouldn't have thought he was the type. Juanita said he was not a churchy person." Or maybe Father Malone meant "seeing" her in a romantic way? Was Madame Genet one of the women Tomas was splashing out on, like the Mavis who Rob Bennett had mentioned?

Father Malone nodded. "When it comes to a person's deepest beliefs, deepest fears, you never know, Mrs. Alwin. This has long been a superstitious place in some ways."

"And Juanita was concerned about this Madame Genet person?"

"She did think her husband was keeping many secrets from her. She's a lady of much faith of her own, and it worried her he might be led astray. And—may I be honest, Mrs. Alwin?"

"Of course."

"There are rumors that this Madame Genet is some sort of front for criminal activity. No one knows much about her. But the archbishop certainly doesn't like the fact that she might be using people's grief to lead them astray."

"You mean she might be bootlegging as well as holding séances?"

Father Malone shrugged. "She appeared so suddenly, and no one knows much about her at all. And odd things have been happening lately. A shipment of sacramental wine from California was stolen before it reached us. This town has never been a haven of law and order, but usually church matters are left alone. And it's rather quiet here at most times."

Maddie nodded, thinking of Rob Bennett and his swanky club. Had one of the well-dressed women there been Madame Genet? "Thank you, Father Malone. You've given me a lot to think about." She rose and straightened her hat.

He stood up next to her and walked with her toward the doors. "Tell Mrs. Anaya I will call on her this evening after Mass."

"I will. She tells me you're helping her find places for the girls at the school?"

He chuckled. "They are certainly clever girls, aren't they? Very . . . spirited."

Maddie laughed. "They are that."

He pushed open the heavy door to let in a dazzle of sunlight and bright-blue sky. "Let me know if I can be of any more help at all, Mrs. Alwin. Mrs. Anaya is a good lady. I will pray for her."

"Thank you, Father Malone." Maddie suddenly remembered what Rob Bennett had said about Tomas's fancy woman, the lady of the evening named Mavis. She glanced back uncertainly at Father Malone. Priests *did* seem to know everything that happened in their parishes. But how did a person delicately ask a man of the cloth such a thing?

"I—you wouldn't happen to have heard if Mr. Anaya had—er, other kinds of friends," she said, feeling terribly clumsy.

He gave her an understanding smile. "I'm afraid not. Mrs. Anaya has concerns, of course, but I don't know of anything in particular. Is there someone you're concerned about then?"

"I'm not sure," Maddie murmured. She would have to keep looking. "Thanks again, Father. I hope I'll see you soon."

"I'm sure you will, Mrs. Alwin."

★ ★ ★

When Maddie got home, she found Juanita cooking dinner in the kitchen and the girls playing with Buttercup on the tile floor. The scents of baking bread and stewing green chili were rich in the air.

Maddie took off her hat and gloves. "I hope there's more you can add to that delicious stew for tomorrow, Juanita."

Juanita looked up, a tiny gleam peeking through the haze of her distraction. "A gentleman caller, Señora

Maddie?" She had often hinted to Maddie that a young woman should have love and children. Juanita seemed so romantic for someone whose own marriage had become such a worry.

"In a way, I suppose," Maddie said. She *did* rather like the doctor, but it wouldn't do to get Juanita's hopes up. Or her own. "It's Dr. Cole. As you know, he's helping us with—things. At the hospital."

Maddie glanced at the girls, who were listening avidly. Juanita frowned and said, "Girls, why don't you go outside and gather a bouquet for the table?"

As Pearl and Ruby dashed outside, the dog barking at their heels, Maddie sat down at the table and reached for some potatoes that needed peeling. She noticed that the box of Tomas's belongings was gone. "Dr. Cole worked as a medic in the war, and as promised, he took a look at Tomas for us since the coroner is gone."

Juanita wiped her hands on a dish towel, her expression wary. "Tell me."

"He thinks Tomas might have been poisoned before he died. He's doing some tests and will tell us for sure when he knows more. Arsenic, perhaps—maybe rat poison or something like that. It would have made any bleeding more quickly fatal, it seems."

"He can't think *I* would do something like that," Juanita said, a sob in her voice.

"I'm sure no one thinks that," Maddie assured her. "But can you think of anyone who . . . ?"

Juanita shook her head, her usual calm slipping into agitation. "I told you, Señora Maddie, Tomas has been mostly away from home lately."

Away with other women? Running gin and cocaine? "I noticed some bottles in that box of Tomas's things. Is it some kind of medicine he took? Something someone could have slipped to him?"

Juanita frowned in thought. "Just some aftershave, I think. And some hair pomade, and—no, wait. There was something. I didn't look too closely, but you know his things have to be gathered up to be buried with him."

She hurried out of the room and came back with the box. Maddie helped her sort through the shirts and handkerchiefs. They found the aforementioned bottle of aftershave and a jar of pomade. They both just smelled of lemons, but Maddie put them aside to be tested anyway.

At the bottom of the box was that strange bottle she'd noticed before. It had sloped sides and a darkened cork and was half-full of some kind of amber liquid. Maddie cautiously sniffed at it, but she could smell nothing.

"Do you know what this is?" she asked.

Juanita shook her head. "It was in his bureau drawer with the other things. I haven't seen it before. He never used to be so concerned with his appearance, not until . . ."

Until there were other women? Maddie held the bottle up to the light. It looked dark, thick, almost syrupy. "I think we should show it to the doctor."

"I suppose so. Is it some kind of drink? That's what I thought, so I didn't look at it very closely."

"If it is, it's not like any hooch I know." Maddie thought of the gassed soldiers and shivered. She carefully wrapped up the bottle and tucked it away to give to David later. She had a lot to think over. "I think I'll do a bit of painting before dinner."

Juanita nodded. She looked deep in thought, but she just turned back to the stove in silence. Maddie went out to the garden. The girls were chasing each other along the gravel pathways, Buttercup barking at them. It was such a beautiful scene, the exuberant girls in the sunlight, the bright flowers, that it made her feel quite sad.

In the studio, she took off her fine suit jacket and put on an apron. She tried to sketch, but her thoughts wouldn't let her focus on her work for once. She thought instead of what she had learned in the morgue, at the hotel, and from the priest. It left her more confused than ever.

A knock at the studio door gave her a welcome distraction. She hurried over to find Gunther standing there, bouncing on the toes of his polished two-tone shoes.

"Maddie, my dear," he cried. "I think I have found that fancy lady Mavis that Mr. Bennett told you Tomas was going around with. There's also a dance at the Golden Rooster Club in a few nights, if you're brave enough to come with me. Someone there might be able to tell you more, as well. All of us miscreants do have to stick together."

Maddie had to laugh ruefully. "Of course you heard something. You know everyone. Come inside and tell me all."

"This is all better than a G. K. Chesterton novel, darling," he said. "I do like something to distract me from my own work."

"It is just like Chesterton," she answered. "Wait until you hear! There's even a priest . . ."

CHAPTER 13

Dinner that night at Maddie's house turned out to be a crowded one and, for an hour or two, a very welcome distraction from worries, puzzles, and grief. With Father Malone, Dr. Cole, and Gunther all coming as guests, Pearl and Ruby insisted on setting the dining room table with Maddie's grandmother's rarely used Meissen china set and gathering a bouquet from the garden. Buttercup twirled and barked at their heels, their excitement infectious.

"But Señora Maddie," Juanita protested as she stood with Maddie in the dining room doorway, surveying the carved antique table and high-backed chairs with their bright woven cushions. "There's no time to make a fine meal! I only have the lamb stew on the stove and a few early asparagus from the garden. I suppose there's some leftover cake for a trifle . . ."

"Juanita, it will be quite delicious," Maddie answered as she swept back the satin-lined curtains to let the light in. "It always is. And it's only a small party. I'll call Kaune's for a delivery of some of their cold salads. It's always fun to have a choice, and the dairy will have cream for the trifle."

"Small, yes, but Father Malone will be here! And a doctor." Juanita's eyes narrowed. "A handsome doctor, I think?"

Maddie bit her lip and pretended to be very busy rearranging the pottery ornaments on the sideboard. "He's not bad-looking. And he's certainly very clever. He'll have a lot to tell us tonight."

Juanita nodded, a sad, faraway look in her eyes. "Everyone has been kind, Señora Maddie. It does give me hope."

Maddie swallowed hard. She too had once needed hope and good friends after her husband died and she felt so alone. "I'll just go see how the girls are getting along."

As she hurried outside, Juanita called, "Don't wear black again, Señora Maddie! Bright colors look so much prettier on you. If this doctor is so handsome and smart . . ."

Maddie laughed. "You and Gunther and all your fashion advice!"

But she did leave the old black satin in the wardrobe and chose a pale-lilac chiffon tea gown and a silver-embroidered Spanish shawl. A bit of color didn't hurt, after all.

It turned out Juanita had more than enough food for a most splendid dinner: the lamb stew with asparagus and new potatoes, macaroni and shrimp salads, fresh greens in olive oil, and the trifle with berry jam and ice cream. Everyone chatted and laughed around the table as they passed the pretty china plates, Father Malone telling them about the trouble he had gotten into during his Boston youth, Gunther sighing over his publishing woes.

"And what about you, Dr. Cole?" Father Malone asked as Juanita passed him another portion of trifle. "What part of England do you hail from? I only visited once, a trip to Canterbury and the 'troublesome' Becket's tomb, but I thought it was very beautiful."

Dr. Cole smiled, and Maddie thought it looked a bit wistful. Homesickness, maybe? A life left so far behind? Maybe it reminded him of his wife. "It's a beautiful place, true, Father. I come from Brighton, near the sea. My own father was a doctor there, as was his, and my mother was the daughter of an apothecary. My parents had known each other since childhood, and I was their only child. But I had plenty of cousins to run with on the beach and eat too much rock candy with on the pier until we were ill with it. My grandfather even remembered when the old prince regent would come there to treat his gout. Granddad was sure that not eating twenty courses at supper might have helped old George more than the sea bathing did!"

Everyone laughed, and the twins demanded more stories about eccentric English kings and queens to add to their fairy-tale repertoire, insisting they would use them in their new doll theatricals and that Dr. Cole had to come be the audience one day soon. David promised he would, and Maddie found herself hoping he would return, once happier times had come to her house and the girls could just be little girls again. When their brother would be home. If that day ever came, as she was determined it would.

"So you were expected to follow in the family business?" Father Malone asked.

"I was. Luckily for me, I always found medicine fascinating," David said. "I loved nothing more than following my father on his rounds, hearing people's stories, helping them when I could."

"It is the same where I grew up," Juanita said. "If your mother made pottery, so did you. If she was a weaver, so were you. I wasn't so good at either of those things, I'm afraid."

"But you *are* a most excellent chef, Mrs. Anaya," David said. "This lamb is wonderful. I haven't had any cooked so perfectly since I lived in France for a time. Hospital food isn't always so palatable, I'm afraid. And this mint sauce—sublime."

Juanita smiled happily. "You must have some more then to take with you. The mint came from Señora Maddie's own garden. I learned this recipe from my grandmother. My own mother never met a piece of meat she couldn't char to bits. It needs a deft hand and good timing."

"I wonder if such talents skip generations," Gunther said. "I don't know anyone in my family who likes to write. Or in Maddie's who can paint. My brother, for instance, is a stockbroker. I couldn't add a line of sums to save my life."

Maddie laughed. "So true. My own brother likes a 'jolly nice' Dutch still life to show his friends after dinner parties

and impress them with the cost of it, but that's about it."
She took a sip of her tea, thinking about families, about
how they were similar or completely different, how such
things could happen even if two people grew up in the
same house.

"Ah, yes. Families," Father Malone said. "Can't live
with them, can't be without them!"

"Did your family approve of you going into the church,
Father?" Maddie asked. "Or did they argue against it, like
my parents and my painting?"

"They would have liked it well enough if I stayed in the
East and aimed for a cardinal's red hat. Not so much when
I came out to missions in the Wild West, though. But we
must all follow our true purposes in life."

Maddie thought of the half-finished canvases in her
studio, the colors and shapes that wouldn't leave her mind
until they came out through her paintbrush. "I hope so."

"You, Mrs. Alwin, are to bring us beauty and truth
with your paints," Father Malone said with a kindly smile.
"Mr. Ryder distracts us and educates us with his pen.
Mrs. Anaya feeds us. And Dr. Cole brings us health or, fail-
ing that, justice."

Maddie suddenly noticed that most of the food was
gone, even the trifle, and the girls were getting heavy-eyed.
The hour was growing late, and they still had serious matters to talk about. "Girls," she said to the twins, "would
you like to bring in the coffee and cheese plate for us? Your
mother has them waiting on the kitchen table."

Once the children were gone, the merry chatter turned solemn. Dr. Cole wasted no time in telling Juanita that Tomas's body would be released for the funeral as quickly as possible, his suspicions about the poison, and the results of the tests that had just come back that evening.

"It looks like something called ethyl biscoumacetate," David said. "A blood thinner. It can have some medical uses, but only when carefully monitored and in very small doses, and sometimes it's in rat poisons. It inhibits the formation in the liver of clotting factors and can bring on hemorrhaging, especially a thin, bright-red, frothy blood, such as Mrs. Alwin here remembers seeing at the scene of the crime. It can cause jaundice, thus the yellowing of the skin, and fever, until even a small cut can cause a person to bleed to death. It appears this is what happened to your husband, I'm afraid."

Juanita's eyes widened with horror, and her hand flew to her mouth. "We keep a box of rat poison in the kitchen," she whispered. "Could his work in the garden—or maybe a mix-up with something else . . . ?"

"Oh, no," David quickly assured her. "He would have had to ingest a greater quantity of it than in such a powder, and over a period of time. Death can occur up to two weeks after discontinuing the drug. No one else here has been ill, so it couldn't have accidentally found its way into food or drink here in your own home."

Father Malone frowned thoughtfully. "When I was a very young man at a mission on the California coast, another priest had a very pretty rosary he once got in the tropics. Red-and-black seedpods, dried and carved into small roses. Paternoster peas, we called them. Sadly, a young child ate one of the beads and bled out in just such a way. Such a small amount. Could it be a similar accident, Doctor?"

David seemed to think about this for a moment and shook his head. "I don't think so. It would take a larger amount and a cumulative effect. Only a tiny amount of the paternoster pea is fatal if chewed. The taste would be rather bitter, though it could be disguised in alcohol or maybe strong coffee. Do you know of any place where your husband regularly eats or drinks, Mrs. Anaya?"

Juanita shook her head. "My husband was not often home of late, Dr. Cole. But I know he didn't drink alcohol, or at least he didn't used to. Ever."

They could hear the clatter of the girls returning from the kitchen, and David quickly said in a low voice, "If you can think of anything at all later, Mrs. Anaya . . ."

"Of course." Juanita leaned closer to him and whispered, "I did notice he seemed very distracted lately, losing track of his thoughts, having fits of temper, things of that sort. His skin and eyes also seemed yellow, but he wouldn't go see a doctor."

David nodded. "Common symptoms, I'm afraid. For how long?"

"Three weeks. A month, maybe," Juanita said.

The girls returned with the cheese platter and coffee set, and there could be no more talk of poisons and murder while they were there. Pearl and Ruby told them instead of the play they were devising for their new dolls, and Gunther suggested revisions and costume changes, making them giggle.

Later, Maddie walked with David to the garden gate. It was a beautiful night, the air soft with the promise of summer, the sky dusty-dark above them. It seemed so strange that something as terrible as murder could happen in her beautiful new hometown.

"Thank you so much for coming tonight, David," she said. "I think hearing this information, no matter how appalling, has done Juanita some good. At least we can feel like we're doing something."

"Honesty is usually the best policy in matters like this, especially when someone is as strong as Mrs. Anaya and can bear it. Hopefully we can use this to help young Eddie."

Maddie nodded. "I do hope so. I'm sorry that you're getting such an impression of our town, right when you first arrive! It's usually not this exciting, I promise, at least not in a murderous way."

He laughed. "I am very glad I came here, Maddie. It's even more than I was hoping." He took her hand and pressed a quick, warm kiss to her fingers. "I'll phone tomorrow if there's any more news. Tell Mrs. Anaya her dinner was lovely."

Maddie watched him walk away into the night and curled her hand tightly in the fringed hem of her shawl, as if she could hold the memory of that kiss there. She glanced up at the moon, rising in a shower of silver in the sky, and whispered, "Don't you dare tell," to its shining light.

When she returned to the house, feeling almost as if her feet floated above the ground just a tiny bit, she could hear the clatter of dishes being washed in the kitchen. She gathered up the last of the used platters from the dining room table and went to add them to the soapy sink.

Juanita was washing the dishes, a small frown on her face as she seemed to look at something—worry about something—that was far away from the cozy kitchen. The girls were brushing Buttercup in the corner, up far past their bedtime.

Maddie took up a dish towel and started polishing the glasses on the drying board. For a moment, there was only the soft splash of water, the girls' giggles, and the hum of insects through the screen door to the garden.

"Dr. Cole does seem like a nice man," Juanita said. "Not many busy doctors would go out of their way to help like that."

Maddie remembered his kiss on her hand, his smile as he said good night. "He *is* very nice. I'm sure that with all of us working with each other, we'll be able to piece together what really happened in no time."

Juanita nodded, and they were silent again for a long moment as they washed and dried, washed and dried. "You were so lonely when you first came here, Señora Maddie, as I was when I first left home. Your eyes were so empty."

"I . . ." Maddie swallowed hard, thinking about her silent house after Pete died, her hollow heart. "Yes. I did feel empty when I first came here. But then I found friends like you and a new home."

"I know how it feels, yes. To be lonely even when you're not alone. Never alone."

"You mean alone in your marriage?"

Juanita nodded. She glanced at the girls, but they were too busy with their brushing task to pay much attention to boring grown-ups. "It wasn't always like that, though. When we first met, he was funny and strong. Sure of himself. He always seemed to know what to do to make things right. I know it's hard to believe now, but I enjoyed being with him then. Would do anything to be with him. And then . . ." Her voice trailed away.

Maddie was fascinated. This was the most Juanita had ever told her about the Anayas' past. "And then?"

"We got older. Things happened to us, made him hard in his heart. Angry."

"But you haven't become hard and angry."

Juanita shook her head. "What use is that, Señora Maddie? It just wastes our time, and there's not enough of that as it is. We have to help each other whenever we can."

"You're exactly right." Maddie opened the cabinet to put away the clean plates. "But it looks like Tomas's anger landed in the wrong place this time."

Juanita frowned. "I warned him to take more care. He stopped listening to me a long time ago. Sometimes grief can blind us, make us not see the important things right in front of us." She laid her hand gently, fleetingly, on Maddie's. "Don't let it do that to you."

Maddie wondered if she meant Dr. Cole or something else entirely. "I'll try not to."

Juanita nodded and handed her the last of the dishes to dry. They put away the remaining crockery, and Juanita herded the protesting sleepy girls toward their beds.

Maddie started to go to her room, as it was growing so late, but she glanced out the kitchen window and saw the tiny red glow of the end of one of Gunther's cigarettes in his own garden. Sure she could never sleep even if she did retire and wanting to have someone to talk to, she wandered over to say good-night to her friend.

"Can't sleep either?" Gunther asked as she pushed open the gate. He gave her a sad little smile. "Darling one, I would have thought you were tucked up safely in bed, dreaming of your handsome doctor."

"Maybe I'm thinking about him *too* much," Maddie said. "I don't seem to feel tired at all."

"Then sit down; have a brandy with me. I don't feel like being alone either."

Maddie drew up one of his wicker chairs under the canopy of trees and took the snifter of brandy he passed to her. It was the very finest, as Gunther almost always had, and she could glimpse the silvery-greenish moon between the canopy of leaves. A soft breeze caught at her hair, and it seemed an idyllic night.

Yet she couldn't quite find the serene contentment that usually fell over her like a silken eiderdown blanket on such night and made her glad to be alive exactly where she was. Her worry over Eddie and his family wouldn't leave her thoughts, and now she worried about Gunther too. His smile wasn't at all his usual merry grin, and his hair was rumpled and ascot untied and hanging over his shirtfront.

"You were quite right," Gunther said at last, breaking the soft silence. "Your doctor is beautiful. No, not beautiful. He's much too rugged for that! But those eyes. That accent. I would ride the trains all the time if I could find someone like *that*."

Maddie laughed. "Pure serendipity. I never thought I would find someone like that either. Even if nothing at all comes of it, I will always be quite amazed."

Gunther sighed. "Serendipity. I put it in my books all the time, yet I don't think I've ever actually seen it."

"It will happen when you least expect it. People used to tell me that all the time when I lost Pete, but I never did believe them. I thought they were just saying what they thought they *should* say." She thought of the Anayas—of Juanita, who worked so hard and loved her children so much and seemed to get so little in return. Of Gunther, who deserved a committed love, a content life, more than anyone she knew. "Of course, serendipity works for bad too."

"Poor young Eddie, you mean?" Gunther said, pouring them another measure of brandy. "At least he has useful friends on his side now. Lawyers, doctors, priests. Most boys in his position wouldn't."

Maddie nodded. What he said was horribly true. There were two kinds of justice in the world for the haves and have-nots. She quickly caught him up on what she had learned so far. "I wish we could all help more. I just feel so very helpless."

"You, darling? Never! Others just sit and wait and wait for things to happen; you go looking for answers. Tell me, what do you think of Dr. Cole's findings? Blood-thinning poison, fatal beatings—just like a detective novel."

Maddie shook her head. "I was never much good at my science classes in school. Always had my nose in a novel. *Jane Eyre* isn't much help now. I can see someone getting angry enough to give him a beating. Bootleggers protect their territory, whether it's New York or New Mexico. But to plan out a poison over weeks or months . . ." She shivered. "That seems to be full of hatred. He wasn't the most likable man ever, sure, but what could he have done to get all of that?"

Gunther stared down into his drink, as if the swirl of the liquid could answer him. "My dearest, I know you don't want to think of it, yet the newspapers say such murders are usually domestic affairs. Would you say the Anayas had a happy marriage?"

Maddie thought of the quarrel she had heard on the day she came home. "Not really. They've been married a long time, I think. Yet Juanita says Tomas hasn't been around much lately, off on some mysterious errands. Juanita claims he mostly ignores the girls, which I've noticed is true, but bullies Eddie. Out of worry, she says, but I saw a bruise on Eddie's face the day I got home."

"Was he faithful?"

"Juanita says he used to step out a bit. I'm not sure how much. She doesn't tell me much about such scandalous stuff. She didn't really seem all that deeply concerned about it when she mentioned it and says men will do what they will. But Pete never did things like that."

Gunther sighed. "She's right about that, your Pete notwithstanding. A lover scorned isn't always thinking straight."

Maddie knew he was right. The papers were indeed full of husbands and wives going after each other in fits of rage. Juanita was too calm for that, too quiet, too stoic. Maybe those were the ones to worry about the most, though? "Aren't those usually lovers shooting or stabbing each other in a sudden quarrel or something? Tomas and Juanita are both so quiet, it's hard to imagine such a thing happening to them. Maybe with one of his fancy women, if he really did have one? She might have lost her temper, whoever the poor girl was." Or even Juanita might have snapped, though Maddie didn't want to consider such an occurrence. "People are such strange, unpredictable things."

"Truer words were never spoken, Madeline, my dear. It makes our work possible, paintings and books and such." He reached into his pocket for his cigarette case and lit up a fresh smoke. "You really don't think it could be the wife?"

"Juanita? No. She's one of the best people I've ever known, kind and nurturing. Rather like the mother I always wished I had. She was angry at Tomas, for sure, and she would always protect her children. She is also very religious, though. I'm sure she thinks marriage is forever."

"Her Father Malone would probably counsel her the same, though he seems a nice sort for a clergyman. A Father Brown sort, even. Could his kindness maybe even lead him to—help Juanita out a bit? Or at least look the other way if someone else did?"

Maddie was shocked. Father Malone, a priest, condoning murder? He certainly would have warned Tomas to cease his activities, if the priest even had a chance, but kill? "Father Malone as a poisoner?"

Gunther shrugged. "Maybe not. My mind does tend to work in novel plots. He would be concerned with sin and all that. Possibly he just thought if Tomas was ill for a while, he would leave Eddie alone, repent his pagan ways."

"Maybe. Then again, lots of people might have thought something like that. *I* might have myself, if I had been back from New York to see what all was going on."

"You wicked girl! So Lady Macbeth." He poured out the last of his brandy bottle. "But I would rather hear more about your doctor now. I do have to live romantically in vicarious ways, you know, since Bertie left."

Maddie laughed and told him more about her trip to Sunmount, her talks with Dr. Cole, even how kind he had been in a most uncomfortable situation at the morgue.

"I do hope he is as nice as he appears," Gunther said wistfully. "You deserve a little fun and happiness, darling."

"As do you! As do we all. Once all this nastiness is over." *And let it be soon*, she added silently.

After the bottle was utterly gone, she made her slightly unsteady way back into her own house. It was quiet now, Juanita and the girls retired to their own guesthouse, the kitchen and the dining room clean. Maddie went through her bedtime rituals of brushes and cold creams, but even once tucked up under the blankets, she couldn't go to sleep. She was too wrapped up in poisons, the state of marriages, priests and Father Brown novels, luck and who got it and who didn't.

She finally fell into a trouble slumber when the sun was peeking over the horizon.

CHAPTER 14

Maddie studied the house. This seemed to be the address Gunther had found for Tomas's woman friend, the mysterious Mavis. It didn't *look* disreputable, which was a bit disappointing. Not that she was sure what she had been expecting. Pink and purple paint? The smell of cheap perfume piped out into the breeze? Whatever she'd envisioned, it wasn't this tidy, pale-yellow Victorian house, windows blanked with heavy curtains against the daylight, tucked behind a low stone fence.

It was midafternoon and quiet there at the outskirts of town, while the plaza a few blocks away was bustling with people going about their business, grocery shopping, banking, and eating lunch. She'd thought surely it was a good time to find Mavis at home before business picked up. Maddie pushed open the gate and made her way up the front walkway to knock at the door.

It opened a couple of inches to reveal an older woman in a green silk dress, maybe a little garish for the afternoon but proper enough. Her gaze flicked down Maddie, taking in her plain gray frock, her blue coat and straw hat with gray striped ribbon trim, her pearl earrings. "We don't need you missionary sorts here again," she said, starting to slam the door.

Maddie blocked it with her foot. "Do excuse the intrusion," she said sweetly. "But I promise I'm not a missionary. I'm here on some urgent business to see a woman called Mavis."

The woman frowned suspiciously. "What sort of business?"

"The sort that might bring the police to your door, if it's not sorted soon," Maddie said. She took a roll of bills from her handbag and offered them. "None of us want that, I'm sure."

The woman took the money and stuffed it into her bodice before she let Maddie in. "No, we wouldn't. Mavis is upstairs, third door on the left. Don't take too long."

"Of course not." Maddie's artistic nature was very curious about what was behind that door, but once again she was a bit disappointed. It was decorated rather like her grandmother's drawing room had been when Maddie was a little girl, all dark wallpaper and heavy walnut furniture, with staid, poorly done landscapes on the walls. Someone played softly at a piano while a girl sang in a warbling voice, but there weren't very many people around at that hour, just a few women in dressing gowns who were chatting idly and watched her with curiosity as she hurried past.

She made her way up the curving stairs to a long corridor, knocking on the third door to the left. "What is it?" a querulous voice called out. "I'm not on the clock yet."

"I'm not your landlady," Maddie said. "I'm a friend of the Anayas. I believe you know them?"

The door swung open. Mavis was a tall, sturdy woman with bright-red hair that matched her satin wrapper, smooth olive skin, and wide, dark eyes. She looked familiar somehow, but Maddie wasn't sure where she had seen her before. She looked anxious and unsure, but also somehow—defiant?

"Tomas Anaya?" she said urgently. Her voice had the touch of a fluid, almost Spanish accent. "You know him? What's happened to him?"

"I—he and his wife work for me," Maddie said. Mavis really did look quite uneasy. Did she not know about the murder? "I'm very sorry if you haven't heard, but he has died."

Mavis stumbled back a step, her fist curling into the edge of her satin wrapper. Her nails were lacquered the same bright red. "Died?"

"Yes. I—well, I'm afraid he was killed."

Mavis's face turned quite pale, and Maddie led her carefully to the nearest chair. She looked around and found a pitcher of water, quickly pouring out a glass and pressing it into the woman's shaking hand. It was a small room, sparsely furnished with only a bed, a wardrobe pushed against the wall along with two chairs, and a dressing table cluttered with bottles, brushes, and pots of rouge and mascara.

"I didn't know," Mavis murmured. "It's been so busy here at work. I knew I hadn't seen him in a few days, but . . . who did it then?"

Maddie watched her carefully. "His son has been arrested."

"Eddie?" Mavis cried. "That kid? It can't be."

"You know his son?" Maddie asked in surprise. She didn't know a whole lot about being a man's girl on the side, but talking about his kids with him didn't seem like it should be part of it.

"Of course I did. Well, knew *of* him. Tomas talked about Eddie sometimes."

"So you did know Tomas well?" Maddie said, trying to keep any hint of judgment out of her voice, any thought of Juanita's worries and fears. She wanted Mavis to trust her.

"Sure, he . . ." Mavis's eyes narrowed. "Say, who are you again? How did you find me?"

"My name is Madeline Alwin. Juanita Anaya is my housekeeper. Also my friend."

Mavis gave a rough laugh. "Friend, is it? Did she send you here? I didn't think she even knew about me being in town."

"I'm not sure she does know," Maddie said, even though Juanita *had* mentioned she thought Tomas was stepping out on her, or used to anyway. "I heard you knew Tomas through—talk."

"This is a gossipy town, no doubt about that. Worse than the pueblo when I was a kid." She took another sip of water, her expression becoming wistful, faraway. "I wouldn't mind seeing Juanita again. Telling her I'm sorry about Tomas."

Maddie was puzzled. "See her again?"

"It's been too long. She probably wouldn't want to see me, though. She was always the respectable sort." Mavis sniffled and glanced up at Maddie. "Say, you *do* know Tomas was my cousin, right? That makes me kin to Juanita, and to Eddie too. I have the right to be concerned."

Well, now, Maddie thought. That would teach her about leaping before she looked. Mavis was Tomas's cousin, not his fancy woman. Interesting. "I'm trying to help Eddie, if I can. That's why I'm here. Trying to see if I can find who really did this."

Mavis seemed to think this over, biting at her lip until a stain of lip rouge came off on her tooth. Finally, she nodded and kicked out the other chair for Maddie to sit down.

"That poor kid," Mavis said. She slid open one of the dressing table drawers and took out a bottle of what looked like whiskey. She added some to her water glass. "What can I do to help?"

"Have you been here long?" Maddie asked.

"At this house, you mean? Only a few months, when I got back here to New Mexico. That's when I met Tomas again. Hadn't seen him for years, but he remembered me."

"You mean you didn't live at San Ildefonso before that?"

"I left when I was nearly fifteen. That's when I met Billy. He was a cowboy, passing through on his way to California.

He was way too handsome and funny too. Lighthearted, y'know? Not like any of the other guys I knew growing up." She took a long drink. "We were going to get married; I know we were. He just had to get some things sorted first. Then he died of the 'flu."

Maddie sighed. So much sadness all around. So much she didn't know, couldn't yet see. It was all hidden behind clouds of unhappiness. "I'm so sorry. My own husband died in the war."

Mavis gave her an understanding little smile. "Tough luck for us, huh?"

"Yes," Maddie agreed, even as she realized how very lucky she really was. Pete was gone, but she could live her own life in freedom, not tied down to a rough job like Mavis. She had a family, as maddening as they were, and lots of good friends. "Was Tomas going to help you get back home?"

"He couldn't even go back himself. Not yet. But I guess he was helping me in his own way."

"How so?"

"I ran into him by accident. I knew he and Juanita lived here in town. I just couldn't figure out how to get in touch with them, see if I could talk to them without embarrassing them." She took another drink. "But then I met him at Madame Genet's shop."

That was a name Maddie had been hearing a lot of lately. "The medium?"

Mavis smiled. "You've heard of her? She's great. I bet she could find your husband for you."

"Maybe so," Maddie said, thinking of Father Malone's suspicions of the woman, both on a spiritual and criminal level. "Did she find your Billy?"

"She's close to it, I'm sure. She says sometimes the spirit you're looking for won't come through at first, that you have to search, talk to your spirit guides. But she knows things only Billy would. Maybe he's communicating through those other spirits for now, like he's shy or something. Not that being shy sounds much like Billy."

"And what was Tomas doing there?"

"Looking for his son, of course. He couldn't do it in the old ways anymore, so he thought maybe this would work."

"Looking for Eddie?" Maddie asked, then she remembered something Juanita had mentioned once. "Oh, yes, the poor baby who died. Forgive me, but Tomas didn't seem like the . . . spiritually seeking type."

"He was sensitive, underneath. We just had such a hard time when we were kids, you know. We had to learn to be tough." Mavis finished her glass. "I think he felt guilty about that baby. He said he hadn't sent for the doctor soon enough. But he did like Madame Genet. He thought she had a gift, like the medicine men from the kivas at home."

"Is that why Tomas and Juanita left the pueblo then?" Maddie asked. "Something about the baby?"

Mavis shrugged. "He says it was because he was a heretic."

Maddie was surprised. "Heretic? That sounds positively medieval. And Tomas didn't seem very religious. Juanita says he wouldn't go to church with her."

Mavis laughed. "Not *that* sort of heretic. Not like the inquisition they used to have right here in town. No, just not with the old ways from the pueblo. He thought people like Madame Genet were really onto something. But that was just an excuse anyway."

"An excuse?"

Mavis suddenly closed up, her expression snapping into boredom as if a curtain came down. She put her glass down on the dressing table. "I don't know, really. I'd left by then. And Tomas wasn't much of a talker. Kept himself to himself, like we all should. But he was nice to me. We would have dinner, talk about when we were kids and things like that."

Maddie nodded. Keep herself to herself—that sounded like advice her mother would give, and it wasn't terrible. But how could she not try to help her friends, if she could? Even if she feared she was useless?

But something else about Mavis's words caught Maddie's attention. Mavis and Tomas used to have dinner together? Did that mean Mavis had had access to Tomas's food and drink and thus could have slipped him something? Did she have a reason to, maybe a reason rooted in their old lives, or resentment that he couldn't help her more now?

"Anyway, I have to get to work, and you shouldn't be here," Mavis said abruptly. Maddie glanced at her, startled, and saw that Mavis's expression had closed down, hardened. She pushed her chair back with a loud scrape and stood up, refusing to look back at Maddie. "Some of us have to earn our keep and can't sit around yapping all day. I'm sorry Tomas is dead, but I don't think I can help you."

Maddie wondered what had changed so fast, why Mavis was shutting her out. "Surely you're the best one who *could* help me!" she said, trying to get Mavis to stay, to really talk to her. She felt as if she was on the edge of something just beyond her reach, but it was slipping away. "I only want to find out what happened. Don't you?"

Mavis shook her head. She reached for a tube of lipstick and leaned close to the window to draw a red line over her lips. Her hand trembled a bit, and she abruptly dropped the lipstick and tightened the sash of her robe. "I can't help you," she said again, her tone hoarse.

Maddie realized she would get nothing else out of Mavis that day. The woman had obviously shut down. But why? Grief? Or guilt? Maddie took a card out of her handbag and put it down on the dressing table. "If you do think of anything else, or if you just want to call on Juanita, there's my address. Come by any time."

Mavis didn't even glance at the card. She just gave a brusque nod and hurried out of the room, so quickly she left the door ajar and Maddie sitting there alone. Maddie could hear the house stirring outside, the sound of voices calling to each other, the slam of doors, and she knew she didn't have much time.

She studied the table where Mavis had put down the glass. There were pots of powder and scented lotions, sticks of kohl, brushes and combs, and a tangle of ribbons. It looked like she lived backstage at the Follies.

Suddenly, Maddie noticed a bottle at the back, a strange shape of sloped sides and flattened bottom, heavy and plugged with a dark cork. It was half-full of an amber liquid. It looked a bit like the bottle that had belonged to Tomas.

She took off the stopper and gave it a cautious sniff. It just smelled earthy, sort of like the lilies of the valley scent her grandmother used to have, with a hint of gin underneath. She held it up to the light and saw a label on the underside. "Tonic," it said in a blocky script, and she wondered if the handwriting could be the same as the note she had received warning her to mind her own business.

She glanced over her shoulder, but no one was there. She quickly wrapped up the bottle and tucked it into her handbag. It couldn't hurt to get David to take a look at the contents, to try to match up the handwriting on the label and find out where Mavis got it. The woman was acting very strangely. If she was Tomas's cousin, if they were friends, surely she would want to help find his killer?

Maddie took another quick look at the table and behind the screen, but she didn't find anything else that looked interesting, and she knew she was running out of time. She straightened her hat and made her way out to the corridor, where one of the other ladies pointed her toward the back staircase. She found herself back outside, away from the heavy air of smoke and stale perfume, in the sunlight again. She was surprised to find it was still afternoon.

She made her way back toward the center of town, wondering if she should stop at La Fonda and think over everything. She did know one thing—it was time to make an appointment with Madame Genet.

As she turned a corner, she glimpsed a crowd of boys coming down the street, noisy and jostling, pushing each other off into the gutter. In their midst, she glimpsed a bright-blond head ahead a tall, skinny figure. Was it Harry, Eddie's so-called friend?

"Hey!" she called and walked faster to catch up with them. "Harry!"

The boy broke away from his friends into a run. Maddie cursed the new shoes she wore and took off after him.

CHAPTER 15

The boy vanished through a doorway, and Maddie ducked after him. How could he move so fast? She was sure it was those blasted long legs and all the exercise he got running around on nefarious errands. She vowed to start walking more.

She found herself in an empty shopfront, but she heard the clatter of footsteps nearby and then a muffled curse as a few crates fell over. She followed the sound and ran down a flight of stone steps into a dank basement. Up ahead, a door slammed.

Maddie forced herself to stop and think, not just act on impulse as she had done too often lately. She pulled open an old, heavy, iron-bound door and faced a narrow passageway.

She was sure it must be the tunnels Gunther told her about, the passages that snaked under the streets and made deliveries easier, especially illicit deliveries. They were more fun to hear about than to actually face alone. In real life, they were rough stone walls that pressed uncomfortably close, cold and damp. She listened carefully for any sound, and she heard more footsteps just ahead, echoing back to her eerily.

She ran after them, thankful there was at least a little light in the small space from a few crude uncovered lightbulbs overhead. Probably the bootleggers had been tired of bringing their own flashlights, Maddie thought as she plunged ahead, her shoes pinching her heels.

Why hadn't *she* thought to bring a torch? she wondered. And maybe some trousers and sturdy boots? Oh, yes—because she had thought she was merely spending the afternoon at a brothel, not chasing urchins down underground tunnels. Just a typical day in the life of a lady.

Brothels, tunnels. How exciting her hoped-for quiet life in Santa Fe was becoming! Maybe it would be a fun story to recount later, she hoped. But for now, her feet hurt, she was hungry, and she cursed "excitement."

She stumbled around a corner and saw a figure up ahead, a flash of bright-blond hair in the shadows. She sped up, hoping he thought he had lost her and would get careless. She summoned up every girls' field hockey game at Miss Spence's, no matter how long ago they might have been, and put on a burst of speed. Just as the boy opened another door, she lunged forward and grabbed his arm.

"Hey!" he yelled as they both tumbled to the floor. "Let go of me, you crazy broad."

"Are you Harry?" Maddie gasped. "Eddie's friend?"

He went very still. "How do you know that?"

"Word gets around town; surely you know that. Did *you* know Eddie was in jail, waiting for bail?"

He had the grace to look shamefaced. Red stained his freckled cheeks, and Maddie realized how very young he really was, just a kid like Eddie, getting mixed up in trouble before he was old enough to know what he was doing. She told herself sternly not to feel sorry for him, to keep view of what she had to do—help Eddie.

"I didn't want Ed to get hurt," he muttered. "I just told him . . ."

"Told him what?"

"There was a job. I thought he could use the cabbage, you see? It was just one little thing."

"Is that how you started? With one little thing?"

He looked away. "I dunno what you mean."

"This job. What was it? I know you make deliveries to all the speakeasies in town. Do you want me to talk to your cousin Tony at the police station?"

Harry rolled over to sit up against the stone wall. Watching him warily in case he decided to scarper, she propped herself up beside him.

The wall was cold and slightly damp through her spring-weight coat. She took a deep breath and noticed things around her for the first time. The cold air smelled of mildew and old beer and something more pleasant underneath, something sweet and spicy, like Mrs. Nussbaum's tearoom's cinnamon toast. She wondered if they were underneath the tea shop. It was like being caught between two worlds.

She shifted her weight and winced as one ankle gave a painful throb. She realized she must have twisted it during her run, and now it was reminding her of that all too painfully.

"This job?" she prompted again.

"It wasn't any big deal. I've had lots of jobs before. Cleaning tables, mixing adobe . . ."

Maddie gestured to the sleeve of his finely tailored striped linen shirt. It was dusty and rumpled now, but that couldn't disguise the fact that he hadn't bought it at the five and dime, nor the polished wingtips on his feet. "I would guess you don't need something like that for adobe mixing."

He twitched away from her. "Maybe I needed money too. I was trying to be a good friend, sharing with Ed."

Maddie thought of the maid at La Fonda, Harry's arm around her as she cried at finding a body in the alley. "Money to buy your girl jewelry, maybe?"

"What girl?" he said. He looked genuinely puzzled.

"I saw you that night at La Fonda. You were walking with a maid, the one who found Eddie's father."

He laughed. "Oh, her. That's my sister, June. I got her that job, back when I bused tables there. Sometimes I wait around to walk her home. It's not always safe out there."

"Oh, I know." Maddie thought of everything she hadn't realized lurked in Santa Fe—violence, danger, things hiding in shadows. "You just *happen* to pop up wherever there's trouble. La Fonda, the new nightclub—you're everywhere, it seems."

Harry shrugged. "I have to make a living, don't I? It's just me taking care of my mom and sister. If I work hard now, I can really go places. Mr. Bennett says so."

The handsome nightclub owner? She could picture him employing the local kids to run errands, but maybe not so much to mentor them. Perhaps she had misjudged him. "Does he give you jobs often too?"

"Just deliveries now and then. He talks to me, though, about running a business. He thinks I could open my own someday."

"What sort of business? Rum-running?"

"There are worse things to do," he muttered.

"I doubt your mother would say that, if you asked her. Tell me about this job you offered to share with Eddie. Was it bringing hooch into town?"

"I offered to split it, not *give* it to him. I'm not that good a friend." He went silent, and Maddie just sat there, waiting. She'd learned that from her mother; sometimes silence was the greatest weapon.

"Okay," he said finally. "It was bringing in a shipment stored in Tesuque. Not even a big load, but the pay was good. I needed someone to help load the wagon."

"And it was for Mr. Bennett?"

"How should I know? There's messengers for that sort of thing, telling you where to get something and where to leave it. That's how it works. I thought that's all this job was too."

He looked away, and for the first time, Maddie saw a flicker of childish uncertainty on his face. "But there was more to it than that? Was the shipment not just alcohol this time?"

"What else would it have been?"

"Maybe cocaine."

His mouth fell open, and he shook his head. "I don't know! I told you, I don't ask questions. I just make the deliveries. Nothing wrong in that."

"Until you get caught. I heard in New York that they've put more federal agents out here in the west to patrol the borders. If you were caught with hard drugs . . ."

He bit his lip. Maddie could see he was scared; his hands shook. But he set his jaw stubbornly. "I never get caught. I know better."

"There's always a first time. Is that why Eddie wouldn't take the job?"

"He was trying to stay out of trouble with his dad again. He'd promised his mother he would."

"So he's been in trouble before?"

"The last time he helped me, his dad caught him. I wouldn't want to mess with a big guy like that when he's angry. Ed had a black eye the next day."

Maddie nodded. She remembered Eddie's bruises when he came to get her at the train station, his quiet remoteness. "What else can you tell me about this job? I won't peach on you. I just want to help Eddie."

"Nothing. I already told you—I don't know what was in it or who it was for."

Exasperated, Maddie wanted to shake the kid until he saw truth. How horribly stubborn he and Eddie were! No wonder Juanita was at her wit's end with him. "Eddie is in jail! The inspector wants to pin the murder on him, so he can close the book and forget about it. You know what could happen to him!"

Harry's face flamed bright red. "I'm sorry for him!" he cried. "Really I am. He's a good friend. But I don't know anything that could help him."

"There must be something. Just come with me, talk to Eddie's lawyer . . ."

"A lawyer! You *are* a crazy broad." Harry jumped to his feet and ran away through the door, slamming it behind him.

Maddie lurched up, trying to follow him, but her ankle gave away beneath her. She stumbled against the wall, cursing as pain shot up her leg. She limped to the door and pulled it open. It led to a flight of stairs, but no Harry. The stony quiet seemed even more oppressive.

She hobbled up the stairs and remembered she had no idea where she was or what she would find up there. It was a bit like *Alice's Adventures in Wonderland*.

At the head of the stairs, there was yet another door, and she opened to find—the bank.

The marble hush of the stone floor and gilded railings, the whispers of tellers at their booths, and people dressed in suits and dresses hurrying past seemed like a whole different planet after the damp tunnel.

"Mrs. Alwin," a man cried. She turned to see Mr. Rosenwald, the manager of First National, watching her with a bemused expression on his face. He gave her a little bow. Like Anton at La Fonda, he was much too professional to show any surprise at his more eccentric customers' behaviors. "How may I assist you today? Is there a problem with the month's dividends?"

Maddie gathered the tattered remnants of her dignity around her. "Not at all, Mr. Rosenwald. It's all quite tickety-boo. I was just taking a little shortcut."

"A shortcut?"

"Yes. Do forgive me. I'll get out of your way now." She started to limp to the glass doors, but she stopped at the receptionist's desk. "You didn't happen to see a boy run past here a few minutes ago?"

The receptionist, a tidy, slender older woman in a dark-blue wool gown and spectacles, stayed as calm and cool as her boss. "I didn't, Mrs. Alwin. But then we always have errand boys coming and going. They're always so fast. Ah, youth."

So fast indeed. And Maddie felt like she was always a step behind. How could she ever help Eddie this way? "Thank you."

She made her way out the door, trying not to gasp at the pain in her ankle. She glanced down to see that the wretched thing was swelling. How was she supposed to get all the way home?

The bank was on the corner of the plaza, catty-corner to the Palace and across from the art museum. It was fairly quiet at that time of day, with only a few people passing by.

"Mrs. Alwin? Can I help you?" asked a deep, smooth voice.

Oh, horsefeathers, she thought. Caught again. She shielded her eyes from the bright sun and looked up to find Rob Bennett staring at her.

Unlike her disheveled, dusty self, he looked like he just stepped out of a tailor's advertisement, in a sharply cut herringbone suit, his dark hair glossy and smooth under a felt hat. "Oh," she said, hating how chirpy her voice sounded. "Mr. Bennett. Lovely to see you again."

"Are you hurt?"

"Just a little tumble." Maddie glanced down at her swollen foot, the tears in her fine new stockings, the scrapes starting to bleed a bit. "Soon mended once I'm home."

"Let me help you. My place is just up the street. You should get that cleaned up."

"Oh, no, I . . ."

"I insist. You don't want to get infected. I'll even throw in an orange blossom, free of charge."

Maddie laughed. "Well, if there's an orange blossom—thank you, Mr. Bennett."

"I thought I told you to call me Rob. Here, lean on me. We'll be there in just a minute."

As Maddie took his arm, she glanced up at the small office just above the grocery on the corner. She glimpsed a pale face there between the curtains, a spangled turban, then whoever it was ducked away. Was that the famous Madame Genet? Why on earth would she be watching Maddie, a stranger?

The club looked very different during the day, empty of revelers. With the lights on and the dance floor deserted, it seemed so much more ordinary. The banquettes were a dull red, slightly worn in patches, the tables marked with rings where damp glasses had carelessly rested. The air smelled of old smoke, spilled wine, and the rich citrus cologne Rob wore as he leaned close to her. It made her head swim.

She studied the array of bottles behind the bar, reflected in the glass shelves. No homemade "tonics" there, only the best. Or at least the containers of the best. He could possibly hide the bad stuff in good bottles, but Maddie knew he hadn't, at least not on the night she was there. The cocktails had been top-notch. Had it all been delivered by Harry? Where did he pick it up?

Rob helped her onto one of the chairs and reached for a cushioned stool. "Here, put your foot up on this, and I'll fetch some iodine."

"You're so kind," Maddie said.

He gave her a wide grin, and she could definitely see why all the ladies in town lined up for his drinks. He looked like a film star indeed. "I'm no philanthropist, except when it comes to pretty ladies with a sharp eye."

"Oh, yes? Then what is your price for assistance?" she teased.

"Maybe another dance? Once your ankle heals, of course, due to my expert nursing."

Maddie tapped at her chin, pretending to think it over. "I think that could be arranged."

He laughed and ducked behind the baize door she knew led to the kitchens. It was also quiet, no cooks there yet, no clouds of steam, no errand boys fetching dirty dishes. She remembered seeing Harry there, running away so fast she couldn't catch him.

She carefully laid her foot on the stool, wincing a bit at the knotted ache, and studied the bar again. Harry said he did errands for lots of people. Did the job he offered to share with Eddie involve this place? Was the cocaine Elizabeth Grover liked so much being run out of the Bennett club?

If Rob had been telling her the truth, Tomas Anaya had been working with a rival gang and run into trouble that way. It was an easy explanation for what happened to him. Yet something about it didn't seem to quite add up.

Rob came back with a basin of warm water and a first aid kit. He knelt down beside her and carefully washed the scratches caused by her fall. As Maddie watched, trying to be brave and not wince, he gently removed some of the tiny pebbles abraded there with a pair of tweezers and dabbed it with stinging iodine.

"You're very good at that," she said. "Did you have medical training?"

He leaned over his task with a serious expression. "Just some in the war."

"You were a medic over there?"

He shook his head. "In training. It was all over by the time they were ready to send me. I learned a few things in the army camps here, though."

"So I see." She watched him press a gauze pad to the worst of the scrapes and then wrap it with a length of bandage. "You should have stayed on and studied to be a doctor."

He laughed. "Owning a club or two is easier money. And I like this work." He glanced up at her and smiled. "I get to meet the most interesting people."

"You could meet them as a doctor too. Surely people confide all their secrets to their physicians."

"They do that when they drink too."

"I guess they do." Maddie glanced around the room, trying to distract herself from the sting of the iodine and the look in his smoky-gray eyes. "It would be fun to work in a place like this."

"More fun than being an artist?"

"Nothing is more fun than that," she said, even though *fun* was not what being an artist meant, not usually. It meant hard work, utter absorption, a sense of meaning, something she *had* to do. It was sometimes wonderful, sometimes terrible, often frustrating. But like being a doctor or a bootlegger, it gave her a glimpse of what lay beneath the surface.

He unwound another length of gauze and gently strapped up her ankle, pulling it tight. "Well, if you ever need another job, I'm always hiring."

Like he hired Harry, and maybe Eddie? "I'll remember that," she said. She admired the neatly wrapped bandage. "You, Rob Bennett, are a man of many talents."

"I try my best." His smile flickered and then turned into a small frown, like a candle going out. "Did you find out anything about your murder case?"

"Tomas Anaya?" Maddie shook her head. "Not really. I did see his fancy woman, but she turned out to be his cousin."

His brows arched. "His cousin? They didn't *look* so—related when I saw them."

Maddie shrugged. Something told her to be cautious, to not share all she knew just yet. Not until she could figure out what it meant. "Who knows?"

"Well, I think my task is done here. And I promised you an orange blossom, didn't I?"

"For being a good patient." She watched him go behind the bar, where he blended the ingredients into a silver shaker and chipped off some ice. She thought that truly he must meet almost everyone from behind that bar. "Have you heard of a woman called Madame Genet?"

The shaker rattled in his hand, and he gave her a distracted look. "Sounds like a circus performer or something."

"Apparently she's a spiritualist medium. Her, er, office is around the corner."

"A medium, huh? I haven't come across one of those in years."

"Still a good living to be made off all the bereaved, I guess. But I haven't met one here in Santa Fe before."

"I don't think I've seen anyone so exotic here in the club. Does she wear a turban, jangling charms, beaded scarves, stuff like that?"

"I haven't seen her myself. I would imagine there's some law of mediums that says they have to."

"I would hope so. Otherwise her clients wouldn't trust her." He laughed as he poured out the drink into two chilled glasses and handed her one. It tasted perfectly sweet and tangy. "What does she have to do with the murder?"

"I don't know. Nothing, probably." Maddie carefully lowered her foot to the floor. "Excuse me for a moment. I feel the need to refresh my lipstick."

He pointed to the baize door. "Just through there, past the rack of glasses, and to the left."

Maddie made her way to the necessary room at the back of the kitchen. It might have been tucked away in a quick renovation, but it was pretty, with pale-pink walls, a brocade fainting couch, and a gilt-framed mirror. Mr. Bennett certainly knew how to build a fine atmosphere for his customers.

She checked herself in the mirror and grimaced at the sight that greeted her. Her hair was tangled, her lipstick vanished, and the sleeve of her coat was torn and dusty. She tidied herself as best she could, using the lipstick from her handbag and repinning her hair. She thought again about cutting it into a fashionable shingle. It would make things much more convenient if she was going to keep chasing through tunnels and going to morgues and brothels in search of elusive answers.

The kitchen was still quiet when she came out, but she could hear the low hum of voices from the club room. Rob and another man, probably the bartender arriving for his shift. Maybe it would give her a minute to snoop around a bit.

She wasn't sure what she wanted to find. Drugs? A note offering Harry a job? A big bottle marked "Poison—To Give to Business Rivals"? She found only pots and pans, crates of produce, unlabeled bottles. She sniffed a few, but none were like Tomas's tonic.

It looked like any other restaurant kitchen, except for an alcove at the back, next to the walk-in icebox. It had room only for a long table, scattered with what looked like a science lab in disarray.

Maddie peered at it closer. There was a length of tubing, some funnels, and a big lidded boiling pot. Whatever this was, it looked like it hadn't been used in some time.

She poked at a few tubes and nozzles and noticed a mark on the back of the stainless steel of a tube. There were some letters, too faded to read, and the outline of a coiled snake. Some kind of manufacturer's mark? It definitely looked like some kind of old-fashioned medical equipment like she used to see at the hospital.

Her nosiness was interrupted by the sound of footsteps echoing in the kitchen.

"Mrs. Alwin?" Rob called. "Are you here?"

Maddie carefully put the bits and bobs back where she found them and hurried back to the main kitchen with a cheery smile. "Here I am!"

A frown flickered over his face. "Were you lost?"

"A bit. I've never seen a *real* kitchen before."

The frown turned into an indulgent smile. "I would imagine it's not a necessity for Astors."

"My mother is the Astor." Maddie gestured to the alcove. "That looks intriguing. Some sort of state of the art chopper or mincer?"

"Just something of my dad's. I haven't even had the chance to try it."

"Your father?"

"From his chemist shop." He took her arm and led her back to the main room, where waiters were setting up the tables for the evening. "Now let me make you another drink and find a car to take you home."

"Oh, I can walk . . ."

"Of course you can't, not on that ankle. You can't ruin my fine nursing. Besides, it'll be dark soon."

"Very well," Maddie answered. "Just one more tiny orange blossom, though, or I'll be one dizzy dame."

It was only once she was settled in the back seat of a cab, speeding toward Canyon Road, that she realized what bothered her. Rob said the strange contraption was from his father's chemist shop. But surely he had told her his family had a grocery?

She was still thinking about that when the car left her off near the end of the street, outside the new post office. She was so distracted, she nearly bumped into one of the postmen coming out with his heavy bag for the evening delivery.

"Mrs. Alwin!" he said. "Glad I ran into you here. You're the only one with a Canyon Road delivery this evening, and I don't fancy facing the Bacas' dog again."

"Glad to save you a trip then." As he went off on his route, she sorted through the small pile of letters, praying one would not be from her mother. That would be the last thing she needed to top off her already straining day.

There was a postcard from her cousin Gwen in California, an idyllic scene of sun, sandy beaches, and a white-washed hotel veranda in the background. *Having a wizard time!* it said in Gwen's almost unreadable scrawl. There was also a bill from the dairy and an advertisement from a new milliner. And a letter from Olive Rush.

Sorry it took me a while to write as promised, but I just made it back to San Ildefonso to find new pottery for the next show. There is a man here whose wife does the most exquisite black work you've ever seen! I've asked around your Anayas, but no one likes to talk about it very much. It seems they were married in the old Spanish church here some time ago, quite against their parents' approval, but haven't lived here for a while.

Juanita Anaya is still quite respected; she always looked after all the pueblo children when their parents were in the fields, and the little ones adored her. But Tomas Anaya is said to have had a drink problem. Such a scourge that is around here! If it was really terrible, no wonder he had to leave. Juanita's brothers still live here; Diego is a farmer and Refugio a rancher whose wife is a weaver. Diego is still a bachelor—quite handsome if I do say so myself. No trouble about either of them that I can see. Diego asked after his sister and her children but not about Tomas.

I'll be back in Santa Fe next week. Hopefully I will have winkled out a bit more by then. I'm not sure we should count on it, though. No white is completely trusted as it is! Do let me know what is happening.

Your friend, Olive

P.S. Finish more paintings soon!

CHAPTER 16

Juanita was working in the kitchen when Maddie arrived home, but she wasn't alone. A man sat at the table, drinking coffee and talking to Juanita in Tewa in low, soft tones.

Maddie paused in the doorway, momentarily surprised. There was never a stranger in her house, and Juanita only ever invited a few of her church friends for tea and cake on Sundays. Maddie had never seen this man before. He was obviously from San Ildefonso like Juanita, tall and lean, his face weathered by the sun but still handsome in a sharply sculpted way, with dark eyes and graying dark hair cut short. He wore a plain denim work shirt and dusty boots; a wide-brimmed felt hat hung beside the door.

Maddie noticed a few suitcases, along with the box of Tomas's belongings—minus the strange bottle.

"Señora Maddie," Juanita said, quickly putting the lid on the pot she was stirring. "There you are! I wondered where you had gone. I didn't want to leave without talking to you."

"Leave?" Maddie asked. She tucked her injured leg behind her, not wanting to answer any worried questions yet.

"Yes. Your nice doctor called, and he said the—that Tomas was ready to be released. He's sending a van to take it to the pueblo to make the trip a bit faster." The man rose to his feet, and Juanita gave him a nervous smile. "And this is my brother, Diego. The girls and I will ride home with him."

"Your brother?" Maddie said. She remembered Juanita said she was estranged from her family. Maybe now that the husband they disapproved of was gone she could mend fences? She smiled at him, unsure if she should shake his hand. Olive had certainly been right when she said he was a handsome one. "How lovely to meet you. Any family or friend of Juanita is always most welcome here, of course."

"And nice to meet you, Mrs. Alwin," he said, studying her closely, quietly, with those dark eyes. "Juanita was just telling me how much she likes her work here."

"I do hope so. I could never do without her."

Juanita arranged some food on platters and put them in the icebox. "There should be plenty here for you to eat, Señora Maddie, until I get back. The milk's been delivered for the day, and Kaune's will bring eggs and vegetables tomorrow. I don't want to find out you were too busy working in the studio and only ate sandwiches."

Maddie laughed. "I'll eat proper meals, I promise. I need to keep my energy up." Especially if it meant that helping Eddie sent her running through tunnels and knocking on brothel doors. She wondered if she should tell Juanita now about Mavis or wait until after the trouble of the funeral rites were over and Eddie was safely back home.

"Juanita says you work as an artist," Diego said.

"Yes," she answered. "Just amateur, though. I hope to work up to more soon. Olive Rush is having an exhibit at the museum, and she's taken a couple of my small pieces."

"The portrait of the girls?" Juanita asked with a hopeful smile.

"That one isn't quite finished yet," Maddie said, "and I'm not sure I could sell it, anyway. I'm sure I'll want it for myself."

"Miss Rush has been a friend to us," Diego said. "Visiting the pueblo, buying pottery. She even gets some of our artists their own shows and makes sure they're paid."

"She's a good friend to everyone, I think," Maddie said, shifting on her aching leg.

Juanita turned away from the stove and gasped when she saw the dusty, messy shape Maddie was in. "Señora Maddie! What happened?"

"I just took a little spill, that's all," Maddie said. "So clumsy of me!"

"Sit down, right now, and let me look at that," Juanita said, taking Maddie's arm and practically pushing her into a chair. She clucked disapprovingly as she examined the swollen ankle and bandaged scrapes.

"It's all right," Maddie said. "Already on the mend. I ran into a friend who helped me out."

"It looks bandaged well enough. But you'll need some of my lavender salve for those cuts," Juanita said. She hurried out the back door, and Maddie saw her crossing the garden to her own guesthouse. The girls and Buttercup ran up to her, clamoring in curiosity, and she shooed them away.

"She hasn't changed," Diego said quietly. "Always taking care of everyone."

Maddie glanced at him, and his stone-sculptured face looked wistful. "She's the kindest person I've ever met."

"It gets her in trouble sometimes, that soft heart. Always has."

"She does try to help everyone, but it's almost impossible to get her to take help in return."

"But she's letting you help her now. She told me about the lawyer and the English doctor you found."

"That's for Eddie. She'll do anything for her children, even accept a little help. It's only a small step to repay her for her friendship." She studied Diego. He seemed only barely younger than Juanita and as quiet and stoic as she was. "I'm glad you're here to help her too. She doesn't talk much about her family."

Diego shrugged. "Not much to tell. Our father didn't have faith in her as he should have, and our mother died a long time ago."

Juanita came back, a jar of lavender-scented salve in her hand. She examined the scrapes again, shaking her head. "I hope you're not talking Señora Maddie's ear off, Diego."

Maddie laughed. "He and you barely say five words in a row, Juanita. My ear is still firmly in place. I was just telling

Señor Diego that I'm glad he's here to help you with the funeral."

Juanita glanced at her brother. "Diego was always my best brother. I used to take care of him a lot when he was a baby and our mother was ill. He was so pretty, I would carry him around to show him off to all the *sa yas, the old aunties.* And he started using the outhouse with no training at all, no diapers."

"Juanita," Diego said, a dull-red flush spreading on his cheeks. "I'm sure she doesn't want to know about that."

Juanita giggled. "It's the truth. You should get your Dr. Cole to look at that ankle tomorrow, Señora Maddie. And use some of this salve every day."

"I will, thank you." Maddie glanced between Juanita and her brother and realized she should tell them about Mavis. The woman was family, after all, and in some trouble. "I met someone today who says she knows you, or once did anyway."

Juanita was taking a loaf of bread out of the oven. "Oh?"

"She says her name is Mavis and that she was Tomas's cousin. She's afraid to come and give her condolences in person."

Juanita and Diego exchanged a long glance before Juanita looked away, straightening the pots and pans on the rack even though they were already perfectly organized. "She can come see us whenever she likes."

"Juanita," Diego said quietly. "There would be gossip. You know she ran off with a cowboy. Who knows what she's doing now?"

"There's always gossip. Even though we left home long ago, it's still talk, talk, talk, and no one knows what they're talking about. No one knows the truth."

"Juanita . . ." Diego said quietly.

"No. She deserves the truth. We all do." She turned to Maddie, her lips drawn tight. "At our home, for many centuries, we've been divided into two clans: the summer people from the squash kiva and the winter people from the turquoise kiva. They each have always had their own cacique, their leader, and also war chiefs. My family is from the summer people, and Tomas was from the winter people. Some of our families didn't like it when we decided to court."

"So you left because Tomas was from a different clan?" Maddie asked. It all sounded so sadly Romeo and Juliet–ish.

"No. That wasn't so good, but it was all right for a while," Juanita said. "They needed as many people to work the land as possible. Lots of us grew sick and died in those days, especially when the 'flu came. But Tomas never could leave well enough alone. He had to follow his own ideas, no matter how harmful they might be."

Maddie glanced at Diego, who was sitting quietly, watching his sister. "You mean things like Madame Genet?" she asked.

"Maybe not her in particular. Father Malone says she's new here," Juanita said. "But even back then, Tomas said he didn't really believe in the old ways *or* in the church." She wrapped her fingers around the silver cross at her neck.

"It was just dangerous talk," Diego said.

Maddie was puzzled. "So his interest in spiritualism got him evicted?"

Juanita shook her head. "That was just an excuse." She glanced again at her brother. "She should know, Diego. She's trying to help Eddie. She's no gossiper."

"Girl Guide's honor," Maddie said. She thought of her mother whispering with her friends over silver tea trays, clucking their tongues about the latest Fifth Avenue scandal, turning other people's lives inside out. She never wanted to become that.

Though she had to admit Juanita's tragically romantic tale was fascinating.

Diego sat back in his chair, his arms folded, and Juanita went on. "It was bootlegging."

"Tomas was bootlegging on pueblo land?" Maddie said. Maybe he did get roughed up for being in a rival gang after all, and it went too far, like Rob Bennett said? Did he know what was going with Harry's deliveries?

"Not him. But he knew who was," Juanita said.

"Juanita, please," Diego said quietly.

"Everyone knew it. They just wouldn't say it. Tomas wouldn't say it either, but he was trying to stop it. He would sometimes have a drink when we first married, you see, and he had been doing just that on the night our first baby died. Tomas hated what strong drink could do to people, but he knew going to the council would only get him thrown out sooner. No one liked him anyway."

"Then who was it?" Maddie asked. "Who got him tossed out?"

"A relative of one of the war chiefs. He was letting the smugglers cross his land, tribal land, for a fee. That's why Tomas could only work in secret, or so he told me. But they got to him first, accused *him* of being the one smuggling."

"How do you know it wasn't really him, Juanita?" Diego said. "He never had proof, and now he's gotten himself killed in an alleyway!"

Maddie remembered how angry Juanita had been when she heard about the rum-running and Tomas's possible part in it. She had even called him a hypocrite.

"I don't think he would have," Juanita said, but her eyes looked doubtful. "He hated it so much. But he hated living in town too. Maybe he wanted to catch the true culprits at last . . ."

"You can't believe that," Diego said. He reached across the table to touch his sister's arm. "He was always a difficult man. Father didn't want you to marry him for good reasons."

"He had his faults, plenty of them," Juanita said, "but he surely wouldn't have dragged Eddie into trouble. He was always so strict with him. He'd already lost one son, and neither of us wanted to lose another."

"So maybe Tomas was trying to catch the culprits for Eddie?" Maddie said. "Because he thought Eddie was running into trouble?"

Juanita rubbed her hand wearily over her face. "He was really angry when he thought Eddie had taken with the wrong crowd. A long plan like that doesn't seem like him, though. Tomas was more likely to fight outright, especially after working quietly at the pueblo just turned around on him like that in the end."

"He was no martyr like your priests say, Juanita," Diego said.

"Probably not. And he blamed me for what happened, of course."

"None of that was your fault," Diego said. "They would have let you stay."

Juanita shook her head. "I couldn't have, not without him. We were married, for better or worse. Even if it meant I had to leave home, find a new way."

Diego snorted. "But he didn't always stay away."

Juanita looked at him with wide eyes. "What do you mean?"

"Someone said they saw him a few weeks back, down by the river. He was talking to someone, but they couldn't see who it was, and then he ran off. But it was definitely Tomas on the pueblo."

"Why would he be there again?" Juanita cried. "When he was in such trouble!"

Diego shrugged. "I don't suppose we'll know now. But I can help you ask around after the funeral. I won't let you down again, Juanita."

"Oh, the funeral." Juanita pushed herself back from the table. "We should be going if we're to have any daylight left."

"You should wait and go tomorrow," Maddie said. "It would be safer."

Juanita shook her head. "We have to finish the rites as soon as we can. Dr. Cole says we can ride in the van, and it should be here by now. It's not a long way home, really."

"Not long." Maddie remembered the happier trip she had made to the pueblo a few months ago with Olive and a couple of other artists, touring the homes and shops, walking in the fields with the beautiful dark mountains in the distance. Maybe being there again would bring Juanita some peace, or at least more answers. And she had to find what answers she could there in town. "Take some food for the trip. You've cooked far too much for me to eat here!"

Juanita squeezed her hand. "I'm sorry I didn't tell you the tale before, Señora Maddie. It's hard to talk about."

Maddie gave her a smile. "Of course. You can tell me anything you like, Juanita, but also you don't *have* to tell me anything. I know we're always here for each other."

After Juanita, her brother, and the girls loaded up their suitcases and left, the house was very quiet indeed. Maddie took a cup of tea and some of Juanita's bizcochitos into the garden and sat on her back portal as the sun slid lower in the sky, turning the evening golden and still. She thought about what she had learned, about Tomas and his reasons for getting into trouble at San Ildefonso, and being forced to leave. Had he been smuggling alcohol, having changed his mind about it all, or was he still trying to stop it?

She suddenly knew what she should do next. She should meet the mysterious Madame Genet and find out what she and her spirits might know about Tomas Anaya.

CHAPTER 17

As Maddie climbed the wooden steps at the back of the building toward Madame Genet's office, she thought that at least the whole misadventure had shown her places in town she hadn't seen before. She'd never even realized this place was here, tucked above the grocery on the corner of the plaza, even though she walked past it all the time. The sounds of everyday business were muffled here, the light shadowed.

At the top of the stairs, she found what she was looking for. A small brass plate on the door read, "Madame Genet, Confidential Inquiries." There was even a doorbell.

Maddie patted her hair into place beneath her hat and smoothed her skirt. She'd worn the fine green suit again and her grandmother's pearls. Surely if she looked like a wealthy, respectable new client, she would learn more from the medium. Maybe even purchase a bit of the "tonic" to be tested.

The door opened, and a tiny, birdlike woman stood there. She wore what Maddie imagined a ghost medium should: a long, silver-spangled dark-blue tunic over a slim black silk skirt. A few wisps of dark hair peeked out from under a feathered turban, and she had dangling, sparkling earrings in the shape of stars and crescent moons. She looked almost Maddie's mother's age, her pale skin creased around smoky-gray eyes, and Maddie was sure she was quite as observant and judgmental as an Astor could ever be.

The woman's gaze flickered over Maddie, and she smiled. "How can I help you, mademoiselle?" she asked in a faintly accented, musical voice.

"My name is Madeline Alwin. I understand you can offer some help to those of who are suffering?"

She smiled gently. "Indeed I do. It is my gift."

"I—I don't know what your business procedure is. Should I have written for an appointment?"

"Not at all. I am very informal. I never know when someone will need me or when the spirits might speak. Do come in." She stepped back and opened the door wider. "I did sense I would have a visitor today, but not that I would meet someone new. How did you find me, mademoiselle? Or is it madame?"

Maddie studied the room. It was small, but as dramatic as any New York stage set. A round table with a white cloth sat in the very center, holding a crystal globe on a brass stand and several boxes of brightly painted tarot cards. A sideboard held various bottles and potions in front of an array of silver-framed photos. The curtains were drawn close against the sunny day outside, and she couldn't tell if any of the bottles matched Tomas's and Mavis's bottles. The light from two small lamps didn't go far into the corners of the room, and there was the sweet, smoky scent of incense. An Asian silk screen stretched across the corner.

Maddie took off her gloves and tucked them in her handbag so Madame Genet could see her wedding ring and easily guess she was a widow. There was a strange, oppressive, almost claustrophobic atmosphere in that room, and she didn't want to stay any longer than she had to.

"Either is fine—madame or mademoiselle," she said. "I felt quite elderly when a waiter first called me 'madame,' but now I rather like it. It gives one a bit of dignity, I suppose."

Madame Genet smiled. "Indeed it does."

"And it wasn't hard to find you. Word of a newcomer does get around in such a small place."

"Yes. I was just passing through on my way to Seattle when I sensed I should stop over for a time. That someone here needed help desperately. Perhaps it is you?"

"Maybe it is."

"Please, sit. Tell me about yourself. Tell me how I can help." Madame Genet offered one of the chairs at the round table and took her own seat behind the crystal ball. "Some tea?"

"Yes, thank you." Maddie slowly lowered herself onto the hard wooden chair. As Madame Genet rang a bell, Maddie studied a painting on the wall, the only artwork in sight. It was a meadow with the sky gray beyond and a distant street of shops and Victorian clapboard houses.

A maid hurried in, a slim figure in a black dress and white apron, pale hair straggling from her cap. Maddie was not really surprised to see it was June, Harry's sister who also worked at La Fonda. Suddenly that group seemed to be everywhere.

"Tea, please, June, and maybe some cake from that delicious tea shop downstairs," Madame Genet said.

June nodded and hurried off again, not even looking at Maddie.

"I've found this such a delightful town," Madame Genet said. "So pretty, and such nice shops, not at all what I expected when I came to the Wild West. I am such a city mouse myself."

"From Paris?" Maddie said, though she knew from the madame's accent that she was no Parisian.

Madame Genet waved her hand, the rings on her long fingers flashing in the lamplight. Maddie saw one was shaped like a snake, a twist of gold with tiny emerald eyes. Madame Genet noticed her looking and smiled. "An old family piece. I am never without it. And no, not Paris. I am a citizen of the world, as I sense are you, madame."

"I've traveled a bit," Maddie said. The maid came back, putting down the tray and leaving again as fast as she came.

"Travel is essential to a well-rounded life," Madame Genet said, pouring out the tea into floral painted china cups. It smelled of jasmine, not the green earthiness of whatever was in those sculpted bottles. "I knew when I was a girl that I had a gift I had to share, but no way of knowing how to develop it, refine it. Only when I left home could I learn what it really meant."

"I often feel the same. Though my gift is painting, not mediumship."

Madame Genet nodded. "I can always tell when someone has that sensitivity. An artistic nature is often the first step to full awareness of the world around us. There is so much we mortals cannot see."

"So you must help them to see it?"

"Of course. Shall we try it?"

Maddie nodded, feeling a bit nervous. Madame Genet stretched out her hands, palms up, and Maddie laid hers lightly against them. Madame Genet closed her eyes and breathed deeply, slowly, for several long minutes. Maddie watched her very closely, but she saw nothing until a frown crossed the medium's brow and her hands closed tighter on Maddie's.

"It is foggy today," she said, her French accent gone, her voice low and rough. "The voices are not coming through clearly. But one is trying. Is he the one who looks for you? He sounds quite insistent. He has been parted from you for a long time."

Maddie glanced down at her gold and diamond wedding ring. Against her will, she found herself almost—almost—hoping. What if her instincts, her education, was all wrong? What if Mavis was right and Madame Genet could find their lost ones? Maddie felt a pang of the old loneliness, the old ache of missing Pete, of feeling not whole without him.

"Is it my husband?" she asked.

"I don't know. His voice is so faint. But he calls out for you. He seems to have so much to tell you. He remembers a battle, I think. There's the sound of machine gun fire, a sense of—of fear. Cold, inescapable. But you are there too, and he isn't scared after that."

"I am there?" Maddie said, puzzled. It was an easy guess that her husband died on a battlefield; there were so many young war widows around.

"Not you, but part of you. A memory? A photo? He is saying he couldn't keep his promise, but he is with you still."

Maddie closed her eyes and pictured the train station where she last saw Pete, so tall and handsome in his khaki uniform as he kissed her. She had pressed a framed photo into his hand, a picture of their wedding day, and he had whispered he would come back to her. He'd promised.

Yet he never did.

"He can see my life now?" she said.

"He is glad you're working. He . . . he likes the people around you, your new friends. But he says you should be very careful."

"Careful?"

"You are always too trusting. Not everyone is worthy of your friendship, your help."

"Who should I not trust?" Maddie asked, thinking of her friends—Juanita, Gunther, David.

Madame Genet shook her head hard, making her earrings jingle. "I can't tell. It's all fading—fading . . ." She suddenly gasped and slumped over the table.

Maddie hardly dared move. Her heart was pounding. "Madame?" she whispered. "Are you all right?"

The medium slowly sat up. She looked as pale as paper under her turban, her eyes bright with tears. "I am quite well. Just a bit faint. It's always that way when I return."

Maddie refilled her teacup and pressed it into her hand. The woman's fingers were ice cold.

"Thank you," Madame Genet murmured, taking a long sip. "Was it him?"

"Him?"

"Your husband, the one you seek. I could not see him clearly. There was such a fog today. But he did seem so anxious to reach you."

Maddie wanted so very much to believe, yet she couldn't quite take that step and give in entirely. Was this how Tomas felt, as he looked for atonement for his lost child? There was so much about people that was an utter mystery. She thought she knew them, and so often she knew nothing at all. "I don't know."

Madame Genet nodded. Her cheeks seemed a little pinker as she finished her tea. "It often takes more than one session for the spirit to truly come through."

Maddie wondered if this was why Mavis kept coming back, searching for her Billy, spending her scant money. Maddie suddenly had the strongest urge to flee that stuffy room, to get away from whatever sticky, clinging energy hung around there. "Should I come back? Tomorrow, maybe?"

"Perhaps next week. I have been tired lately, and it makes it harder for me to see what I must. But wait here for a moment. I have something that might help you."

Madame Genet rose from the table and made her way unsteadily to the door where the maid had vanished.

Maddie waited for a moment, but she couldn't sit still. Something about the session made her feel restless, uncomfortable. She carried the tea tray to the sideboard and studied the bottles arrayed there. Herbs floated in amber liquid, but none she recognized. A large silver vase sat on the corner, filled with branches of white and yellow flowers.

Behind them were a few framed photos. A man and woman in white Edwardian summer clothes in a meadow much like the painting. A graduation group outside a schoolhouse. And one was a little girl in a ruffled dress and enormous hair bow holding a baby in a long gown on her lap. They seemed to be in a garden, a summerhouse behind them. The girl had Madame Genet's large eyes.

The photo next to it was of the same girl, alone this time, standing in front of a shop window of some sort, the camera's flash bouncing off the plate glass. Maddie could faintly see some kind of contraption inside the building and the last few painted white letters of a name: IST & CA. The girl looked very serious, almost as if she disliked having her photo taken. Maddie could sympathize.

Next to the table was a wastepaper basket, half-full. Maddie took a quick glance through it, wondering if she would find anything that looked like the dark, block letters of the threatening note she had received telling her to stay inside and paint pictures. It was only a couple of bills and an envelope with madame's address on the outside. She stuffed it into her purse to look at it later and compare the handwriting.

Madame Genet came back in a swirl of spangled robe. She seemed a bit startled to find Maddie not at the table, but she quickly smiled. "I see you are admiring my younger self."

"I do miss those hair bows. They made getting ready in the morning so much faster."

"No pins, no combs, just the tie of a ribbon," Madame Genet agreed. "Yet when we're young, we can't wait to be older, to steer our own course."

Maddie remembered her nursery, high up in the Fifth Avenue house, and how she would spend hours staring out the window at the real life of the street below. "Yes."

"That was my father's business," Madame Genet said, gesturing to the photo of her by the window.

"And this one?"

Her lips pursed. "My brother. Long before he was—lost to us. He was the one who first showed me my gift."

"I am sorry. I have one brother, but I always wished I had more siblings myself."

"It was long ago. I have hopes of leading him to the light again." She held out a bottle. "This is for you, madame. To help build your strength. The stronger we are, the more we are able to see our lost ones and the hidden world around us."

"Thank you," Maddie said. She took the glass cautiously. It was plain and round, not like those Tomas and Mavis had, and the liquid was paler than theirs.

"Take a small dose every evening and come back to see me next week. I am sure your husband will come through then."

Maddie tucked the bottle into her handbag and hurried out of the stuffy room. It seemed to press closer and closer around her. The bright day outside, the people on their ordinary errands, seemed very far away even as she walked the familiar streets toward her house.

Reentering her home, the rooms seemed very silent and empty without Juanita and the twins. Maddie took off her hat and gloves and left them on a side table. She felt quite tired, as if she had indeed been wandering around on the Other Side. The real world was so bright and strange. She turned toward her bedroom, intending to take a long, hot bath, but a clatter from the kitchen made her freeze.

"Who is there?" she called, her heart pounding.

Eddie appeared in the doorway, a half-empty milk bottle in his hands. He looked rumpled and pale, shadows beneath his eyes, his hair tangled. "It's just me, Miss Maddie."

"Eddie!" In her relief, Maddie rushed forward to hug him tightly. Usually he would have pulled away with teenage disdain, but now he hugged her back. "Oh, Eddie, I'm so happy to see you."

"And I'm happy to see you. But where is everyone?"

Maddie smoothed his dark hair, her heart aching at all he had gone through, all that he still had to get through.

Surely he was too young for all this. "I'm afraid they've gone to the funeral. Dr. Cole got your father's body released."

Eddie pulled back with a scowl. "Without me? But I should be there! There are things I have to do. I'm the son."

"And you can do them very soon. The important thing is you're not in jail. Here, let's get out some of the copious food your mother left, and you can tell me what's happened . . ."

★　★　★

It turned out Mr. Springer had gotten Eddie out on bail. As he ate some of Juanita's lamb stew and a large hunk of buttered bread, he told Maddie what had happened, the way the inspector and his deputies let him out right away when Mr. Springer mentioned his senatorial connections. He would have to go before the judge in a few days, but at least he was home for the moment.

Maddie took a bite of one of the bizcochitos and let the cinnamon and sugar melt deliciously away before she said, "So we have only a few days to find out who the killer is."

Eddie made a scoffing sound through a mouthful of bread. "It'll take longer than that. Lots of people didn't like my dad, you know."

"So I'm finding out. But he had a few friends too." She thought of Mavis, who had cried for him. But it was undeniable that he had interfered in matters some very dangerous people had thought he shouldn't. Why? How? "Speaking of friends, I ran into your old pal Harry. He seems to make deliveries all over town."

Eddie frowned. "He's not my friend. I used to run around with him and his gang, but that was one thing my dad was right about in the end. They're more trouble than they're worth."

"I'm glad you found that out then. Harry said you turned down a job he offered."

"I knew there was something shady about that. I'd done some delivery jobs before, just kid's stuff for pocket money, but this one didn't sound right."

"How so?"

Eddie shrugged. "Harry didn't tell me much about it, and the money was too good for just a little pickup and drop-off like the usual. I thought about it. Ma could use the money if the girls are going to school. But I didn't want to get into trouble." He poked at the remains of his dinner and frowned. "Of course, I got in trouble anyway, didn't I? Might as well have done the job."

"Of course you shouldn't have. If some intuition was holding you back, you were absolutely right not to do it. And this trouble will soon be over."

"I hope so. That jail was crackers."

"I know you and Tomas quarreled. What was it really about? Your mother says he didn't like you running with the wrong crowd, but was that all?"

Eddie snorted. "He didn't like my friends, and that was really ripe of him. I saw him, y'know. With that fancy woman, and then on the corner with that bootlegger. He got mad at us all the time, but he was never any saint."

"Maybe not. But that one particular lady was nothing to be angry about. She is your father's cousin. I just met her myself."

"Cousin?" Eddie said doubtfully.

"Yes. It seems she got into some trouble years ago and ran away. Tomas was trying to help her."

"But what about the booze? I heard he was smuggling it, same as anyone else."

Maddie thought of what Rob had said, that Tomas had worked for a rival bootlegging gang, and then the arguments that he had been a teetotaler and that was what had got him into trouble on the pueblo. "Now that I can't say. Hopefully we'll be able to find out a lot more tomorrow. You should go to bed now, get some sleep. You looked exhausted."

He nodded. "That'll be nice. My own pillow and blankets. That jail is no place for quiet. They shine lights every hour, and the guy next door liked to scream his wife's name all the time. Ugh."

"I would imagine it was no fun at all. But you're home now." And if Maddie had anything to say about it, he would stay there. But it felt like time was running out, faster and faster, like a silk scarf slipping through her fingers.

She sent Eddie off to bed with some lemon drops and more milk, but she knew she wouldn't be able to sleep for a while herself. She fed Buttercup the scraps and went to rinse the dishes in the sink, going over everything she had learned in the last few days.

As she put away the dishes, she noticed a slip of paper tucked up by the phone. *Dr. Cole called,* she read in Eddie's messy, penciled scrawl. *Dinner tomorrow at La Fonda, lots to tell.*

She felt her cheeks turn warm, and she had to smile a bit despite everything that was going on, the worries swirling in her head, the tiredness that pulled her down. She was going to see David again—tomorrow! She took down the note and folded it carefully before she made her way to her room, Buttercup at her heels. She had a feeling she might sleep well after all.

CHAPTER 18

The New Mexican Restaurant at La Fonda wasn't too crowded when Maddie made her way to her own little table in the corner, beneath the bright murals of Spanish dancers and colorful bullfights. Most diners were still sipping their aperitifs in the bar or gossiping in the lobby.

She was a little early, so luckily she had time to settle herself before the handsome doctor arrived. She patted her hair into place, smoothed the skirt of her bronze satin cocktail dress, and went over all the places she had been that day, trying to retrace Tomas's steps on that fateful night. She hadn't had much luck, and there had been no sign of Harry, his sister, or his pals at all. Probably they were all laying low after the trouble.

She took a quick peek in her compact mirror and adjusted her lipstick. She just wanted to get David's advice on what she had found so far, surely that was all. There was no reason to be nervous. But she still couldn't quit fidgeting with her long necklace of jet beads, trying to make them fall just right.

"Mrs. Alwin," Anton called, hurrying past the red-painted chairs and turquoise-draped tables of the dining room. "I'm so happy to see you again. I hope you've recovered from that terrible unpleasantness the other night?"

"It was not at all fun, I agree," she said. "But I am completely recovered. I hope your staff has, as well. It's not the sort of thing anyone expects in their everyday world, I'm sure."

"They are doing splendidly—such bricks. La Fonda is usually a safe place, and I have assured them nothing has changed in that regard." His smile flickered into a quick frown. "One maid is rather tearful still, but then she's young. She probably reads those hideous novels about ghosts and vampires that are all the rage now. Last year, she wouldn't use the elevator because she was sure it was haunted by a ghost bride."

"Really?" Maddie said with a grin. "How intriguing. I'll have to ride the elevator sometime soon to see if she appears."

"I wouldn't count on it, Mrs. Alwin. Ghosts are notoriously shy. But you may need to use the elevator soon anyway. Mr. Ryder is planning a palm court dance on the roof this summer."

"How delightful! I do look forward to it. We could all use a little distraction right now."

"I certainly agree."

Maddie remembered the sobbing maid, Harry's sister, the one who worked at Madame Genet's and couldn't be found that day. "The maid who was upset—is her name June?"

Anton looked surprised. "It is. Do you know her?"

Maddie shook her head. "I just happened to see her after the terrible discovery. She was crying, and seemed most understandably upset."

"Of course. Aside from the tears, she seems well enough. She's still doing her duties on time."

So she *had* come to work. "I'm glad to hear it. If I can do anything to help . . ."

Anton sighed. "I fear no one can help. Such things must fade away on their own. If the unfortunate event was solved, I'm sure it would put a lot of minds at ease! A murder on our own doorstep. Who would have thought such a thing? It must have been a passing maniac."

"I'm sure it was."

Anton moved on to speak to the next table, and Maddie studied her menu, even though she always ordered the same thing, the lobster thermidor. Anton was right. If the murder was solved and the culprit safely put away, everyone could move on with their lives in town, their minds easier knowing the villain was gone. The strings tied up with a clever explanation, just like in a Chesterton novel. Sometimes she felt like she was within grasp of what happened, but then she felt further away than ever. Tomas Anaya had lived in her house, and now she saw she hadn't known the man at all. Nor did it seem like anyone else had, even his wife. He had too many secrets.

She looked up to find David standing in the doorway, very tall and smart in a sharply tailored charcoal-gray suit, his blue eyes scanning the room. She waved at him, and he smiled. As he made his way toward her, past the other groups of diners, Maddie saw how the ladies stared at him as he walked by. One or two even patted their hair or reached for their compacts, just as she had.

He *was* quite good-looking, she thought as she watched him. Very distinguished, and with a smile that brightened the room. And he was dining with *her*. She wanted to laugh, to twirl with excitement—and she hadn't felt that way in so very long. It was like waking up after a very dark night.

"I'm so sorry I'm late, Madeline," he said, taking the chair across the table. He put a folder down on the turquoise-colored cloth. "I wanted to make sure I had all the reports to give you."

Maddie tapped at the thick pile of papers. "It certainly looks thorough. Would a novice like myself even understand it, or will it just look like random words?"

He laughed. "It might very well. Lab reports have a way of doing that. I did type up a summary. It's there on top if you want to take a peek."

Maddie opened it and scanned the neat columns. "How exciting."

"You won't think so after you read it. Toxicology is interesting in its way, but seldom exciting."

"This will be. I was just thinking how everyone will rest so much easier once they know what happened."

"Sometimes knowing *how* something happened doesn't tell us *why*. It just makes for more confusion."

"Sounds like life. One step forward, two back."

"Sometimes, yes."

"At least this is one step, right?" Maddie smiled at him. "It was so kind of you to send a van to take Tomas back to the pueblo. Juanita will feel better once she can have a proper funeral."

He nodded solemnly. "It was the least I could do. I remember in the war, it was nearly impossible for anyone to have a proper funeral. So many families were left feeling incomplete."

"Of course. Oh, I forgot to tell you! Eddie is home! Mr. Springer got him out on bail. He's very upset he can't do his part in the funeral rites."

"I'm sure he is, poor kid. But it will help his mother more in the long run if he's there with her for good. Jumping bail wouldn't help him now."

"That's what I told him. I left him with some work to do in the garden; hopefully that will keep him busy and at the house for a while. Out of trouble until his name is fully cleared, anyway."

"Good idea. Idle hands and all that, as my grandmother used to say."

"Your grandmother?"

"A doughty Cornish lady. She had a different saying for every situation."

Maddie laughed and bent her head to study the pages in the folder. David examined the menu. The restaurant was getting busier, the sound of chatter and laughter winding higher, but Maddie felt as if she was in her own little world, tucked away in the corner with David and the strange words she tried to decipher. Only when the waiter arrived did she look up to give her order and watch as he poured out some sparkling water.

"So it was the ethyl biscoumacetate in his system, just as you suspected?" she asked after the waiter had departed.

"Yes. Commonly called warfarin. It would be easy enough to obtain for someone in the medical profession or who knows how to derive it from common rat poisons."

Maddie sighed. "It makes sense. I was hoping it would be something terribly exotic, though. Something there was only one source for. Even I have rat poison in my own garden shed."

"A civilian would have to buy a lot for it to have the effect it did on Mr. Anaya."

"Maybe one of the shops in town could help us, if they keep a record of sales?"

"If it was bought locally. Someone could derive it themselves too, if they had the supply and a little knowledge. The taste could be disguised in something strong, like a coffee or cheap liquor."

"Interesting. What about the bottles from Mavis and Tomas?"

"That was rather curious. Mr. Anaya's did have some trace amounts of the warfarin. Not really enough to kill him quickly unless he had taken several bottles of the stuff, and it doesn't sound like he did. More of it might have accumulated in the liver, though, and diminished the vitamin K we need for clotting. The other two bottles were just a bit of parsley water. Mavis had a bit of whiskey in hers too. It looks to me like someone else got hold of Tomas's bottle."

Maddie nodded, feeling a bit relieved she hadn't been handed a poisoned apple by Madame Genet. But Tomas had—unless the poison came from elsewhere, and the tonic was just a convenient receptacle. Those bottles seemed to be all over town, delivered by Harry. But where did he get them? "So maybe the poison combined with the beating led to a lethal effect?"

"That could very well be. A symptom of ethyl biscoumacetate poisoning would be increased bleeding, especially of that bright-red, frothy sort you described. So we might be looking for two culprits working independently of each other, whether or not they knew their combined work would be deadly. Where exactly did the bottles come from?"

Maddie told him about her visit to Madame Genet and how the woman was wound together with Tomas. She also told him about how young Harry delivered crates full of the things all over the place and that Tomas was not known as a drinker. "However, I can't figure out a reason why the medium would want to kill her regular clients. Her income surely depends on people coming back for repeat séances."

"Maybe Mr. Anaya found out she was a fraud and she was afraid he was going to spread it around."

"Very possibly. But Tomas wasn't much of a believer, or so I used to think. He seemed convinced enough by Madame Genet to make Juanita confide in her priest, she was so worried. And Mavis seems to believe in the spirits too."

"What did you think of the madame?"

Maddie thought of the dark room, the woman's cold hands and faint words. "She was pretty good. Everything the public thinks a medium should be, I'd say. There was even a crystal ball. But she didn't have much to say about Tomas."

"Discretion is probably as much a part of the job as crystal balls. Wouldn't want anyone spreading rumors from the other side."

Maddie laughed. "Of course not. Who would? I just wish *I* could communicate with the other side. It would make things so much easier."

Their food arrived, and as they ate, they talked of more pleasant things than murders and spirits. They chatted about travels and their families, of favorite art and books read lately. She quite forgot everything else as she laughed at his stories of his grandmother and all her sayings. His funny stories made his blue eyes glow and made Maddie feel ridiculously happy.

When the dessert arrived, she looked up in surprise at how long they had been sitting there. Talking and laughing with David had made the time fly by. Only a few people were left at their tables, but she could hear a crowd in the lobby.

She saw two people standing outside the door, a man with his back to the restaurant as he talked to a woman in a bright eau-de-Nil dress. Maddie recognized her as Elizabeth Grover, but her blonde hair was tousled, her mascara smudged. She waved her hands and seemed to be angry, but the man in the cheaply shiny evening suit just shook his head.

Maddie remembered Elizabeth in the ladies' room with her white powder. "Excuse me for a moment, David," she said and slid out from behind the table. By the time she reached the lobby, Elizabeth was hurrying away, and the man was nowhere to be seen.

"Elizabeth," Maddie called. Elizabeth turned to face her, a determined, overly bright smile on her face. "Elizabeth, are you okay?"

"Absolutely wizard, Maddie. Why do you ask?"

"You just—when I saw you just now with that man, you seemed a bit upset."

Elizabeth waved her hand. "What, him? He's been after me for ages, trying to get a date, and I found out he's engaged to some chambermaid here! I was just giving him what for, telling him off for treating a girl like that."

"He sounds like an odd bird."

"He is! Men. They're the worst."

Maddie thought of David, who was waiting for her in the dining room, his smile, his attentive eyes. "Sometimes. Are you sure you're all right? Should Anton ring for a ride to take you home?"

Elizabeth laughed a bright, brassy giggle. "It's so early, Maddie! Don't be a fuddy-duddy. I'm just off to the ladies' room, then going dancing. We're only young once, you know."

"Elizabeth," Maddie began, worried by the bright sheen to her eyes. "Do be careful. If you need anything . . ."

"I don't need anything at all," Elizabeth said, her voice shrill. "Or nothing you can get for me. Won't everyone just mind their own business? Isn't that why we came west? To do as we please?"

She rushed away down the hall, and Maddie slowly turned back toward the restaurant. On impulse, she went instead to the front desk and asked for June. Maybe Harry's sister would know more about what task her brother had worked on or about the mystery man arguing with Elizabeth Grover.

"She's just finishing her shift," the desk clerk said. "She should be leaving soon. Maybe she's downstairs in the maids' cloak room?"

"Thank you," Maddie said. She thought of her waiting dessert and David but decided she would just get a quick word with June before the maid left work.

She made her way downstairs and through the narrow labyrinth that let the staff move quickly through the hotel. A few waiters and chambermaids hurried past with covered trays and stacks of towels. One of them pointed her toward the cloak room.

She could hear voices—a soft murmur—as she turned the corner that led to the staff cloak rooms, and she caught a glimpse of June's blonde hair at the end of the hall. But the girl wasn't alone. She was talking quietly, intimately, with a man Maddie recognized as the one who had been arguing with Elizabeth just a few minutes ago; he wore the same cheap evening suit, had the same slicked-down dark hair. This time, she could see his face. It was Mike, the waiter from Rob's club who she'd met chatting with Gunther.

June put a beseeching hand on his arm, and he shook her off. Maddie ducked behind a row of laundry carts and tried to creep closer to hear what they were saying. Their voices were too low for her to understand more than a few muttered words.

". . . won't do us good now," the man was saying. How very different he was from the man she met at the club, his accent now rough. ". . . missing sales and that."

"Harry says it'll be soon," June answered. "Things just have to calm down a bit. There's . . . much attention now. All that blood . . ."

"We'll lose business! Our boss says . . ."

But Maddie wasn't to know what the boss said. Two girls in laundress smocks came clattering along the corridor, their arms full of sheets and towels, their laughter loud. They teased June, whose cheeks turned bright red.

"I have to go to work," Mike said. "Tell Harry. He knows what he has to do if he wants his money."

June tried to catch his arm. He shook her off and strode away. June watched after him for a long moment, biting her lip as if in indecision, and then she went inside the cloak room.

Maddie made her way back upstairs and found David sorting through the autopsy papers at the table. Their coffee and cake were waiting.

"Sorry that took a while," she said as she slipped back into her seat. "I saw something a bit interesting." She quickly told him about Elizabeth, June, and the man from the club.

"Cocaine, eh?" he said. "Here in Santa Fe?"

"Could it have something to do with the poison?"

"Maybe. It's been a while since my toxicology class. I would need to . . ."

Maddie suddenly realized a few tables near theirs were watching them with interest. Town gossip did love a new romance—or even better, romance and murder. "Maybe we could talk about it later?"

He followed her gaze and nodded with a knowing smile. "I see. I think you are quite right, Mrs. Alwin. This isn't the best subject for such a lovely evening. Maybe you would walk with me around the plaza?"

Maddie smiled. "I would love to."

Elizabeth was right about one thing—the night was young, and the plaza was crowded with people enjoying the warm evening as Maddie strolled its gravel pathways on David's arm. A band played in the lacy iron gazebo, and a few couples danced on the flagstones in front of it. She almost felt like she was tiptoeing on clouds, it was all so nice.

She glimpsed a light on in the second-floor office of Madame Genet. She wondered if there was a séance tonight.

But the beautiful Santa Fe evening seemed far away from anything as frightening as ghosts sending warnings from the other side and from smoky clubs and drug smuggling. The air was soft, just touched with the first warmth of spring, and everyone around her was laughing.

David made her laugh too, with stories about his English childhood, and he listened closely when she answered with tales of her own New York upbringing, playing in the park with her brother, classes with her school friends. It felt good to remember such days, mostly good days really, and to perhaps look forward to more good days to come. Maybe there really was happiness yet to have for all of them. It had been too long since she felt that way, too long since she could remember the past without pain.

But when he left her at her door with just one sweet lingering kiss on the cheek, she had to admit she felt a bit disappointed. Yet he had promised to come back for tea the next day to talk over everything in the lab reports, so all was not yet lost.

It was rather amazing to feel that excited little flutter once more. Maybe she was still young enough after all.

CHAPTER 19

The next day, Maddie was in the kitchen, trying to stir up a batch of drop scones that her mother's cook in New York had once taught her. It wasn't quite as easy as Mrs. Brown had made it look, but Maddie had invited David Cole to tea, promised a treat for Eddie, and also sent a note to Gunther inviting him, and for some reason, she wanted to impress them all with her domestic wizardry. If only she had any domestic skills to speak of, she thought ruefully as the dough slid like liquid through her spoon. Even Buttercup, sitting next to the stove, didn't want to eat any stray lumps. They all obviously missed Juanita.

At last she was able to mix up a batch that held together, prettily spotted with dried currants, and she sat down at the table as they baked. As she waited, she got out the threatening note she had received and the letter she'd taken from Madame Genet's office and laid them next to each other. The letter was unsigned and was mostly about the office that was for rent and someone urging Madame Genet to come to town soon to help with "some matters." The hand-writing wasn't quite the same, the block letters of Maddie's note being an obvious ruse, but the paper and very dark ink looked similar. She wondered who had brought Madame Genet to Santa Fe in the first place.

She took out a notebook and tried to write down what she knew so far about their sad predicament. She realized she had actually found out rather a lot in the last few days, but none of the details seemed to stick together to make a whole story.

People who had a grudge against Tomas seemed legion. Maddie jotted them down as she thought of them. Rob Bennett said Tomas had belonged to a rival bootlegging gang and had a few run-ins with Bennett's employees. But Mavis said Tomas had been against drink, and even Juanita and her brother said his teetotal opinions had gotten him thrown off the pueblo. But even if Tomas had eschewed drink, it hadn't seemed to make him very sweet-tempered. He'd quarreled with his own family, especially Eddie, as well as with his in-laws. Maybe even Mavis only pretended to like him now. She had said they sometimes dined together, a chance to lace his drink with the poison. So—all the bootleggers in town, the whole pueblo where he used to live, his relatives. Who else had he rubbed the wrong way?

Maddie tapped her pencil against the page. *Someone* disliked the man enough to feed him poison, which had made a painful beating fatal. Who had given him the poison? The medium seemed like the obvious choice—the trace of warfarin was in her "tonic"—but if Tomas had gone, she would have lost the money she made helping him look for his lost son. She didn't seem to be a mad poisoner, just a charlatan. And her bottles were the same as the ones delivered all over town. What if the medium had a friend who *was* a poisoner? A friend who had a grudge against Tomas and who'd used his trust in Madame Genet against him? The church didn't like her work. Did the police? What would they do to discredit her and run her out of town?

Harry had tried to get Eddie to help with the smuggling operation. Eddie had said no, but what if his father hadn't known that and had been driven into a rage thinking of his son bootlegging? She thought of June the maid and her boyfriend, Mike, who worked at the club. Where did they figure into it all?

So—there was Tomas's own family; Juanita's family, who might want to save her from her great mistake at last; Rob Bennett and his network; Harry and his gang; Madame Genet, for some as yet unknown reason; and Mavis, though Maddie couldn't figure out why, unless maybe he'd promised to help her in some way and then reneged, which was quite possible. Mavis did have a hard life and felt abandoned by her family. Two separate groups, maybe, who didn't even know about the work of the other? A poisoner and someone who'd delivered a revenge beating, both of them meeting in one fatal moment.

Buttercup barked, and Maddie suddenly smelled the acrid tang of burning bread. She looked up, startled, to see clouds of smoke billowing out of the oven.

"No!" she cried and jumped up to run across the kitchen. It was too late to save her scones, though. They looked like pitiful lumps of coal.

Maddie sighed and went to the door to look for Eddie, who was watering and weeding in the garden. She had hoped the work would take his mind off everything, but he still looked distracted and terribly young and fragile.

"Eddie!" she called. "An emergency, I'm afraid. Can you run to Kaune's for some cakes?"

★　★　★

By the time David and Gunther arrived, she'd managed to cobble together a decent enough tea. A plate of iced cake and cookies from the grocer's, some small sandwiches with Juanita's leftover bread and potted ham spread, and even some scones she'd salvaged. She was making a pot of tea, trying to stop Gunther from adding a dollop of rum to it, when Eddie answered the knock at the door to let the handsome doctor in. She had to laugh when she saw he'd even brought flowers. How much more lovely could he get?

The four of them sat down to dig into the makeshift repast, talking about what was going on in town, general chat, and gossip. Once the cakes were gone, Maddie took out her notebook and went over what she had learned.

"I'm afraid your handsome writer-waiter seems to be engaged to June the chambermaid *and* chasing Elizabeth Grover," she told Gunther. She told them what she had seen at La Fonda, the lovebirds' half-heard quarrel. "Could they both be working for whoever is smuggling in the drugs and then supplying them to hotel customers?"

"June, Harry's sister?" Eddie said. "I've never heard of her doing any job but the one at the hotel, making beds and such. She's never been arrested or anything. But she *has* been engaged at least three times lately. Harry wishes she'd just settle down. But I've never heard of this guy."

"Mike. He works at Mr. Bennett's club," Maddie said. "And Bennett admits Tomas had some run-ins with his men, but he said it was because Tomas was some sort of business rival, trying to undercut the bootlegging racket in town. Yet your uncle says Tomas was such a teetotaler, it got him into trouble at home."

Eddie frowned. "It's true that I never saw him drink. You know he walloped me good when he thought I was smuggling, even though I wasn't."

Gunther took a quick nip from his flask. "And the handsome Mike might be perfidious, but he is also a chatterbox when he's been purloining the orange blossoms. I was at the club just last night, and he told me Mr. Bennett doesn't just smuggle in his booze. He makes it himself, top-notch stuff."

Maddie remembered headlines when she was in New York of people collapsing and dying in the streets, poisoned by bad booze. "That sounds dangerous. David, could homemade hooch have been what poisoned Tomas?"

David looked thoughtful. "Possibly. There are so many things that can go wrong with homemade stills, of course.

Blindness, insanity. Who knows what people put in their bathtub gin? Yet that's not what seems to have happened to Mr. Anaya. It was warfarin that showed up in his tests. It thins the blood so it can't clot. Even a small cut could then be fatal."

Maddie thought of the strange equipment she'd seen in Rob's kitchen, the seemingly random pile of pots and pans and funnels. He'd said it came from his father's chemist shop, even though he'd told her before that his father was a grocer. It had looked disused, but she wasn't really sure what a still in use would look like. Maybe that was what he used to make his "top-notch stuff" but something had gone wrong? Yet no one else had died.

"The warfarin was in the bottle he got from Madame Genet, at least traces of it," she said. "I just can't understand why she would do such a thing and thus lose a regular customer."

"Maybe she knew him before?" Gunther said. "She could have some grudge against him?"

"But I can't figure out how or when. There is the connection to Mavis, though, who's his cousin."

"Maybe she didn't like him?" Eddie said. "Ma's family didn't."

"Her bottle was clean," said David. "Just some herbs and a bit of whiskey. But of course that doesn't clear her. She could be using the same bottles herself to throw off suspicion."

"Madame Genet could also be using Mavis to get to him, if she *did* have a quarrel with him," Gunther said. "But no one in town knows who she really is, do they? Even the priest doesn't know, and the church always makes it their job to know about everyone in town."

"Father Malone did seem to only be concerned about the state of his parishioners' souls if they went in for such hoodoo," Maddie said. "He said nothing about her bringing in booze." Though there was something else, something lurking in the back of her mind that she couldn't quite remember.

"We're never gonna find who did this, are we?" Eddie whispered. He buried his face in his hands, his wiry shoulders shaking as if he struggled to hold back tears. "It's all going to be blamed on me!"

"No, Eddie," Maddie said, patting his shoulder. She felt so helpless, so lost. She only wanted to help Eddie, to clear his name so he was free to live the rest of his life. "We *will* find who did this, I promise. We already know so much more than we did before."

And all the things she had learned seemed to confuse her even more. How unknowable another person's life was, especially when they were gone! But she was determined. She would find out what was happening and free Eddie, if it was the last thing she did.

CHAPTER 20

That night, after an impromptu garden dinner with David, Gunther, and Eddie, where Gunther brought out his Victrola and she danced with David under the stars and even Eddie laughed and forgot his troubles for an hour, Maddie found she couldn't sleep. She lay awake in her bed, watching the moon rise in the sky through her window, turning everything over in her mind again and again.

Surely it all had to fit together somehow. There was something, some detail that she had overlooked. It seemed the harder she tried to grasp for it, the further away it went. She would make a terrible assistant in a detective novel! She was certainly no Watson.

She closed her eyes and tried to picture the story like a painting, or a tapestry that flowed along, telling its tale. A sort of twentieth-century Bayeux Tapestry.

Tomas and Juanita met, fell in love, fought her family's wishes, married, had a child, lost a child, then made a new family with Eddie and the girls. But the loss struck Tomas with some sort of guilt. And then, despite having tried to make a life at their home, they had to leave after Tomas couldn't stop making waves. She knew the pueblo was a small, close-knit community, one that depended on each person and his or her relationship to everyone else. Had Tomas still been angry with the people who sent him away? Was Juanita? She seemed to have a chance to mend fences with her family now, as evidenced by the recent arrival of her brother.

And had Tomas's enemies considered him gone for good just because he was made to move—or had they now wanted to make sure of it? How did Mavis fit into that story? She was an outcast too. She said she loved her cousin, but what if it was more complicated than that? If the Anayas had been involved in her leaving—or even just refused to help her after—would she still be angry?

Maddie thought of how Mavis was when she visited her. Hardened by life, but tearful when she heard about Tomas. Wonderfully hopeful of Madame Genet's powers to bring her back her lost love, the lost life she'd once hoped for. If she was faking that, surely she'd missed her calling as an award-winning actress. No, Maddie now didn't really think it was Mavis—poor, downtrodden Mavis—and she'd seen no signs of old enemies from the pueblo stalking Tomas in the time the Anayas worked for her. Not that it meant they weren't out there, of course. She knew there was much below the surface she wouldn't be allowed to see. She would ask Juanita more when she returned from the funeral, but she didn't think anyone would tell her very much else.

The next figure she saw in her tapestry was the bootlegging scene. Rob Bennett's flashy club; Mike the waiter and
his fiancée, who was Harry's sister; the Golden Rooster.
They all were involved in smuggling alcohol and maybe
even the drugs supplied to people like Elizabeth Grover. It
was Rob Bennett who'd told her about Tomas's activities
with some rival gang, Tomas's run-ins with his own men,
but that didn't ring entirely true. If he was teetotaler, as
Juanita said, he might very well have gotten into trouble
with the town's purveyors of hooch. And that seemed to be
everyone, who got the same stuff in the same bottles.

Had Tomas really caused them enough trouble to make
them go after him? Maybe he'd had some way to disrupt
their supply routes or turn their lower-level workers like
Harry against them. It seemed possible.

And where did Madame Genet fit in? Tomas and Mavis
seemed to believe in her powers, even take comfort in
them. Yet she had popped up in town so suddenly. There
didn't seem to be enough bereaved souls in Santa Fe to
make it profitable as a long stop for her, not like in a big city
such as Los Angeles or New York. Father Malone had said
the church was worried about her spiritual influence—but
enough to plant poisoned "tonic" on her to get rid of her?
Maddie thought of the Borgias with a laugh. She could see
the affable Father Malone paying a visit to Madame Genet,
warning her away, but nothing so Machiavellian.

But could the medium be here for a reason other than
séances? Could she be part of the drug ring? Madame Genet

was in a good position to know who in town would make a good scapegoat. It would take some knowledge and skill to distill the poison and administer it in such a way to divert suspicion. To make sure Tomas died at a distance in some different way. Mike had said he "didn't mean for it to happen" that way. Was he the one who beat Tomas up, only to see him bleed to death in that alley?

Maddie thought of Madame Genet's small room and went over every detail of it in her mind. The white tablecloth, the crystal ball, the Asian screen, the heavy curtains blocking the light. The pot of tea. The woman's sparkling rings, her face pale with powder, her piercing gray eyes that seemed to see more than Maddie would wish. The sideboard with the framed photos, the flowering branches in the silver vase. White ones. Could poison be distilled from that?

She thought of the photos. The little girl with the baby. The same little girl standing outside a shop window in her pinafore. What was it about the shop? *Make it a painting*, Maddie told herself and focused harder.

Yes. The window. The letters. When she was looking at the photo, it was only a fleeting moment before Madame Genet interrupted her. Now she remembered those letters. It was a chemist shop with the outline of a snake painted there. A snake like the ring Madame Genet wore? Surely the daughter of a chemist would know what to put into her own tonics to make them lethal? But what did she have against Tomas? If Mavis was right, he was a good customer to the medium.

A chemist shop. Maddie sat straight up in bed. Of course. Rob Bennett also had a father with a chemist shop—or a grocer, depending on the day. What if he and Madame Genet were in league? What if they'd both decided Tomas was too much trouble and had to go? Would Tomas have been able to disrupt the flow of business enough to make murder worthwhile? He *had* been very rough with Eddie when he'd thought his son was involved with smuggling. Maybe he did that with more of the young errand-runners, perhaps in a runaround way to atone for the loss of his other son?

Maddie thought of the strange equipment in the kitchen of the club. Surely it was indeed a homemade still, yet it had looked so much more intricate than the ones her friends kept in their basements in New York. Maybe it was a chemist's equipment. Something to do with Madame Genet's childhood shop. If only she had taken a better look at the stamps on the back of the contraption when she was in Rob's kitchen . . .

She had to see, to make absolutely sure before she took such evidence to the police. That arrogant inspector wouldn't listen to her otherwise. He might very well not believe her anyway, but she had to try. She had to find a way to *make* him listen.

She rolled over to peer at the clock on her bedside table. Almost three. Surely the club would be empty, and no one would come in for several hours. She could pop in, take a look at the still, maybe get some kind of sample David could test against the tonics, and then pop out again.

She felt a quiver of anxious excitement deep in her stomach as she pushed back the blankets. Surely she was crazy to be getting out of her comfy bed in the middle of the night to go prowling through town! But it was a crazy thing she knew she had to do if she wanted to end this quickly.

She swiftly dressed in a pair of black wool trousers and an old navy-blue pullover of Pete's. She pinned up her hair and tucked it under a black cap.

As she put on her sturdiest lace-up boots, Buttercup peeked out from under the sheets and gave a whine.

"I know," Maddie whispered to her. "You have to stay here, my girl. I'll be back before the sun rises." Just in case, she took out Pete's old service revolver and some ammunition from her dressing table drawer.

Buttercup went back under the covers, and Maddie made her way to the kitchen. She was sure Juanita kept a torch there for the too-frequent times when the electricity went out. She found it in the cupboard and quickly scrawled a note for Eddie in case he woke up before she was home.

The night was perfectly still in that deep, dark hour, the only sound the wind through the trees and the faint, ghostly cry of birds in the distance. All the houses and shops were still shuttered and blank as she made her way through the streets. It didn't feel quite real, as if she moved in a dream, the familiar world distorted around her.

She made her way down narrow, winding side alleys, trying hard not to think of Tomas and what happened to him in just such a place. It was so silent, the air seemed to hum with the quiet. A bird swooped down overhead, and she nearly cried out.

She forced herself to take a deep breath and kept walking. She couldn't go back yet.

The club building was just as quiet as the rest of the town, the revelers all gone home to sleep off their Pink Ladies and orange blossoms. The doors were locked, of course, but Maddie found a small window at the back that she could wiggle open. She pulled herself up and over the ledge and tumbled to the tile floor of the kitchen.

She sat up slowly, holding her breath as she listened carefully. Just more quietly.

She turned on the torch and tiptoed through the empty room, past stacks of pots and pans, racks of glasses, and a basket of dirty linen. Just an ordinary kitchen.

The still was where she last saw it—in the back alcove, seemingly untouched. Yet as she shined the light over it, studying the details, she caught a whiff of something herbal, almost earthy. It reminded her of the "tonic." Was this really used to make the stuff then? What else was concocted there?

Maddie found the faint mark on the back of a metal funnel she remembered glimpsing before. It was rather tarnished and faded, the letters too faint to read. Yet she could see the image of a twisted snake. Some sort of business trademark?

It did indeed look like the one on the window in Madame Genet's old photograph. And the ring she wore. *An old family piece*, she had said.

"I know I said to visit the club anytime, Mrs. Alwin," a voice said behind her. "But this is an inconvenient hour."

Maddie's heart leaped precipitously to her throat, and she gasped. Feeling like a 100 percent chump for not paying attention, she pulled out Pete's service revolver and spun around to face Rob Bennett.

He wore his pristine white shirt sleeves, his hair slightly rumpled, a faint smile on his face that was more frightening than fiery angry. And the gun he held was smaller, newer, and more accurate than hers.

"I see you're interested in my father's old business equipment," he said, as friendly as if they were sipping drinks at the bar again. "It's a bit of a clunker, sort of old fashioned, but it gets the job done. They don't make such quality nowadays."

Maddie swallowed hard past the dry lump in her throat. "The job of distilling nerve tonics?"

He laughed. "That's more in my sister's line of work these days. I'm more interested in being able to make a spot of gin when we run low."

"Your sister?" Maddie whispered. Of course—it made sense. The baby in the photo, the chemist shop. The gray eyes.

His own pale-gray eyes narrowed. "Yes. I thought you knew. The fantastical Madame Genet. You visited her, yes? And were sort of nosy about the premises. Emeline is a big help sometimes and a bloody nuisance at others. Typical big sister."

"And which is it when she's poisoning people who give you trouble? A help or a nuisance?"

His laughter turned to a fierce frown. "That sounds like a long conversation, Mrs. Alwin. Why don't you take a seat, and we'll have a little chat? You'll have to give me that gun first, of course."

"I don't think I will," Maddie said. She held the gun level in her hands, surprised it was so steady. She felt rather distant from the whole thing, like it was a movie reel. He gave a small nod, and she was suddenly seized from behind. Her breath was knocked from her lungs in a great whoosh, and her heart pounded.

"I'm sorry to have to treat a lady like this, but I don't seem to have a choice," Rob said sadly. "You really should have just stayed home and painted your pictures. Lots safer for a lady like you."

"It was you," she whispered. He had written that note telling her to mind her own business. Maddie was utterly furious with herself. G. K. Chesterton wouldn't think much of her secret sleuthing skills at all.

CHAPTER 21

Maddie sat facing Rob Bennett on a chair in the quiet club, her hands tied as she watched him pacing. He still held the gun, but he kept shaking his head, as if he was arguing with himself. His henchman was gone, probably outside the kitchen door to make sure no one interrupted.

If he *was* going to kill her, surely she deserved to hear the whole story first. Maybe if she could keep him talking, like some reverse Scheherazade, she could figure a way out of the stupid mess she had gotten herself into. She surreptitiously worked at the ropes on her wrists.

An image popped into her head of David's smile as they'd waltzed in her garden. She would definitely like to see him again. The thought made her work harder.

"Was Tomas really such a dire threat to your business?" she asked.

Rob shook his head. "You really don't know? Even though the man and his family live in your own house?"

Maddie thought of her own mother, her haughtiness toward servants who got above themselves, and Maddie decided to try to imitate her. She lifted her chin and looked down her nose at him, even though she was sitting and he was standing and continuing to pace. "The personal lives of the staff are none of my business."

He laughed, and it sounded shaky. He ran his hands through his hair, leaving it standing on end, and she hoped it was a sign of indecision rather than desperation. "Only when they're dead, huh? Then you go snooping into their business all over town."

"Eddie is just a child. He needed my help."

"A child! Where were excuses like that when my father died and I had to take care of Mother and Emeline? But I did it. Better than he ever could. Then some Indian came around causing problems for business, trying to get my contacts out at the pueblo in trouble. I needed that trade route. I couldn't let that go. There's too much income at stake."

"Why not? Like you said, he was just one man. He had no power, especially to a man whose clients include senators and Grovers and people like that."

"Some of my shipments have to cross pueblo land. I have a man there who facilitates business, someone high up who can make things invisible. He warned me about Anaya. It seems the man caused trouble years ago and was fixing to start up again now. He'd been to visit some relative of his, someone whose land we needed to cross. If more marshals were out there . . ."

Maddie remembered the story Juanita and Diego told about Tomas getting into trouble by exposing bootleggers at the pueblo. And Diego had said someone had seen Tomas at the pueblo recently, though Juanita had been shocked by that. "After all this time?"

"My mother said a leopard keeps its spots no matter what. Anaya interfered enough that some of my sources were taking notice. Some of them were thinking twice about letting us use their land for our crossings. I told you, I couldn't have that."

"So you got Madame—Emeline to poison him with her tonic? After he turned to her for help in his grief?"

"At first we thought he would be susceptible to her medium gig. Those pueblo sorts are superstitious, right? My contact told me about the man's baby. Emeline said she could find out his secrets, and maybe we could blackmail him or something. That's worked a treat before."

Maddie's fingers curled into fists as she remembered how, just for a moment, she had actually hoped Madame Genet was genuine. That her husband was really there. It had been hooey all along, and she should never have been fooled. She had been fooled about too many things lately. "But not this time?"

Rob slammed his fist down on a table, making her jump. She twisted harder at the ropes, feeling them loosen a bit. "He didn't give up any useful dirt, and neither did his cousin, that whore. So we decided to make him sick, just a little. Get him out of the game for a while."

Maddie wrapped her fingers around the rough rope, managing to slide her thumb under the knot. She tried to remember what she had learned about knots in the Girl Guides at Miss Spence's. "That didn't work either?"

"Worse luck. But we'd just started. Emeline said not to give him too much, to be patient. She'd used it before, see, to cause a few hallucinations in her séances. Just a tiny amount. If you use too much, they can bleed out."

"You couldn't afford to be patient, though, could you? Not if shipments were being held up and costing you money. People like Elizabeth Grover need their fix. Did you send your men to beat him up then?"

"I told you! I didn't mean to kill him. No one did. Not unless it was necessary. Mike and the boys decided to give him a sample of justice, that's all. They did it because sometimes we have to get tough with people, and I told them to do it. Justice has to be rough sometimes, you know."

Maddie doubted people like that would be shocked at any amount of blood. "But you're the one who pays them. You told them to do it."

He ran his hand through his hair again. "They're hot-headed kids. They get bored when not much is happening. A little fighting never hurts. It gets people off our backs, sends them a message."

"Unless someone was being dosed with blood thinners first." Maddie forced herself to give him a gentle smile as she worked harder at the knot. "I do understand. Sometimes things get out of hand in a Western town like this. I can see you're a good man, just trying to run a business, to take care of your sister."

His eyes narrowed, and he nodded. "That's true. It doesn't help me when people get themselves killed. Bad for business to get attention like that."

"Of course not." She smiled again. "I can help you. I'm an Astor, remember? And I know what it takes to make a living too. I could never run a club like this. You're very good at it. But I can't help you if I'm dead like Tomas."

"I did try to warn you to mind your own business," he said, his voice softer. "On that note. You should've listened."

"Yes," she said. So it had been him who'd written that note after all. The jerk. "I should have. But that's all in the past now."

He reached down and loosened the knot, almost as if he moved in a dream, his eyes cloudy. She didn't have an instant to hesitate. She suddenly remembered things she'd thought long forgotten, fighting techniques some of the soldiers recovering in the hospital had once taught her. She had only been trying to distract them then, but it was very useful now.

She twisted in Rob's grasp, simultaneously kicking back with her boot and bending her head to bite his hand. He howled and let her go, and she started running. She didn't know where she was trying to go or where his henchman was lurking; she only knew she had to get away, to hide.

She saw her torch lying on the floor and swept it up. She heard Rob shout at her, and she tipped the still over in his path to block him. It clattered apart, a loud metallic clash on the tile floor. He cursed and shouted out for Mike.

Maddie managed to get the back door open and plunged out into the night. She didn't have much of a head-start, and she glanced around frantically for a hiding place. There were only trash cans and a few vegetable crates. Then she remembered—the tunnels.

She found the empty storage space where she'd chased Harry and ran down the steps into the stone passageway. Just like the first time she saw it, she was in too much of a hurry to notice where she was headed in that subterranean world. She just kept running, praying that Rob hadn't seen her go that way and that her torch would hold up.

The weak light wavered on the rough stone walls, and the air smelled dank and stale. She turned and turned again until she had no clue where she was in relation to the streets above. But she couldn't hear anything behind her, so hopefully she had lost her pursuers.

She dared to take a moment to catch her breath, leaning against the wall. She couldn't let herself get overwhelmed, couldn't let herself think about how close she had been to the murderers. How close she had come to losing her life just when she had found it again.

She sucked in a deep breath to keep from crying—and smelled a faint sugary yeastiness in the chilly air. The tea room! Of course. That was where she and Harry had sat talking, under the tea room, near the bank. Surely she was close to an exit.

She plunged ahead, only to freeze at a clattering sound in the darkness behind her. She glanced over her shoulder and saw a shadow flicker on the wall, coming closer around the corner. She broke into a flat out run again.

"Madeline!" Rob shouted, and she realized she hadn't lost him after all. She ran faster, her legs aching and her lungs about to burst. She found another flight of stone stairs and tumbled up them.

She found herself in one of the shops behind the tea room, just as her torch flickered and went out. Rob managed to catch up to her, reaching out to grab her sleeve, so close she could feel his breath on her neck. She punched him in the face, aiming for his eyes with her manicured nails, and as he howled, she managed to break open the shop door and rush out toward the plaza.

"You witch," he yelled. He grabbed for her arm again, and that time he caught her. She tripped and fell into the road, the breath knocked out of her. He loomed over her, his face nightmarish in the moonlight.

"That's not very ladylike behavior, is it? Not very Astor-like," he said with a hoarse laugh. His fist came up, but he never had a chance to land the blow. A pale blur shot out of the night and fell on Rob with a ferocious growl. As he screamed, Maddie scampered away and pushed herself to her feet.

"Buttercup!" she cried when she saw, to her astonishment, that it was her sweet little dog on the attack.

"Buttercup, no!" she heard someone shout. Eddie ran over to grab the dog by her collar and pull her away. Behind him was David, his shirt pale in the night, his face twisted in anger.

"Sorry about that, Miss Maddie," Eddie panted as he held onto the struggling dog. "I thought maybe Buttercup could help track you down."

"But what are you doing here? Both of you?"

David kicked Rob as the man tried to struggle to his feet. He landed another blow, which kept Rob down, and Maddie was sure he hadn't just been a medic in the war. The fury on his face was astonishing to behold. "Eddie came to fetch me at the hospital when he found your note. Luckily, I hadn't gone back to Sunmount yet. He was worried about you being out here on your own. And quite right he was, I see." He looked down contemptuously at the now sobbing club owner, holding the man down by twisting his arms behind his back. "I take it you found the murderer then?"

"Yes," Maddie gasped. "It was him and his sister, the medium. Tomas was threatening to impede their booze highway. He . . ." She suddenly felt so shaky, all the adrenaline of her flight draining away, and she nearly fell down. Eddie caught her, and she hugged him and Buttercup close.

"I suggest we get him to the jail right away," David said, hauling Rob to his feet. "Then it's a headache powder and some sleep for you, Maddie. You're the heroine of the night, but I'm afraid it won't feel so glorious in the morning when all the excitement wears off."

Maddie swayed on her feet. "It doesn't feel so tickety-boo right now either." Every muscle in her body ached. But he *was* right—at that moment, knowing Eddie was safe and justice was done, she felt just the tiniest bit glorious. Maybe she wasn't quite Father Brown or even Watson yet, but she was learning.

CHAPTER 22

The beautiful late spring day seemed all wrong for what was happening around them, Maddie thought. Not right for visiting a grave at all. Just like the day of Pete's memorial service at St. Thomas Church on a hot New York afternoon had seemed all wrong, with the heady scent of lilies making her head spin and the swell of the organ drowning out every thought.

Today wasn't quite like that, though. They were outside, for one thing, with a fresh, pine-scented breeze in the air and no noisy city clamor pushing around them, intruding on grief. The sky arced endlessly overhead in bright, sunny yellow and blue, not a cloud in sight. The cry of birds gave the only music. Just the black clothes of the small group gathered around the fresh mound of sandy dirt in the churchyard gave any hint of what was really happening.

Tomas's memorial service.

As Father Malone chanted his words of office for the dead, his black cassock and purple stole as dark as the crows perched on the picket fence nearby, Maddie studied the village beyond.

San Ildefonso, only about twenty miles from Santa Fe, was not a large place, with only a few narrow dirt lanes leading out from the large central plaza lined with small adobe homes. A few of them sometimes opened as shops, selling the beautiful, distinctive, black-on-black pottery, but today they were all shut and silent in respect for a man they had once sent away.

Yet now his family and friends were welcomed back. The old Spanish church—by far the largest building at San Ildefonso with its second-story gallery and bell tower, freshly painted white walls, and large graveyard—was quiet except for the group gathered at the new grave. Juanita, Eddie, and the girls stood beside the small wooden cross, written with Tomas's name and dates. Beside it was a much more faded marker for the Anayas' long-lost baby.

They were all still and silent, Juanita's veiled head bowed as she held the twins against her. Beside her was her brother Diego and another man who looked so like Juanita he could only be her other brother, Refugio, the rancher. Once in a while, Diego would gently touch her hand, and she would nod at him.

Most surprising of all, Mavis stood there too, though apart from the others. She lingered by the fence, a lonely figure in a dark-blue dress and veiled hat, her red hair shimmering as she cried. Juanita waved at her, and Mavis slowly, hesitantly, waved back.

The only others present were Olive Rush, who had brought them in her own car out to the pueblo, and Maddie. She knew she could never have come to Tomas's funeral and his releasing rites, but Juanita had insisted she come with them to put the cross into its place and say a final good-bye.

"If not for you, Señora Maddie, we would never have known what really happened to Tomas," Juanita had said when the killer was revealed. "And Eddie might not be back with us. Please, come home with us. Let me show you where we came from."

So Maddie had agreed, and she was glad she had, despite the somber veil that seemed to wrap around them all in that silent graveyard. It was important to say good-bye properly, to know at least a measure of peace had been achieved.

She clutched her black handbag in her gloved hands and watched the mountains in the distance as she listened to Father Malone's words. It was a beautiful place, with the thick, green orchards along the river, the purple mass of the Jemez Mountains in the west.

She knew that the Puebloans believed that all spirits who belonged to the mountains and waters returned there to become one with the earth again, to be reunited with all the other departed spirits. She hoped that was true for Tomas, that his restless, angry spirit had found stillness there. She hoped it was true for Pete too.

And maybe, just maybe, one day they would all be together again, part of the land they loved.

Father Malone said his amens, and Juanita crossed herself. Eddie scattered a handful of cornmeal over the grave, and the twins laid small bouquets against the cross. Their little faces looked sad and pale under their black hair bows.

"My wife has made a small luncheon," Refugio said. "If you can all stay?"

Juanita glanced at Olive, who said, "Yes, of course. My car is entirely at your disposal, Mrs. Anaya."

"It's very kind of you," Maddie said. She glanced around and saw that Mavis had gone.

As their little group made their way out of the gate that led from the churchyard, Maddie noticed that one of the shuttered windows of the nearest house was open a small crack. Someone peered out. It snapped shut when whoever it was noticed her, though, and she wondered if whoever was in there was one of the people who allowed smuggling across their land. One of the people who'd led to Tomas Anaya being tossed out.

Father Malone had said Inspector Sadler had promised to investigate the smuggling, but Maddie had seen little evidence of effort so far. Maybe the inspector thought San Ildefonso was too far from Santa Fe to matter to his rich patrons. But she had the feeling that one day the matter would come around again, one way or another. If Tomas's death had taught her one thing, it was that no secret stayed hidden forever.

Juanita took her arm as they walked toward the house where Refugio's wife waited, the enticing scent of fresh tortillas and spicy stew wafting toward them.

"Did you hear, Señora Maddie?" Juanita said quietly. "Father Malone has found the girls places at the Loretto school! Starting in the autumn term. They can live at home and be day students. He thinks Pearl especially has a real talent for mathematics, though they are going to need tutoring in history this summer."

"That's wonderful, Juanita!" Maddie said. "Of course I will help them study." Though she feared the house would be much too quiet without their hijinks all day.

"They will have a good future. Or at least the chance of one." Juanita glanced back sadly at the churchyard, those two lonely graves.

Maddie squeezed her arm. "Could you come with me for a moment, Juanita? I want to show you something."

Juanita looked cautiously curious, but she nodded and followed Maddie to where Olive's dusty old roadster was parked in the shade of a cottonwood. Maddie took a package from the boot.

She tore off the brown paper wrapping and held it up to show Juanita. It was the portrait of the twins, sitting together in her studio, their arms linked. Their white dresses and pink hair bows were all that was proper for young ladies, but their smiles shone with mischief. With joy in the hope of the future, just as their mother hoped.

Juanita pressed her hand to her mouth. Her dark eyes gleamed with unshed tears. "Oh, Señora Maddie. It's beautiful. Just like them. My lovely, lovely little girls."

"It's for you," Maddie said. She held the canvas out to Juanita. "A little thank-you for everything you do."

Juanita gasped. "Oh, no! All your hard work? It is too much. It should be in the museum show."

"You know I could never bring myself to sell it. It's rightfully yours. Only once I knew that could I finish it."

Juanita stared at it in silence for a long moment. Finally, she nodded. "Only if we can hang it in the sitting room for now."

"Right over the fireplace, of course." Maddie quickly kissed Juanita's cheek and smiled. "Now let's go try some of that delicious-smelling stew. You need to eat and keep up your strength, and I can't wait to hear all about your lovely family."

EPILOGUE

"Are you sure, Señora Maddie?" Juanita said. Her reflection in the dressing table mirror was deeply worried.

"Absolutely sure," Maddie said decisively. "Just do it, Juanita."

"Perhaps you should wait until next week after the party. If it goes wrong . . ."

"How can it go wrong? I'm as ready as I'll ever be."

Juanita sighed and reached for the scissors. She frowned, lifted a long lock of Maddie's dark hair, and cut it off.

"You see?" Maddie said. "Easy peasy."

"If you say so." Juanita went about the rest of her task with careful concentration. In only a few minutes, Maddie's long hair lay on the sheet under her feet, and she had a crisp, chin-length bob.

She turned her head, examining every angle. It felt so light, the bare nape of her neck so cool. She shook her head in delight and laughed. "Oh, it's wonderful! I can see why it's so fashionable. We should do yours now, Juanita."

Juanita shook her head. "Oh, no. I like my hair just as it is. But it *does* look becoming on you, Señora Maddie."

Maddie slid a diamond clip into one side and examined the effect. "What do you think, girls?"

Pearl and Ruby sat on her bed, watching the proceedings with wide eyes as they petted Buttercup's ears. After all her heroics, the dog had happily gone back to being a spoiled house pet, growing fatter on all her special treats.

"You look like you're in a movie," Ruby said.

Maddie laughed. "Then you must help me choose the right film star gown. The party's starting soon."

As they sorted through the wardrobe, making piles of "no" and "maybe" dresses, Maddie watched them with a smile. Somehow every moment felt brighter now, as if a cloud had lifted and the sky was an endless blue again.

Once Eddie had been cleared, he had gone back to San Ildefonso with his uncle Diego to visit Juanita's family for a while. He was supposed to return when Rob Bennett and his sister, Madame Genet, who had been caught trying to flee town with the proceeds from her customers' phony séances, went on trial. In the meantime, Maddie had worked on new paintings and Juanita had cooked far too much food for their dinners, which meant that David had to be invited to share in it rather often.

And tonight he was going to escort her to the first public viewing of her work. Maddie couldn't remember ever feeling quite so excited—or so nervous. Whether it was the thought of having people look at her paintings or having a date for the first time since Pete, she didn't know.

There was a knock at the door, and Juanita smiled. "I'll answer it, Señora Maddie. You finish getting dressed. Girls, come along and let her decide on a frock."

Maddie gave her a shaky smile. "Are you sure it's okay? My hair, I mean. Do you think he—well, people—will like it? I'm not sure . . ."

Juanita laughed. It was the first time Maddie had heard her laugh, really laugh, in quite a while, and it sounded good. Very good. It sounded like—for the moment, at least—things were right in their little world.

"You look like someone in the fashion papers," Juanita said. "And anyway, it's too late to change your mind now." She hurried to answer the door, and Maddie stood up to examine herself in the mirror.

She chose her pink silk and chiffon again, with a new gold cashmere shawl and her grandmother's rope of pearls. With her hair shorter, she felt so light and young that she was sure she could twirl and twirl up into the sky.

She glanced at Pete's photo and gave him a smile. "I know you would approve, my dearest," she said. And he would. He would love to see what she was doing now—the art, the hairstyle, even being chased by villains. All of it. She knew she didn't need a medium go-between to talk to her husband. He was always there when she needed him. And now he wanted to see her go out and have a lovely evening.

She picked up her beaded evening bag, tucked in her lipstick and compact, and hurried out to meet her date.

David was laughing with the girls, who were skipping around and telling him all about their latest doll theatricals as he stroked Buttercup's ears and made her wag her tail. They all seemed to like him so much and were so comfortable around him, Maddie thought as she watched them. He seemed to bring light and laughter into the room whenever he was there. Even the sad shadows she had once seen in his own eyes seemed lessened. She didn't want to get her hopes up, to crash again to the cold, hard earth as she had too many times before. Yet he made her smile too. And that was good enough for today.

He looked up and saw her standing there in the doorway. His jaw dropped just a bit.

Maddie laughed nervously and gave a little twirl. "Do you like it? I decided to join the modern age at last!"

"Are you sure you're an artist and not a vamp?" he said with a laugh. "I would think I was looking at Theda Bara!"

Maddie laughed harder. "It's just me, plain old Madeline, I'm afraid. A few pounds lighter, though."

He took her hand and spun her in a foxtrot step that made the girls applaud in delight. "You look stunning with any hairstyle you choose. I'm a lucky man tonight."

"You should go on now," Juanita said, "or you'll be late. All your paintings will be sold before you even get there."

Maddie wrapped her shawl around her shoulders and kissed the girls good-night before she headed out into the evening on David's arm. Spring was sliding into summer already, and the breeze was warm and soft.

"I thought we might walk since it's such a lovely evening," he said. "But I can call a car if you're tired."

"Not at all! A walk would be wonderful; it's so warm tonight. And the stars are coming out!"

He smiled, and they walked hand in hand toward the plaza, chatting companionably about his day's work at Sunmount, the progress of her newest painting, and gossip about their friends in town.

"Maddie," he said, suddenly serious as they made their way through the evening's promenade on the gravel pathways and the soft green grass of the plaza. "Are you sure you're recovered from everything that's happened?"

She glanced up at him to find him watching her with a worried glint in his blue eyes. "Of course. Your friend Dr. McKee at the hospital examined my scrapes and bruises and proclaimed me quite well."

"But how do you feel? It's not every day most of us get chased through the streets by a murderer."

"I guess not. I admit I do sometimes have a bad dream or two. But we're all safe now. Work helps me forget." She glanced back over her shoulder at the crowds of the plaza, the young couples smiling shyly at each other, their mothers fanning themselves and chatting, the ice cream cart and the band playing from the wrought-iron stage. "It doesn't seem like such a dark cloud would be lurking under the surface here, does it?"

He smiled. "Surely you know from your detective novels that darkness lurks everywhere. All we can do is try to dig it out into the light. It dies in the sunshine. And that's what you did for this town by getting rid of Bennett and his gang."

Maddie sighed. "I hope so. I don't feel brave at all, though. Just rather silly. At least Eddie's safe now, and Juanita and her children can start to rebuild their lives. It's a shame, though."

"A shame?"

"Yes. He really did make the best orange blossoms in town."

David laughed, and they hurried up the steps into the art museum. She'd just been there the day before, helping Olive with the last pictures to be hung for the sale, but now it all looked transformed. Chinese lanterns cast a soft golden light on the flagstone floors and the pale-tan walls, giving the jewel colors and rich textures of the paintings a life of their own. The galleries were already crowded with people in evening clothes, sipping from Venetian glass goblets and chattering over the work.

Maddie glimpsed Olive, a tall figure in her red velvet Navajo skirt and heavy turquoise necklaces, explaining a scene of a tin-roofed farmhouse and improbably green-colored horses in the blue grass yard to a group of buyers, her hands waving dramatically in the air. David was stopped by two of his patients, so Maddie drifted through the rooms, examining the works, sampling the spiced cider, and munching a tiny lobster roll from a waiter's tray.

Among the bright, merry crowd, Maddie glimpsed an incongruous figure—Inspector Sadler in his tweed coat. The man munched on a tiny crab cake and studied one of the paintings with a frown on his face. Maddie made her way toward him, determined to be friendly now that the real killer was safely caught. Even if the man *did* set her teeth on edge.

"Well, Inspector," she said. "Lovely to see you here. I hope it's not a threat to any of the artwork that called you out?"

He glanced down at her balefully, the crab cake held in his hand. "Not at all, Mrs. Alwin. Our department has been tasked with a bit of—community outreach."

Maddie bit back a laugh. "Community outreach? Whatever is that?"

"Meet the people in town, get to know them. It will make connections easier to spot when crimes happen. One of the newest techniques in modern policing."

"I see. It does sound rather useful." Maddie glanced around the gathering, wondering about the "connections" between all the people there, what would happen next. "All's well that ends well, eh, Inspector?"

"I suppose it is," he said in a grudging tone. "But I have to warn you to be more careful in the future, Mrs. Alwin. You never know what's really going on in your own backyard."

"No," Maddie answered slowly, thinking of everything that had happened, all she had learned. "You really don't." She gave him a smile and left him to his crab cakes, drifting through the galleries.

"Darling, there you are!" Gunther called. His green-and-white polka-dotted cravat gleamed as he kissed her cheek. "Here, have some more of this delicious planter's punch. Not much punch to it, I'm afraid, but I added just a touch of my own."

"Gunther, you are an angel," Maddie said and took a drink from his glass. "I do need a bit of courage before I look at my own paintings, hanging there for everyone to see."

"No fears there, my love! You've already sold one, and I've seen several plump collecting pigeons eyeing the other."

"Really?" Maddie cried.

"Would I lie to you? Come on, you can see the little red dot for yourself."

They made their way through the crowd, past large portraits and landscapes, to find her two small scenes on one of the most prominent partitions. There was indeed a "sold" dot on the image of her house and garden, and a small knot of people gathered around the other painting, talking together in low voices.

Maddie took a long moment just to watch it all, to let the warm, happy glow erase her fears for just a moment. She had done what her family said she couldn't—created something beautiful from her own mind and paintbrush that other people could enjoy. She had said something with her imagination, declared that despite everything the world and life could be worthwhile.

"You see that man there?" Gunther said, gesturing to a portly gentleman who was studying her paintings with a monocle. "He's from the Santa Fe railway. Rumor has it he's looking for images for the new calendar."

"Really?" Maddie gasped. "They pay hundreds of dollars when they use a print."

"And your work is just as good as Blumenschein's or anyone else's. If we both keep fingers ever so tightly crossed . . ."

Maddie laughed and held up her hand to show her crossed fingers. "Dreams do come true sometimes."

"Darling!" he cried, seizing her hand in his. "You took off your ring."

"Yes." She studied the narrow white shadow on her finger where her diamond wedding ring had been. "I hope Pete would understand."

"How could he not? You're young; you have a new life now and years to live it. Even bootleggers can't bring you down! It doesn't mean you've forgotten him. We never forget them, do we?" He gave her a sad smile, as if he understood loss and remembrance.

"Of course I do remember him. I always will."

"Speaking of a life to live, how is the gorgeous English doctor?"

Maddie smiled. "Very well. He's over there talking to the Hendersons. His patients, as well as big patrons of the arts here."

They both turned to study David, whose hair shone in the golden light. He gave them a wave and a broad smile, and Gunther sighed.

"You are lucky, darling," he said and took a sip of his punch.

"I'm beginning to think so."

"Did I tell you I've started a new novel?"

"No! What happened to the last one?"

He took her arm, and they walked along the line of paintings, studying Olive's portrait of the Martinez couple and their gleaming black pottery. "It just wasn't working. I'm not in the romance mood, I suppose."

"Then what's the new one?"

"A detective novel, of course. An English lad who comes West to take back his family's silver mine from a terrible villain. Until he's wrongly arrested when there's a murder."

"It sounds terribly intriguing."

"I thought so. We can't let Father Brown have all the fun, can we? Three chapters are done so far. My editor seems interested."

"Oh, Gunther, that's wonderful!"

"But I need you to solve some more cases. It's such marvelous inspiration."

Maddie shook her head. "No more of that for me. I'm settling down to a calm, quiet life now."

"No, darling! You are never meant for calm. You would be bored in a day. We both would. Now what do you think of this painting? I love the storm coming over the mountain."

They stopped to examine a large scene of distant purple peaks and roiling dark clouds. "I think I prefer sunshine now. But this is very dramatic."

She was absorbed in examining the elegant brushstrokes of the sky, the tiny hint of gold light in the corner, when she heard someone calling her name above the murmur of the crowd. "Maddie! Oh, Maddie, there you are. Finally."

Madeline whirled around, startled. She saw a petite, waifish woman with silvery-blond hair cut in an Eton crop pushing her way through the knots of people around the paintings. Her elfin face was so familiar to Maddie, but it was usually laughing, alight with mischief. Now it was pale, the eyes shadowed by purplish crescents, her fine tweed travel suit and silk blouse rumpled.

"Gwen?" she cried as her cousin threw herself into Maddie's startled arms. The last time she'd seen Gwendolen Astor, Maddie had been waving her off from the train station at Lamy, watching her continue their planned trip to California while Maddie stayed in Santa Fe. "What on earth are you doing here?"

"Oh, Maddie," her cousin sobbed. "I'm in such trouble . . ."

Author's Note

Thank you so much for spending some time with me in my beloved hometown of Santa Fe! Even though we've lived here only a few years, I've been visiting northern New Mexico since I was four years old, and it always felt like "home" to me, a beautiful place with a special magic. I've also always loved the 1920s—the clothes, the cars, the films, and even the silly slang—so this series is a dream come true for me!

Maddie, the Anayas, Dr. Cole, and their friends (and their foes, like Inspector Sadler!) are fictional, but Santa Fe is filled with a rich history, and I loved using just a few real people and places in the story.

Olive Rush (1873–1966) was an artist, muralist, teacher, and great advocate for Native artists. A Quaker from Indiana, she moved permanently to Santa Fe in 1920 and was instrumental in opening the Museum of Fine Arts (where Maddie has her own first art show). It was meant to give a venue to local artists, especially Native Americans, and she herself painted numerous murals that can still be seen all around the country. Her house on Canyon Road was left to the Quakers and is still there in its mostly original condition.

Frank Springer (1848–1927) was an attorney, rancher, railroad millionaire, and artist and archaeologist, as well as a quintessential Western character! The town of Springer is named for him, and his wife was known as one of the most famous hostesses in Santa Fe.

Alice Corbin Henderson (1881–1949) was a poet who met her husband, the painter William Penhallow Henderson (1877–1943) at the Institute of Fine Arts in Chicago. They came to Santa Fe in 1916 when she contracted tuberculosis and stayed on, becoming leaders of artistic life in the city and another great support for Native arts.

The poet Witter Bynner (1881–1968) spent most of his early life traveling Europe and Asia until he moved to Santa Fe with his companion, Walter Johnson, in 1922 and became another leader of local society, hosting people such as D. H. Lawrence, Georgia O'Keefe, Willa Cather, Igor Stravinsky (who led a concert in the cathedral), Robert Frost, Edna St. Vincent Millay, and Martha Graham. His beautiful house is now the Inn of the Turquoise Bear.

La Fonda Hotel is still a gorgeous centerpiece of downtown Santa Fe! It's said that an inn of some sort has stood on the spot for over four hundred years, but the place Maddie would have recognized was quite new, redesigned by Mary Colter and meant as a luxury accommodation. The open central courtyard is now an elegant dining room and the bar newly remodeled, but the margaritas are as good as ever, and they say the ghost bride still rides the elevator! Just outside is the plaza, where there are musical concerts in the summer and magical lights at Christmas and where young people still meet and flirt and tourists buy jewelry from the merchants under the old portal of the 1600s Palace of the Governors. The tunnels under the main plaza were real, and a few remnants can be seen in shop basements.

I still do some of my grocery shopping at Kaune's Grocery, though it's moved a few blocks away since it opened in 1896! It's said to have been the first place in town to sell Coca-Cola and to deliver for free. (Sadly, Mrs. Nussbaum's tearoom, said to serve delicious cinnamon toast, is long gone!)

Sunmount Sanatorium was considered the height of luxury and excellent health care when one of New Mexico's greatest industries was caring for TB patients. The fresh mountain air, abundant sunshine, and good food of the hospital (a central, Spanish-style main hospital and cottages with sun porches) brought in many artists who made the town their home after they were cured. Gerald and Ida Cassidy, Sheldon Parsons, and John Gaw Meem, were just a few. Nothing of it remains now, but the old St. Vincent's Hospital still stands beside the gorgeous nineteenth-century French Gothic cathedral built by the famous Archbishop Lamy. The hospital is now partially a hotel, but watch out for the basement's ghosts! The school of the Loretto Sisters, first opened in 1852, is no longer standing, except for their famous chapel with the spiral staircase. The school was closed in 1968 after educating countless young women, and their chapel is now used for concerts and weddings.

San Ildefonso Pueblo, first built around the year 1300, is north of Santa Fe, near Los Alamos, and can still be visited at certain times. (Don't miss the January 23 feast dance day, when the public is invited!) If you love the beautiful pottery of Maria Martinez and her family, a visit to her home is a must.

Maddie's own house on Canyon Road is based on El Zaguan, originally built in the 1850s and enlarged over the years. Today, it houses the Historical Santa Fe Foundation and is not open to the public, but the garden is always there for everyone to see. The portal and shady walkways are the perfect place to take a break from gallery hopping.

Many thanks to the art tours at La Fonda, the walking tours of Ghost Walks Santa Fe, and the librarians at the Archives at the History Museum for the great information and time spent answering all my questions. (The Archives keeps an online register of thousands of photos at palaceofthegovernors.org/library.) I highly recommend a visit to any of these when you come to town!

A few books I found useful include the following:

Taos and Santa Fe: The Artist's Environment, 1882–1942 and *Artists of Twentieth Century New Mexico*, Van Deren Coke (1963)

Frank Springer and New Mexico: From the Colfax County War to the Emergence of Modern Santa Fe, David F. Caffey (2006)

Turn Left at the Sleeping Dog: Scripting the Santa Fe Legend, 1920–1955 (2006)

The Inn of History: An Account of La Fonda Since 1610, La Fonda Hotel (1977)

La Fonda: Then and Now (2016)

Olive Rush: Finding Her Place in the Santa Fe Art Colony, Jann Haynes Gilmore (2016)

Chasing the Cure in New Mexico: Tuberculosis and the Quest for Health, Nancy Owen Lewis (2016)

Literary Pilgrims: The Santa Fe and Taos Writers' Colonies, 1917–1950 (2007)

Loretto: The Sisters and Their Santa Fe Chapel, Mary J. Straw Cook (2002)

Lamy of Santa Fe, Paul Horgan (2012)

Death Comes for the Archbishop, Willa Cather (1927)

Taos Artists and Their Patrons, 1898–1950, Dean A. Porter (1999)

Light, Landscape, and the Creative Quest: Early Artists of Santa Fe, Stacia Lewandowski (2011)

The Santa Fe and Taos Art Colonies: Age of the Muses, 1900–1942 (1983)